ANCHORED

Brigitte Quinn

Represented by:
Katherine Fausset
Curtis Brown, Ltd.
10 Astor Place, 3rd floor
New York, NY 10003
(212) 473-5400 ext. 182
kf@cbltd.com

ISBN-10: 0692473513
ISBN-13: 9780692473511

This above all: to thine own self be true,
And it must follow, as the night the day,
Thou canst not then be false to any man.

Shakespeare

December 2000

CHAPTER 1

Figures, she thought, the one day she hoped to sleep in, some knucklehead celebrity had to up and crash his plane. Barbara King propelled herself through the glass revolving door and into the lobby of the Phoenix News Channel.

Her old friend and producer Rip Danko was waiting for her, leaning against the lobby's security desk where the Saturday morning guard reclined in his chair holding a transistor radio tuned to a sports station. Danko, also seemingly oblivious to the blockbuster story their cable television station was about to cover, was slowly paging through a copy of *Rolling Stone* magazine. He looked up as Barbara charged over to him, her long, red hair falling out of its inadequate clip.

"Reading up on the plane crash?" she joked.

"Officially, it's not a crash. Not yet." Danko rolled up the magazine and squeezed it into the back pocket of his jeans. "Walk with me; talk with me," he said, taking Barbara's arm as he steered her through the lobby.

Barbara, still in her winter warm-up suit and sneakers, wanted to break into a run. This would be the biggest story their lowly third-ranked channel had ever covered: Grant Danes, acclaimed actor and amateur pilot, and his pseudo-celebrity new bride, were likely dead. If Barbara handled herself well in the breaking news shitstorm, she might be able to rise in the ranks at the Phoenix, or at least prove to her boss that she was cool in a crisis.

But running wasn't in Rip's repertoire. "Slow down; it's only cable!" was his flirtatious warning to bodacious interns scampering about the newsroom. As Barbara walked with him, she detected the unmistakable whiff of the Pepperpot (the Phoenix staff's favorite watering hole) emanating from Rip's paisley print shirt.

"Go mano a mano with Johnnie Walker last night?"

"Jack Daniel's, actually. And he won," Danko sighed, running a hand through his longish blond-grey hair. "So. Danes decides to pilot his Cessna to the Hamptons for a showbiz shindig. He and the wife never show up."

"When did they disappear?" Barbara asked. She wasn't going to ask, "When did they go missing?" as the writers at the channel would have it. That phrase would have given her high school English teacher fits: "You don't *go* missing."

"The plane was off the radar after 8 o'clock last night—it was supposed to be a Teterboro to East Hampton, or, technically, Wainscott flight," Danko replied. "We're sending reporters to the airport, to Danes's mansion in Southampton. The weather was lousy and he was a rookie pilot. Thinking is there might have been ice on the wings and he lost control. Don't listen to any crap about them paddling to a beach waiting for a rescue boat. Water temps are in the 40s."

"Should have stuck to playing a pilot in the movies, huh?" Barbara said, trying to sound like a cigar-chewing news veteran who'd seen her share of pretty flyboys crack up their airborne sardine cans. She certainly didn't wish Danes dead; she'd enjoyed his movies, especially the one where he played a bipolar, one-armed Gulf war pilot who learns to fly, and love, again, thanks to a comely copilot. But Barbara had to admit she was giddy when Danko had paged her to come in, even if her beeper had awakened her from a dead sleep at 6 a.m. and spoiled her day of ice-skating with her husband and little boy.

"You're on at 8," Danko said, as they reached the end of the long lobby where one set of doors led to the newsroom, the other to the station's offices.

"Eight," repeated Barbara. "Yikes." She needed to get to the newsroom for the conference call, then dash to her office to prep. She had to print out and speed-read every iota of information she could dig up on Danes: his early showbiz days playing a transgender serial killer on a 1980s nighttime soap, his snub by the Academy but Golden Globe nod for *Broken Wing, Mended Heart,* and his foray into directing. Barbara also needed to research the wife: her solo CD, which included a dreadful duet with a screechy-sounding Danes, her "friendship" with a rapper that led to a brief break up with Danes, and her blatant lip-synching at an awards show which effectively ended her singing career.

"And Barb," Danko said, his hand on the door, "You're gonna have to yank Spencer out of the anchor chair." Of course, Lois Spencer, Very Important Anchorwoman, had beaten Barbara onto the set.

"I could take her," said Barbara, making a fist and flexing a bicep.

Danko grinned lasciviously. "I'll bring the creamed corn for your wrestling match."

"Roger that."

Barbara flung open the frosted glass doors and entered the newsroom. It looked like a pinball machine, with pods lighting up as writers and producers flipped on overhead fluorescents and slammed into their work corners. They ricocheted across the room to the satellite desk where phones were blinking red and ringing.

Next, they bounced to the bookers' pod at the head of the newsroom to linger for a few moments before shooting back to their desks.

If the pinball game had a space-age theme, the rotating round news desk would be the floating mother ship. It was elevated, its height setting it apart from the rest of the newsroom, and it rotated at an infinitesimal speed, even slower than a merry-go-round coming to a stop. Barbara's boss, Cal Carmichael, the Phoenix News Channel's cheery leader, thought it would be a slick bit of showbiz aesthetics to have the set spin. This way the anchor desk's backdrop would be a constantly changing shot of the newsroom in all its frenetic glory. Cal, a former soap opera actor attuned to stagecraft, thought the astronomically priced set was worth the money and would generate buzz. Others pointed out that no one ever went home from a Broadway show humming the set. Sitting on it as it turned, Barbara felt like a rotisserie chicken.

Just as Danko had warned, Lois Spencer, with her long-necked 6-foot frame, was roosting in the anchor chair. As Barbara walked by, she made a point of not looking in her direction. Barbara headed straight for the conference room where producers and writers and production assistants were swarming in advance of the planning meeting and Cal's call. With everyone in sweats, scrunchies, and baseball caps, it looked as if the Phoenix staff had assembled for a station softball game.

Barbara took a seat at the conference table and glanced at the giant elementary school-style analog clock on the wall. 7:13 a.m. She'd set a new record in her drive into Manhattan on the Long Island Expressway to the studio that morning, but even if this meeting got going soon, she'd have a meager 40 minutes to change her clothes, research, print, read, and get hair and makeup before running over to The Rotisserie.

The conference room had filled up and was now standing-room-only, as producers and writers nervously eyed the old-fashioned clock. Barbara stared at the space-aged, winged, conference call phone, willing it to life. It looked like a plane, with speakers in its nose and wings, and control panel buttons in its fuselage. The plane. Damn. She needed to research Danes's model, its safety record, and the details of the instruction he'd received in piloting (apparently not enough). Where was Cal? Barbara tapped her foot.

7:15 a.m. "Good morning, campers!" came the voice crackling through the phone. Finally. Cal calling from his office on the 25th floor of their building. He never attended the meetings, probably wanting to preserve his image as the unseen "Charlie," communicating with his news "Angels." She'd never met the man herself as he was on a mysterious medical leave when she was hired a year ago and few at the channel had. But she'd seen his publicity shot. He was somewhat Charlie-esque: a white-pompadoured older man, still dapper, if not a bit puffier since he'd played a doctor in soaps. Cal had moved on to directing and then left the soap operas altogether to work as a producer in a then new genre—the television talk show—where he turned a pudgy everyman host into a star. Cal's new frontier was cable.

"What have you got? Southampton, you're up first!" Cal sounded chipper as ever, even though he had to be feeling the pressure: he was delivering marching orders for covering a story that could actually get ratings.

A producer who'd been rushed to the Danes's cordoned-off compound up-talked her update. "The reporter's with the, um, truck? At Southampton hospital? In case, they're like, okay? And maybe swam to shore? I can't get into their like, mansion, so I'm outside? I'm trying to get someone? From the family?"

This girl sounds 16, thought Barbara.

"Alrighty," chirped Cal. "East Hampton, you there?"

A deep-voiced young man who'd mumbled incomprehensibly into Barbara's earpiece when he'd produced her show last week signed in.

"We'reattheairportliningupanofficialmaybeapilottoo."

Cal, undaunted by what was to Barbara a nearly unintelligible response, continued, "And New York?"

Barbara's eyes turned toward her rookie producer du jour, sitting across from her in the conference room. Jimmy O'Byrne, was it? The poor kid's face was a map of anxiety prompting the stage crew to nickname him Zitty O'Breakout. He began, "King starts at 8 and we'll rotate every hour with Spencer/Topper."

"I didn't notice young Will on television this morning," Cal interjected.

Will Topper, Lois Spencer's co-anchor, was a mess. The channel's wardrobe mistress and minions were constantly in his office, collecting his frayed pants or ties that were stained with Lord knew what. He got away with a lot because of his cool Australian accent, but his malapropisms and mangled grammar irritated Lois to no end, what with her flawless English and fluent French. But Cal hired Will because he "popped" on television, and chalked up his linguistic difficulties to "cultural differences." One of those differences was that he wouldn't let work get in the way of an all-night rave. So now, while Spencer was anchoring the missing- plane story, Topper was likely still on the dance floor, pressing the heels of his hands skyward.

"Not sure of his status, Mr. Carmichael," Zitty gulped. "We have a live shot from midtown, where we'll be doing a little man-on-the-street, asking folks 'How will you remember him?' and..."

"Careful not to kill him before he's dead!" Cal said brightly.

"Right. Right. Of course." New, angry red pin-points were probably already pushing their way up to the surface of the producer's skin.

"Make sure, however," said Cal, "that the Specials Department puts together a Danes obit package. And have someone do a side-bar package on the wife—she was an actress or a model, wasn't she?"

"A singer," answered Zitty. "Sort of." Zitty gave a nervous smile as his quip produced a titter in the conference room.

Rip joined the call from his office. "Cal. It's Danko."

"Good morning, Clarence!" The boss was the only one allowed to call Danko by his real name; they went way back.

"An entertainment print reporter who's covered Danes since his TV days is on his way in to the studio," said Rip. "He can help the anchors fill."

"Terrific!" Cal dropped his voice. "Now, before we go...."

But before Cal could begin his inevitable pep talk, Lois Spencer cut in. From the set. Only she could have maneuvered her crew to punch in the conference call during a commercial break.

"Good morning, Cal. Lois Spencer here. Just wanted you to know that I got an exclusive. I'll be interviewing the wife's childhood friend in the 9 a.m. It's an exclusive and the control room should monitor so they can record and replay the exclusive during prime time."

Thanks, Lois, because we hadn't heard the word "exclusive" the first two times, Barbara thought.

"Great work, Lois!" Cal exclaimed. "So before we go, let me say a few quick words." When Cal started his missives, Barbara always wondered if they should genuflect, like a ball team before a game.

"It would seem that Hollywood has suffered a tragic loss. If this is so, the Phoenix News Channel wants to be first with the news. But always remember and never forget, our competition would be all too happy to accuse us of negative coverage. For now, stay away from any of the seedier aspects of the showbiz... shall we say...*lifestyle*." Assuming this referred to rumors of cocaine consumption on the part of Danes and his bride, the conference room crowd emitted a mild rumble of laughter. Cal continued, "Let's focus instead on a star who had great box office and was certainly loved by his fans." There were a few "mmm's" of agreement, but most of the assembled were already bolting out of their seats as Cal signed off, "Go make some great TV!"

CHAPTER 2

After the sprint to her office, Barbara slammed the door, turned on her computer, tore off her clothes, and searched the wardrobe rack in her office for a dark suit. Danko was right—no way had Grant Danes survived. She put the phone on speaker and called hair and makeup.

"Where in fuck's name are you?" Jane's accent, an unfortunate mix of British and Irish, sounded even more clipped than usual.

"Can you and Ang do me at the same time?" Barbara glanced at the clock on her desk. *7:19*. "I'm on at 8."

"8 o'fucking clock? Chip chop!"

As her desktop lighted up, Barbara grabbed a pair of panty-hose from a drawer and pulled them on, as she read the latest urgent wire copy about the plane off of the screen. Even though she didn't like to watch Lois, she had to turn on the television to hear what the Phoenix was reporting.

The Associated Press is quoting an FAA source as saying the plane is still officially listed as missing at this point...

Unsurprisingly, the Phoenix's crackerjack teenage producers out in the field hadn't gotten any information from their own sources, meaning Barbara would have to rely on the wire copy. She zipped up her skirt with one hand and hit the "print" button with another. Before she even finished buttoning her blouse, she poked her head out of her office door to make sure her unreliable printer was working. She scanned the wires, printing out story after story but also ignoring another rumor: that Mr. and Mrs. Grant Danes were *not* living happily ever after. The newlyweds deserved an un-fractured fairy tale when they were newly dead, didn't they? Barbara slipped into a pair of pumps, grabbed an earpiece from her desk, seized the stack of copy from the printer as it churned out the last piece, and ran like hell to hair and makeup.

Jane was at her station, furiously powdering Rip's entertainment reporter guest, holding his jaw closed to prevent amiable chatter. With her black lab coat, oversized black glasses, and white hair pulled into a severe bun, she looked like a mad scientist. The guest's presence prevented her from launching into her fuck patois (*What took you so fucking long? What fucking took you so long?* or the more generic *What in the fuck?*) when Barbara arrived.

"Angelica's waiting for you," said Jane. "I'll be in shortly."

Barbara decided to dispense with any niceties with the guest who couldn't talk anyway, and pulled back the thick velvet curtain that separated Jane's room from Angelica's.

Angelica was standing at attention next to her leather barber chair, hand already on the trigger of her water spray bottle and her other weapons—mousse, brushes, blow-dryer—lined up on her console, ready for deployment. Her uniform, a black lab coat, was the same as Jane's. But on Angelica, it looked like a mink. Runway-tall and elegant, with light brown skin and green eyes, "Tyra," as in Banks, was the nickname bestowed upon her by male producers who always seemed to need a trim. "We're pushing it, girl," Angelica warned Barbara, nodding toward the television on her console. On the bottom left corner of the screen, underneath the station logo—which was supposed to be a Phoenix but more closely resembled a turkey—was the time: *7:27.*

"Damn conference call," Barbara said as she plunked down into the chair while Angelica misted her hair.

"Don't worry," Angelica said, grabbing her blow-dryer. "We'll get you out in time."

Barbara started speed-reading her copy. In first grade, she and her best friend had been placed in an advanced reading class, their teacher bestowing upon them the privilege of walking down the hall to the *second*-grade classroom to make their book selections. Barbara thought she was supposed to read a book a day. When halfway through the school year, she confessed to her best friend that she found the reading assignment tough, her friend clarified that they were only supposed to read a book a week, silly. Barbara felt like a sucker, but racing through all those chapter books had taught her how to read in a hurry.

Barbara now plowed through the copy on her lap, as Jane ripped open the curtain, pushed Barbara's chin up, and started applying foundation as Angelica continued styling.

Jane threw the foundation sponge into the trash, powdered Barbara; gave her contour and blush, eye shadow, and liner; and then started rifling through the plastic yellow makeup box labeled "KING."

"Someone stole her fucking mascara!" Jane cried. Although Jane hadn't lived in the U.K. for more than 30 years, she still saw palace conspiracies everywhere. She threw Angelica's curtain back to go solve the case of the missing mascara.

Angelica rolled her eyes and started pulling Barbara's hair into Velcro curlers. She tapped at the television screen with her teasing comb. "That one," she said. Lois Spencer was glaring at her viewers, daring them to miss a word of the Very Important News she was imparting.

With freezing rain falling on Long Island, Danes likely encountered an ice buildup on the wings of his plane...something even an experienced pilot might not be able to contend with..."

"She comes running in here at 5:45 this morning," Angelica began. "Tells me and Jane that 'her people' wouldn't be in 'til later and we need to get her done for the 6 o'clock."

"Did Cal call her to come in?" Barbara asked, wanting to know where she fell in the pecking order. On weekdays, Barbara had the 9–11 a.m. shift, and Lois and Will, the 11–1p.m. Barbara liked to think that being up first gave her the edge, but she wondered: in a crisis, was Lois the favored anchor?

Angelica blow-dried the curlers on low so she wouldn't have to shout her gossip. "Hell, no! She said she got the scoop from a friend in the business."

"Her boyfriend," added Jane, who'd located the mascara and was back in front of Barbara, holding the tube before her so she would stare at it without blinking while Jane applied.

"You mean her *old man* friend," said Angelica. It was no secret that Spencer's agent boyfriend was getting on in years.

"Her elderly gentleman caller," Jane put in.

"So she races in here," Angelica continued, "And tells the crew, 'I'm taking the reins at 6!'" Barbara thought of large Lois looming over the hapless weekend morning anchor; she surely relished big-footing him.

"Jeez. I only got the page at around 6..." Barbara said, feeling guilty for being slighted that her planned family day hadn't been disrupted sooner.

Jane shushed her and started lining her lips, not drawing the lines outside their natural boundaries as she usually did. "No blow-job lips today," she said. Boy, Danes and the wife had to be dead, if hair and makeup had been told to *not* make the anchors look sexy.

"Don't sweat it," said Angelica. "Least they found you. Heard Topper was at some throw-down. A guy from graphics said he was still there when he left the bar at 2 a.m."

When she was allowed to speak again, Barbara joked, "No gloss? This *is* a huge story."

"Oh for fuck's sake!" said Jane. "You'd think he was a great stage thespian."

"He's a big deal, Jane." Angelica removed Barbara's curlers, not stopping to pick up the ones that tumbled off her console. *7:47*. "Sad. All that money—coulda *hired* a damn pilot."

"You couldn't pay me to get into one of those flying death traps," Barbara said.

Angelica had teased Barbara's hair into Don King proportions and was now starting to style it using her long, rhinestone-studded fingernails. "Hold your breath," she ordered, pointing the spray can at Barbara's head. "You need extra spray—if they blow the breaks, we won't be able to touch you up."

"Thanks for the hustle, Ang."

"Anything for you."

Barbara often wondered why Angelica was so good to her. Was she truly her friend or was she just playing it smart politically, figuring that if Barbara had a big future at the channel, she could hitch her wagon to her star? But Angelica was no anchor ass kisser; in fact, she seemed entirely unimpressed by the on-air talent. What did register with the former high school sprinter was that Barbara was also a teen track star and still tried to run several miles a few days a week. Angelica's remark upon hearing Barbara's fastest time for the 100-meter hurdle: "Not bad for a white girl."

"I better run," said Barbara, unsnapping her robe as Angelica clipped Barbara's earpiece to the back of her jacket collar and gave her a push toward the door.

"You look great," Angelica called after her.

As Barbara opened the door to the newsroom, she glanced at the wall of clocks from the various time zones. The only one she cared about was the one that read *7:55*. As she zipped toward the set, she was nearly knocked over by her pimpled producer, who, hand shaking, thrust a piece of paper into hers.

"Your first guest. Former FAA guy. Pronouncer's on there. Gotta get in the control room. Oh, we're starting with the live shot from East Hampton. I think. Not sure..." With that, he chomped down on a powdered doughnut.

Someone should cut him off from that sugar, Barbara thought, as she paused at the foot of the rotating set so the audio guy could hook up her microphone pack. She could see Zitty still at his desk, throwing papers around before finally finding his headset.

7:57. A minute away from Lois' toss to the two-minute break and then Barbara was up. Barbara's underarms felt moist—she was nervous. In the year since she'd been hired at the Phoenix, she had earned a reputation for being "unflappable" (a description Angelica had overheard) during breaking news. Cal would definitely be watching closely today, and perhaps auditioning her for bigger and better.

"Mornin', beautiful. It's your friendly audio department." Her cue to whisper into the mic to make sure it was working.

"Top of the morning, guys. Check. Check one, two..."

"Have a great show."

7:57:50. Lois was winding down.

When I join you again at 9, I'll have an exclusive interview with a childhood friend of Grant Danes's bride...

Ten seconds to tease into the break and instead of giving the audience a quick recap, or, God forbid, mentioning that Barbara was up next, Lois had instead plugged herself. Lois rose from her seat, and let out a satisfied sigh. Barbara sat down in the chair and should have said, "Nice job, Lois." It *was* proper etiquette to pay a compliment to the anchor who'd just finished a particularly hectic hour, even if you didn't like her. But Barbara couldn't muster it. Lois nodded to her and walked off the set, ducking as her black bob barely cleared a jib camera. She then disappeared, without a word of thanks to the crew.

Barbara's stage manager, Tex, who could usually compensate for any control room deficiencies, was putting his headset on. He stroked his long mustache and rasped, "Comin' back in 90."

Surely within those 90 long seconds, she'd get some direction from the control room about where they were going first, which reporters or satellite interviews or phoners were ready.

Silence. Tex, a former ambulance driver, tried to cut the tension.

"I tell you what, there's no way those two are alive. If that plane hit the water, they probably smacked their heads into the controls. Woulda split open like melons. And if the crash didn't kill 'em, they probably froze. Or drowned." He coughed. "Slow death, drowning. Not how I wanna go." He shook his head. "One minute. Quiet on the set."

Barbara scribbled a few more bullet points onto her stenographer's note pad. There would be no scripts today.

Tex said, "Thirty seconds, boys and girls." And then, to Barbara. "Control room talk to you yet?"

Barbara shook her head and Tex fingered the cigarette he had in the front pocket of his shirt. He was no doubt longing for the days of a smoky newsroom and a set that didn't spin. He cupped his hand around his headset mic and said, "Someone in there please tell the anchor what the hell is going on?"

An aged stagehand looked desperate. "Where are we going?!"

"Don't crap your Depends, I'm trying to find out," Tex said. He then shrugged apologetically to Barbara. "Twenty seconds."

Nothing. Barbara checked her laptop computers to see if the wires or the channel's in-house "urgent" cue had any new information. A bulletin was crossing from the Associated Press. *A Suffolk county radio station is quoting a police official as saying the wreckage of a small plane has been found off the waters of Long Island.*

Barbara's eyes widened. Tex threw his hands up in the air. "Fifteen. Sorry. They're all screamin' in there. Friggin' *out-of-control* room."

Wreckage, Barbara thought. So she'd be the one to break the news they were dead.

"Ten seconds," said Tex.

Barbara took a breath.

Tex counted, "Five...four..." and then gestured with three fingers for the final, silent "Three, two, one." The red light flashed on and the Phoenix news bulletin sounder whooshed.

Good morning. I'm Barbara King with a Phoenix news flash. We have brand-new information on the possible fate of a beloved movie star. Grant Danes's small aircraft, which he himself was piloting, disappeared last evening...and now the AP is reporting that the plane might have been found....

Tex brought the fingertips of both of his hands together and then pulled them apart slowly. Stretch.

We want to emphasize that we haven't confirmed this information yet...

As Barbara took a breath, Zitty the producer finally spoke into her headset, "Um Barbara, we have a...." but then stopped.

Barbara kept talking.

The Associated Press is quoting a Suffolk county radio station. Our reporter on scene, with whom ***we should be speaking shortly,*** *is working to confirm this report.*

Barbara was trying to send the control room a message but they probably weren't listening to what she was saying on air.

Zitty the producer came back in her ear. "Okay. Here's the deal. Wait. Uh...." Barbara continued vamping, while he kept talking to her. And he neglected to take his finger off the button he pushed to talk to her when he shouted at someone in the control room.

"Give me a fucking second, okay?" His voice broke. "I'M FUCKING TELLING HER NOW!"

What we do know is that the plane was reported missing late last night. That "missing" classification has not officially changed.

No one would ever guess that the Phoenix's coverage was rudderless and that the anchor was swimming, trying to reach the safety of a live shot. No one, except maybe Danko.

Bastard was probably in his office, lights off, taking a record album out of its sleeve and placing it on his office turntable. He was done getting the schedule on track, and if his television was on at all, it was probably muted. But if he bothered to look at the screen, maybe to check out what she was wearing, he'd have to notice that the channel wasn't on a live shot yet. Barbara sent him an instant message on the Phoenix computer system.

King: HEEEEEEEELP!

If he saw that, he'd stroll into the control room and ask, where's your goddamned live shot? Rip liked to say that a cat is only interested in pawing a ball of yarn because it moves when swatted. Humans also like to watch things move; get it?

The producer put his finger back down on the button to talk to Barbara, but this time she heard Rip's voice.

"Scram."

"I'm turning things over to Rip!" Zitty quaked.

We want to update the viewers who might be just joining us. Actor Grant Danes and his wife are missing this morning and a

Long Island, New York, station is now reporting that the, quote, "wreckage" of a plane has been found.

As Barbara took a breath between sentences, Danko whispered in her ear, precise and pissed. "Phoner ready. Miletto. Talk cops' work at scene of wreckage."

Joining now is former NYPD detective Anthony Miletto.

Miletto was the head of Phoenix security and a great guest in a pinch—Danko must have called him before he even got to the control room.

Detective, thanks for joining us this morning.

"He can also talk about the security detail they had as celebs."

If a small plane has been found in the waters off Moriches, Long Island, it would have to be the missing aircraft, right?

As Miletto answered, Danko told Barbara: "Rerouted the truck and reporter from the hospital to the mansion. I'm getting the Southampton producer on the phone. She'll have a Phoenix News Flash confirming the plane found."

Christ, thought Barbara. The teenage? Up-talker? But they needed someone from near the scene.

Rip continued smoothly, "When you're done with her, intro the reporter at East Hampton airport. One hit and I'm moving him to the scene of the wreckage. Tag with that."

Barbara continued her interview with Miletto, but Rip came back suddenly: "Cut him off!"

Before he even finished saying "off", the bulletin sounder whooshed. And in the seconds it took for the screen to be filled with the Phoenix News Flash graphic, Danko whispered: "Phoenix confirms from a cop source—wreckage of plane found."

A Phoenix News Flash: The Phoenix News Channel is confirming the wreckage of Grant Danes's missing jet has been found in the waters off Morriches, Long Island.

Rip said, "Cop says bodies, too."

And our team in Southampton is now being told by a police source that the bodies have also been located.

"New phoner, Barb: Phoenix producer...

Let's go live now to a Phoenix producer....

"Amy Street in Southampton,"

...to Southampton, outside the Danes mansion, and producer Amy Street. Amy, can you tell us the precise location of the wreckage?

Within minutes, the Phoenix graphics department had replaced the *MISSING* montage (a plane, a map, the couple's wedding picture) with a close-up shot of Grant Danes in a tux and beneath it, the dates *1960–2000*. The bride's middling, fleeting fame as a singer had been posthumously trumped by, grand thespian or no, her movie star husband.

CHAPTER 3

5:59:00 p.m. Barbara was about to start her sixth and last hour of the day's Grant Danes death coverage before the evening news anchor, Bill Hunter, aka "Ironsides," took over. He was the channel's senior anchor and managing something-or-other, wheelchair-bound, old, and one-thousandth Cherokee. Cal had stolen him from one of the networks and thought he brought "cachet" to the channel. To Barbara's mind, Ironsides' droning delivery and tendency to lick the corner of his mouth as if to prevent some invisible drool from settling in his mustache, made him damn near unwatchable. But even if Cal got sick of him, he couldn't fire a disabled Native American. Still, Barbara hoped that one day Ironsides would bore himself to sleep on air—certainly grounds for dismissal—and she could get the coveted 7 p.m. time slot.

Rip had gone home, so Barbara was anticipating a new voice in her ear as she waited on the set. The adrenaline rush was gone. The story was now just a blur of snippets from the various categories of coverage (*Danes's love of flying, his ascent from small screen to silver screen, his storybook marriage*), which had progressed from glowing to subtly critical (*a possible lack of pilot training, his box office flops, his prior romances with actresses and models).* After interviewing everyone from pilots to paparazzi and mostly ad-libbing her 6 hours of coverage, Barbara was now drinking coffee to stay energized.

"Hello, Barbara *Konig,"* said the female voice in her earpiece. "Looks like you're going to be my anchor for the next hour."

Who was it? Who would know Barbara had changed her German surname to its easier-to-pronounce English equivalent after she got her first job in big market radio? And what was this "my" anchor business? Nervy broad, whoever she was.

Barbara just nodded; with 45 seconds to air, she didn't have time for conversation. She looked down at her scripts.

"You there, Barbara?" the voice persisted.

Barbara looked directly into the camera and gave a thumbs-up, assuming the mystery producer was watching Barbara from the control room. Leave me alone, I'm trying to read, she thought.

"Okay, 30 seconds to air!" the mystery producer announced. "We're starting with the compound, then the scene of the wreckage, then your first interview, which will take us to the first commercial break. I'll remind you as we go!"

Barbara looked at Tex, who, in a nod to Zitty's morning producing debacle, said, "At least this one's not pissin' herself."

The show went smoothly, with Barbara reading the copy this producer's team had meticulously prepared but ignoring the interview questions that someone (probably the pesky producer herself) had put in the prompter. The producer's voice was in Barbara's ear constantly.

"The reporter at the mansion is ready." *I know. You told me that. Twice already.*

"The guest's name is John O'Brien. O' Brien. John." *Yes. I've interviewed him twelve times today.*

"The commercial break is coming up in 30 seconds. Make this the last question." I *know how to tell time and I already said, on air, that this was the last question.*

And then, during Barbara's interview with a reporter who covered celebrities in the Hamptons, the producer whispered in Barbara's ear, intoning as if *she* were the anchor, "There were rumors that Danes held cocaine-fueled parties at his mansion, no?" *Um, excuse me? Remember Cal's instructions not to indict the guy when he's barely cold?*

Barbara ignored her and asked the guest if Danes was a regular on the Hamptons social circuit.

The producer tried again, "In his failed efforts to move behind the camera, to direct, didn't Danes visit Cuba? And once there, didn't he cozy up to Castro?" *Okay, the movie was a stinker, but there were no pictures of Danes sharing a smoke with Fidel. Who was this woman?!*

Barbara asked instead, "Might Danes have pursued more directing projects in the future?"

When the hour was over, Barbara couldn't pull her earpiece out of her ear quickly enough. She slammed it on the console and went directly to Jane's station to get a baby wipe to take off some of her makeup before her drive home. Rubbing the back of her neck to try to loosen the knots that had formed there, Barbara walked slowly into the greenroom, and surveying the molasses-like substance in the coffee pot, decided she'd take a pass; her irritation during her last hour on air would be enough to keep her awake for her drive home. It was time to wind down, to think about getting back to her son, Rory—if there was no traffic, maybe she'd make it home in time to tuck him in.

Barbara heard the click of heels coming down the hallway, seconds before the greenroom door flew open. A compact woman in a chic suit but sporting a boyish haircut, stood before her. She looked familiar to Barbara. She had a white patch of eyebrow and hair above her forehead—vitiligo, probably—which made her look like either Susan Sontag or Pepé Le Pew, depending on your point of reference.

"Barbara, Sloane Davis," she said, extending a hand that was no bigger than a child's.

Barbara smiled politely as she cycled through the Rolodex in her head. High school? College? One of the newsrooms where she'd worked?

"WAMS?" said Sloane. "Amherst?"

"Oh, gosh, right. Sorry," said Barbara. "Nice to meet...see you again." That was it. Barbara's first job out of college, reading news updates at a classic rock station.

"I'm producing weekends here—that's why we haven't bumped into each other yet. I started here last year as a booker, then wound up running the department, and then got a shot at producing." Sloane folded her arms, striking a confident pose, and continued, "But it all started at WAMS."

Barbara remembered now. She'd been just a couple of weeks away from leaving WAMS for a radio station in Boston, when she was asked to give a station tour to a new disc jockey and aspiring programmer. A mousy-looking girl named Sloane, whose improbably hunky boyfriend shuffled behind her, peppered Barbara with questions for the better part of the hour.

"I gave you the tour," said Barbara.

"I became station program director 3 months later." Sloane smiled. "I took the station to #1."

Barbara remembered the stories about Sloane she'd heard from the DJs with whom she'd stayed in touch. Sloane's first act as PD was to change the station's format from album rock to Top 40. It was of no concern to Sloane that her staff and Amherst locals had the collective musical taste of a hippie commune. George Michael replaced George Harrison. Big Brother and the Holding Company was usurped by Kool and the Gang. And it was goodbye, Richie Havens, "Hello," Lionel Richie. One disc jockey quit by ripping up the cover of a Duran Duran record, unintentionally, yet ingeniously shearing the moussed hair clean off one of the band members. "That's our only Duran Duran album!" Sloane had shrieked. As legend had it, the DJ shouted back, "Duran Duran? Fuck You Fuck You!"

Sloane put her hand on her hip and took a step closer to Barbara. "I have to ask. Were you okay with my style tonight? I tend to give a lot of direction."

Barbara wasn't about to defer to a DJ. "Since you asked," she said, "I would have preferred less."

"Really?" Sloane chuffed. "Because my anchors usually like to get helpful reminders," she said, adjusting the pencil behind her ear. Who'd she think she was, Lou Grant?

"Well, you know, I'd been on the air since early this morning, so I knew the story pretty well," Barbara said, trying to be diplomatic.

"Most anchors also appreciate the questions I provide for them."

"Do they?" Barbara's temper was rising.

The greenroom door opened again; Rip sauntered in and wordlessly poured himself a mug of muck.

"Indeed they do," said Sloane. "I can't understand why you wouldn't want to ask about his coke habit and communism. Our viewers think Hollywood is sleazy and that actors are crazy liberals—they would have eaten that up!"

"Communism? Are you serious?" Barbara gritted her teeth. "The man's lifeless body just washed up on shore. And besides, I don't think our viewers should be *fed* rumors or innuendo..."

"Listen, boys," Danko broke in, taking a step toward them. "It's late. Sloane, I need Barbara." He grabbed Barbara by the arm and led her out of the greenroom, looking over his shoulder, explaining, "Gotta prep for Monday morning."

"What are you doing?" Barbara asked as soon as the door closed behind them.

"Come have a smoke with your old Uncle Rip."

"But she was picking a fight with me over not asking these ridiculous questions she put in the prompter!"

"You don't wanna tangle with her. She's a little climber. Keeps calling me to put her on the weekday schedule," said Rip. "I haven't, but Cal likes her. A lot."

Barbara and Rip reached his office. Its door, as usual, was covered with pictures: Ringo Starr's face superimposed over a keffiyeh-wearing Yasser Arafat; Jerry Garcia's visage matched with Einstein's hair; and photos of Danko replaced the faces of both Page and Plant as they riffed, backs arched, in a red-tinted poster from their '77 tour.

Barbara leaned against the doorway as Rip waded into the darkness of his office, snapping on his desk lamp so he could find the cigarettes and hooch he kept in his desk. He poured a shot of Wild Turkey into his coffee cup.

"I won't have what you're having. That's disgusting, Rip."

"Hair of the dog—can't be picky about the dog," he said, snatching his pack of Marlboro Lights off the top of his desk.

Once in the "smoking lounge," a corridor that bridged the gap between the Phoenix and the Pepperpot, home of the extra-spicy Bloody Mary, Barbara took off her pumps and let the concrete cool her feet. Holding her sling-backs in one hand, she reached for one of Rip's cigarettes with the other.

"Unlike Sloane, you performed magnificently in the control room today, Rip."

"Thanks," he said, pulling a Bic lighter from his jeans pocket and lighting her cigarette. He nodded toward the Pepperpot. "Don't suppose you have time for a pop?"

"Nah, I gotta get home," she said, taking a drag so deep it almost made her cough. She shouldn't even be hanging around to chat with Rip, but she should probably be grateful to him for breaking up her fight with Sloane and for his earlier control room heroics. "Wasn't it a rush this morning?" she asked.

Rip leaned against the wall, one foot propped up against it, looking like a surly teenager defying the lunch monitor to make him put out the butt. "Don't start," he said.

"Come on, I had to deal with everyone from pizza face to that pesky little Sloane today. Why can't you just be my producer?" She playfully batted her eyelashes at him.

"Don't do that," he said, grinning.

Barbara met Rip in 1992, her first year at *The Buzz,* an all-news blowtorch of a radio station, the New York City flagship owned and operated by one of the big-three networks. She was the morning anchor, and he was a roving correspondent who also filed syndicated commentary called *Rip Reports,* a name updated from its pithier teletype-era moniker, *Rip and Read.*

At their station Christmas party that year, Rip, a drinker with a legendary hollow leg, had just knocked back a third gimlet, scribbled a few notes on a cocktail napkin, and left the bar to call in his commentary from a pay phone near the restrooms. Barbara happened to walk out of the ladies' room and past the phone when, still using his announcer's voice as he finished his report, Rip grabbed her arm.

...and so we'll see if the nation really will get a two-for-the-price-of-one president when the first couple-elect moves into the White House in the new year. That's your Friday edition of Rip Reports. Rip Danko reporting.

Rip hung up, crumpled his "script" and pulled Barbara into a room on the other side of the phone bank. Who knew there was a coatroom in the bar? Rip didn't say a word, just started kissing her, rather forcefully, she thought, for such a laid-back hipster. Within seconds, Rip had untucked the gold satin blouse from her black velvet skirt, unclasped her bra (how'd he know it was a front-open?!), and was reaching for the door to lock it. Instead, the door pushed open.

"Filing your report from the coatroom again, Danko?" asked one of their reporters who'd come to claim his jacket.

After agreeing with Rip that they "blow this popcorn stand," Barbara found herself in the less-than-cozy confines of his Chelsea studio. It exhibited even less decorating panache than a dorm room with one exception: a skeleton wearing a safari-style reporter's vest and a purple scarf, perhaps a trophy from a sexy refugee. Rip picked out a Dead record to play on his 70s-sized speakers, placed two filmy glasses filled with Wild Turkey on the milk crate full of records that served as his nightstand, and pushed Barbara onto the bed. A waterbed.

"Surf's up, baby."

The next morning, party shoes in hand, Barbara waded toward the shore of Rip's apartment door.

"No need to leave so soon." Rip had rocked himself upright and was reaching for a cigarette.

"I better go. I know you have to hit the road," she said, knowing Rip was leaving for D.C. that day.

He patted the bed, creating a ripple. "You can hang here if you like, have some breakfast, take a shower..."

"I saw your bathroom. I'd only feel dirtier afterward," Barbara said, as she sat back down on the bed. "And I'm pretty sure the bourbon's all you had in your kitchen." Raising her arms to put "kitchen" in air quotes made her lose her balance and pitch backward like she was falling into a crashing wave.

Rip threw an arm around her and released a cloud of smoke as if to capture the song lyrics he recited, about a longtime bachelor trying to catch a girl named Althea.

"But you're not trying to catch me, Rip, are you?" she said.

"No," he admitted. "I'm not."

Barbara pecked his cheek and got up. "We're probably better off as friends." Rip was too old for her and a womanizer to boot—guys like that never changed.

"Friends with an asterisk," he'd added, blowing a smoke ring and poking his finger through it.

In the Phoenix corridor, Barbara studied Rip, figuring he had to be 55 by now. But he was still the sharpest guy in the control room and she wouldn't rest until he agreed to be her producer. "Not even for a *friend with an asterisk,* Rip?"

"I'm managing the producing staff," he said.

"You'll get bored."

"I'll get another ulcer if I'm in the control room." The first one was why he gave up the road and agreed to be a producer and unpaid consultant and confidante to Cal when Cal started his channel. "And besides, Barb—we both know you're gonna move up and out of dayside."

"Not if I have to navigate a minefield every day. Think of it, Rip. We'll do it together—come up with a whiz-bang show, get the channel some numbers, take our act to prime time and then, on to the networks..."

The radio station where they'd worked together was owned by one of the big-three networks and at a luncheon one day, the network television president took a shining to Barbara and gave her an audition and then a job hosting the network's early morning television news broadcast. Barbara was thrilled and figured she was on her way up to the network's later-in-the morning talk show, and then, one day, the pinnacle: the network's evening news desk. But her show was unceremoniously cancelled and now Barbara hoped that moving to prime time, cable's more prestigious time slot, would get her noticed and hired by one of her former network's rivals.

"And you get to stick it to the assholes who dumped you," said Rip. "But you'll have to get Cal to get rid of Ironsides first."

"He can't be happy with him—watching him's as good as taking a sleeping pill!"

"Cal likes Ironsides. And his ratings are solid." Rip took a long, last inhale before using his thumb and index finger to launch his cigarette butt in the direction of the Pepperpot. "Cal's actually going to be taking a good look at dayside soon."

"Really? What do you know?"

"Nothing specific."

Barbara narrowed her eyes. "You know."

He had to know. He and Cal were tight, as their friendship dated back to a weekend of heavy drinking when they were both in Los Angeles for the Simpson trial. It was a Lennon/Nilsson lost weekend of sorts for Cal who'd had a falling out with the missus. And while they didn't get kicked out of the Troubadour and no Smothers brothers were heckled, Cal and Rip did a substantive bar crawl that ended at the apartment of a "stewardess" acquaintance of Cal's. Rip "had the pictures," so to speak.

"Honest. Nothing solid," Rip said, crossing his heart. "Just that he wants to make some improvements. Look, just do your thing, baby. If you're going to ascend to the throne, you need to show Cal you can handle breaking news. And you did that today. He was probably watching. Maybe even with the volume on."

Barbara placed her shoes on the ground and, using Danko's arm for balance, slipped back into them. "Okay, Danko," she said, flicking her cigarette away, too. "But I'm not giving up on you."

CHAPTER 4

An hour later, Barbara pulled her Honda into the driveway of her split-level home in Bayville, Long Island. At work, she had tried to push thoughts of 5-year-old Rory out of her mind, hadn't let herself imagine holding him or skating with him at the pond where she'd skated as a girl. But now, she couldn't turn the key in the front door quickly enough; she took the small flight of steps up to her living room two at a time. She surveyed the room: mittens now soaked by melted ice, a skate's blade poking out of a worn canvas bag, and a Styrofoam cup rimmed with chocolate and tiny teeth-print crescents.

Barbara took the next flight of stairs more quietly; it was past 8 and Rory might be asleep already. She stopped in the doorway of his room, always startled by the life-size poster of Spiderman adhered to his bold blue walls. Rory was splayed out on his denim-blue sheets, his comforter only partially covering his white waffle undershirt. Out cold. She sat on the edge of the bed and saw his hand, small, but no longer a baby's, clutching a picture frame. Pale blue and adorned with sea shells and glitter for sand, it held a shot of Barbara and a 2-year-old Rory at the ocean. He liked to hold it, he said, "When you have to go on TV." Barbara sighed and kissed his warm cheek which had probably been bright red and ice cold at the pond. She gently pried his fingers from the picture and placed it back on his nightstand.

Barbara walked into her bedroom and the man from whom Rory was seemingly cloned was in their bed, propped up on pillows, a book of poetry resting on his hairy chest, his eyes closed. "Oh, no, you're passed out, too?" she said as she sat down on their bed and took off her suit jacket and pumps.

Ben opened his eyes and smiled. "Hey there," he said, reaching for her. They kissed. "Little man passed out early. Sorry, I know you wanted to see him."

"It's okay. I wish I could have gone with you guys," said Barbara, reaching for the glass of wine Ben had set on the night table for her. She looked up at the television in their armoire; Ironsides was on. "I would have been home earlier if they'd wheeled him in sooner."

Ben plucked the remote from the bedspread and turned the television off. "You were great." He took his wine glass and toasted her, "To the next Baba Wawa!"

Ben wasn't well-versed in pop culture, but ever since she'd clued him in to the old *Saturday Night Live* parody of her namesake and idol, Barbara Walters, he liked to please her by referencing it.

She rolled her eyes. "I wish."

"You were solid. You had lots of detailed information and you didn't fawn over him...or trash him. I was wondering how your station was going to handle the story, given that he wasn't a family values kind of guy."

"Well, one of the producers tried her best to piss on his grave before it's even dug, but I ignored her." Barbara shook her head at the thought of Sloane. "Chick worked at my station in Amherst, if you can believe that."

"No kidding?" asked Ben, sitting up, and placing his John Ashbery on the nightstand. "Small world."

"Too small," said Barbara, standing to take off her camisole and skirt and pantyhose before walking into the bathroom adjacent to their room.

"Too bad about Danes," said Ben. "It's never what you expect, is it?"

"A shame really," said Barbara, emerging from the bathroom. She picked her wine glass back up from the night table and settled into bed next to Ben. He looked good, with that dark hair of his set against the white sheets.

"I heard you mention Princess Diana. It was a similar story, in a way—people so glamorous, so famous—they probably think they're immortal, that nothing mundane could ever end their existence."

"Interesting," said Barbara. "I didn't get to delve that deeply on air, though."

"'Mundane'—probably not the right word for a plane crash," Ben seemed to be thinking aloud. Despite working for a hedge fund, he was a wordsmith, a poet, at heart. While supportive of her ambitions, he didn't have high regard for cable news as an informational medium. He preferred the depth provided by a PBS documentary, or best of all, *The New Yorker.* Once, after finishing an epic piece on the swallows of Capistrano, Ben said he "wanted more."

Barbara leaned back into her pillow. "Tell me about skating," she said.

Ben rubbed his chin where a beard had once been and smiled. "Rory was funny. Some woman at the pond noticed him picking his nose and told him he shouldn't do that or his nose would get big. You know what he said?"

"Oh, no."

"He said, 'You must have picked yours a lot.'"

Barbara and Ben laughed. "Our boy," said Barbara. "A visitor from the Planet Honest."

They'd just been getting romantic last night when Rory visited their room, asking for a drink of water and *hey, why are you kissing?* Maybe they could pick up where they'd left off, thought Barbara, just as Ben pulled her to him.

She put her hand on his leg and meant to explore, but as Ben kissed her neck, she felt herself drifting and her hand came to a rest midway up his thigh.

Ben took her hand and placed it at her side. "You've had a long day, Baba," he said and turned off the light as she fell into a deep, dreamless sleep.

CHAPTER 5

On Monday morning, the ratings for the Danes crash were in and Danko was the man who had them.

As Barbara knocked on his door, taking care not to disturb the rock 'n' roll collage, she heard the twitchy guitar strains of Hendrix's "Foxy Lady."

"I'm playing your song," Rip said as she walked in.

Barbara took the seat across from his desk. "Can I see the ratings?"

"Well, good morning to you, too," said Danko, slowly reaching behind his chair to turn the turntable's volume down. She was being aggressive, but she also knew how it went in television: you needed to capitalize on ratings success. She'd been at the Phoenix for a year and largely because of the lame stories they covered so amateurishly, she had failed to attract ratings or Cal's notice.

The phone rang and Danko frowned as he picked up. "Their wedding was in May."

As he hung up, a second extension lit up and Danko answered, "The plane was his—he owned it."

"Lazy little shits," Danko muttered as he hung up. But he was regarded as the guy in the newsroom with encyclopedic knowledge—why look something up when you could just ask him? It had been the same for him when they worked at *The Buzz.*

Spiro Agnew, dead or alive?

Danko: *Dead*

Capitol of Ethiopia?

Danko: *Addis Ababa.*

A writer, irritated by Rip's instant monosyllabic answers, threw down the gauntlet.

Fluffer Nutter sandwich. One part nutter, two parts fluffer?

Danko: *You should know that one, seeing as you're the expert on fluff, asshole.*

Barbara smiled at the memory as the phone rang again and this time, Rip let it ring, saying, "I'm not answering another Grant Danes trivia question."

"Good," said Barbara, rising from her chair to stand behind him so she could see his computer screen. "So how'd we do?"

"Down girl," said Danko, his round glasses at the tip of his nose now as he scrolled through seemingly indecipherable columns of numbers.

The Phoenix's daytime ratings often registered "hash marks" because the viewership hadn't even reached 100,000 people to be recorded as the lowest possible rating of a ".1." Cal's "No Filters, No Fluff" news channel had launched two years ago but was only now getting press because the blatantly political (with the exception of Ironsides' 7 p.m. straight summary) prime-time shows were threatening their competition. Cal had been prescient: he had recognized that cable television would be the home of niche programming. Phoenix viewers were grateful to see stories they couldn't find on other channels: reports on children who refused to stop saying "God" when pledging allegiance, profiles of Up-With-Abstinence teens, interviews with citizens who refused to remove neon crèches from their lawns at

Christmastime. Cynics teased that the Phoenix transmitted its signal from a lair inside a volcano where an eye-patch-wearing Cal, sitting in a motorized chair, programmed his hosts' every word. But Cal just chuckled, telling the critics his prime-time pundits were merely the television equivalent of a newspaper's editorial page.

Barbara was skeptical when she was first offered her job anchoring dayside at the Phoenix. Every news operation she'd ever worked for—from her high school newspaper to her all-news radio station—prided itself upon being apolitical, and she ardently believed in presenting both sides of a story, playing it down the middle. Before accepting the job offer from the Phoenix, she watched the daytime coverage and was soon convinced there was no diabolical plan afoot to spread conservative politics. It seemed the channel was just desperately trying to fill 8 hours of programming.

The folksy segments were balanced—two guests with opposing opinions would fill more time than just one guest with a conservative viewpoint. Daytime pundits didn't have to be Republican, just blonde and feisty. Foreign affairs experts gave neutral assessments on international imbroglios, not because they were trained diplomats, but because they were thrown on the air before they had time to compose cogent thoughts.

So the *No Filters* part of Cal's slogan was true enough. Not so much though for the *No Fluff* claim. D-list actors' desperation for the spotlight was the perfect fit for a channel that sorely needed guests. Problem was, the more washed-up they were, the worse they behaved. Some refused to talk about the role for which they were famous. An aging nighttime soap star, best known for her fight scenes in pools, insisted on talking only about her *art*, her novel. A former pop sensation who used two names now and only wanted to be interviewed about her animal rights activism stormed out of the station when a booker told her she'd be asked about her singing. The truly hard up pilfered food from the greenroom: a formerly famous dancer was spotted leaving the Phoenix with a couple of crullers peaking out of her pocketbook.

The only comforting thought was that few were watching.

"Let's see," said Danko, pointing at the numbers on his computer screen. "You started Saturday morning at 8 and...." But Barbara had already processed the numbers for her on-air hours. "I got a .8 in the noon! That's better than Spencer's hours and tied with Ironsides' 7 p.m.!" She slapped Rip on the back, saying, "And you produced the noon. Told you we were a good team!"

"Easy, baby," he said, leaning back in his chair. "You know my philosophy on ratings: Don't take credit, don't take blame."

"Yeah, yeah," she said, heading for the door and stopping to give Rip a little shimmy. "Hey, Ironsides, *I'm comin' to get ya!*"

After that morning's show, *Grant Danes: Icy Wing, Doomed Flight,* Barbara decided to pay Cal a visit, not to complain about the tasteless play-on-movie-title a writer had chosen for the continuing coverage, but to tout her weekend ratings. This way she'd get Cal to think of her as an anchor who drew viewers, an anchor who would deliver numbers in prime time. She rode the elevator up to the 25th floor, and walked confidently toward the security guard who returned her big smile. He must have recognized her from television.

"Good morning, young lady, may I help you?" Surely this guard, probably a former cop who had to trade toughness for obsequiousness, was making a little joke, pretending not to know her.

"I'm here to see Mr. Carmichael?" she said, certain that would trigger recognition. Who, but an anchor, one of the Phoenix's talent, could stroll in and expect to see the boss.

"And you are?"

Barbara, holding her shoulders back, refusing to admit defeat, continued to smile at the guard when he told her that Mr. Carmichael's assistant "suggests you call for an appointment."

Barbara returned to her office and closed the door, finally able to frown. She punched in Cal's extension to set up a meeting and he himself picked up after the first ring.

"Barbara King, so sorry I missed you. Meetings! They keep me in meetings all day!" Whoever *they* were surely couldn't force him to do anything, but it was a charmingly humble stance. And he wanted to talk to her. He'd probably been dazzled by her fluent ad-libbing and intelligent interviewing during the Danes coverage and was going to tell her, *Thatta girl, Babs! Looks like you're well on your way to anchoring prime time!*

Barbara sat up in her chair, crossed her legs and smoothed out her skirt as if she were on the set. "Cal, I wanted to talk about those weekend numbers...they were really...."

"Spectacular!" he boomed. "They were spectacular! Our prime time's within a whisker of the competition now, and I'm glad you called, Barbara, because I have some terrific news for dayside. We've hired Jack Stone away from the competition and he's going to co-anchor with you on dayside!"

Prime time's ratings were good? Jack *Who*? And did he just say *CO-ANCHOR*?

"You mean co-anchoring, as in anchoring another show on dayside or..."

"Oh, ho ho, no, he's going to be anchoring the 9 to 11 with you! He'll be your new partner, your television husband, if you will. Think of it, Barbara. Any of those eyeballs who used to watch him on the competition will follow him to the Phoenix."

Barbara sagged in her chair. "But I thought my hours were doing well...I've been meaning to talk to you about..."

"Barbara, dear, you're doing a marvelous job for us. No one believes me when I say this, but we are on our way to number one. And part of our success, aside from solid journalism, of course, is casting."

"But Cal, I'm...."

"Disappointed? Now, Barbara, I know anchors don't like to share the spotlight. But you and Jack are going to be swell together. Trust me."

"It's just that..."

"You weren't expecting this. I know, I know. But perhaps there's something I could do for you to soften the blow?"

How 'bout not giving me a co-anchor?, Barbara thought. But Cal obviously wasn't asking her, he was telling her how it was going to be. She sat up.

"It would be wonderful to have a designated producer, Cal. On Saturday, during that hour when my numbers were as high as prime time, Rip Danko was producing and I thought..."

"Oh, you're the crafty one, Barbara, bringing Clarence out of his semi-retirement. Ho, ho! I'll see what I can do. Now, in the meantime, I'm going to put you on with my girl who'll fill you in on the new co-anchor arrangements."

Arrangement was right. Her *TV husband*? The Phoenix hadn't even auditioned them together to see if they were compatible—it was an arranged marriage, for crying out loud!

At other stations, pairing anchors was a serious business, a near-scientific process. Several combinations of anchors would read together, on camera, and then, after a scrupulous review of the tapes, management would decide which two had the best chemistry, and audition that couple further. Once christened "The Team," the anchors would have their publicity shots taken, with their arms folded or, if they had a more playful relationship, leaning against each other, one posed with hand-in-pocket.

Promos would be shot with cameras trailing the anchors as they walked determinedly through the newsroom, stopping to put on their reading glasses and examining copy, and then turning to the camera to spew profundities such as *News matters. You matter. We know you know news matters. And that's why we matter to you.*

When she heard Cal's assistant come back on the line, Barbara asked her when she and her new co-anchor would start.

"Tomorrow," she said. "But first, Mr. Carmichael wants to spice up your look a bit. Hair and makeup's been told."

Before heading down to hair and makeup, Barbara called Rip.

"Sold me down the river," he said when he picked up.

"Oh, come on, Rip, it'll be fun. Did you really want to do schedules and have to explain to teenagers in the newsroom that Jethro Tull isn't a hillbilly?"

"I guess not," he laughed. "It won't be the worst thing, being around you again."

"Being around me and this Jack Stone character, whoever he is. By the way, did you know about this?"

"About what?"

"About what," she mocked.

"Stone? Nah. Cal mentioned something about a 'player to be named later' on dayside but he never said who it was and he never mentioned your slot."

"What do you know about him?"

"Hosted some weekend crime show for the other guys. One of these reporters who tags along with the cops, rides with 'em. Fill-in anchor too, I think. I'll find out what I can about him, okay, baby?"

"Okay," she sighed. "I'm going to work my own sources now."

CHAPTER 6

Barbara charged into hair and makeup where Angelica and Jane were already waiting for her, black lab coats on. Angelica handed Barbara a robe and started combing her out. Jane, the operating room nurse, gathered up a handful of foils to hand to Angelica. Angelica expertly pulled strands of Barbara's long red hair and held them taut, dipped a small paintbrush into a vat of a white paste and coated the hair, then wrapped it in foils which she folded into neat rows.

Barbara didn't mind the makeover. She'd been given a "look" before; her previous network had sent her to a Madison Avenue salon where the shop's half-poodle, half-man owner promptly told her she needed to be redder. "Think Nicole Kidman." When she weakly joked that Nicole would resent the comparison, he said, "I *know* you could never look anything like her!" And when she added she couldn't wear her hair too long, she was a news anchor after all, he yipped, "I don't care what you do for a living! I'm telling you how you can look good!"

"They want you to look spicy. Cinammon-y. You cool with that?" asked Angelica as she tamped down a foil with her teasing comb. "They want you lighter 'cause the new guy has dark hair."

Jane pushed her Buddy Holly glasses up her nose and looked at Angelica apprehensively, probably wondering if Barbara was going to throw an anchor "how dare you objectify me" hissy fit.

"It's fine. I know you'll make me look great," said Barbara. "So come on, give it up—what to you know about this Jack Stone?"

Jane exhaled and postulated a conspiracy: "Could it be they only gave you a day's fucking notice because he has a...past...a bad reputation?"

Angelica took another foil out of Jane's hand and, shaking her head said, "Not true, Jane. Girlfriend of mine freelances at the competition and did him a couple of times."

"Shagged?!" asked Jane.

"Did his makeup," Angelica corrected.

"Oh," Barbara and Jane said at the same time.

"Says he's okay. Doesn't fuss over his looks. Polite. And does not *shag* around on his wife." Despite her catwalk looks, Angelica was prim; Barbara sometimes found her in her leather chair, reading a well-worn Bible during breaks.

"Not to challenge your sources, Ang—but how does she know that?" asked Barbara.

"Well," said Angelica, calmly coating another lock of hair, "This friend of mine is...well...she's built like Jane."

To demonstrate, Jane ran a hand over her own ample chest which made her look like a buxom bird filled with song. F-bomb-laced song.

"And unlike those of us who cover up with our robes," continued Angelica, "this girl likes to shove her chest into the talent's face when she's powdering them."

"Naughty minx," said Jane.

"But she says Stone never looked twice at her," Angelica explained, as Jane handed her the last of the foils and retreated to her station.

After Angelica set the egg timer for Barbara's hair, she studied Barbara.

"I'm not happy about this," said Barbara.

"It's not gonna take away from you." Angelica knew of Barbara's ambitions. "If you play along, Cal won't forget."

"Well, I just don't want this guy to jump the line. I don't want to wind up as his sidekick, you know? I don't want him to think I'm some sort of anchor-bimbo. He needs to know I'm a force to be reckoned with!"

The greenroom door opened and Barbara heard footsteps, then a man's baritone. "Anybody home?"

Barbara gasped. That sure sounded like an anchor voice. With her eyes wide and head full of foils, Barbara looked like a giant sunflower. She grabbed Angelica's arm and they listened as Jane walked into the greenroom and said, "May I help you?"

"Hi. I'm Jack Stone, the new anchor. I'm supposed to have a publicity shot taken and Mr. Carmichael's office sent me down here for some powder and spray."

Barbara grabbed the hair spray from Angelica's console and shoved it into her hand and started pushing her toward the curtain as Jane said, "I'm Jane. Makeup. But you'd best get your spray first—let me introduce you to Angelica and...your new co-anchor."

Barbara furiously shook her foils "no," creating a rattling sound, but Jack was already opening Angelica's curtain.

"I'm Angelica, Mr. Stone and this," she said, extending a graceful arm toward Barbara, "is Barbara King."

Barbara tried to strike a sophisticated pose in Angelica's reclining chair by crossing her legs. She tried to rise, but her robe hitched up and she had to tug down on it.

Jack bent down. "That's okay, don't get up," he said, looking at her as if trying to place her. He was tall, not like so many

Lilliputian television people who had to sit on phone books behind the anchor desk. His hair was nearly ink black and pin straight. Oh, and he was handsome; plenty of television anchors were just shy of out-and-out handsome. He was not shy of that at all.

"Nice to meet you, Jack," said Barbara. Instead of getting up to shake his hand, she turned on her side, probably looking like she was posing for a nude portrait.

"I'm sorry to interrupt," he said. "I can see you're...."

Barbara pulled on one of her foils, holding it in the air, "Trying to make contact with Mars?"

Jack looked at her quizzically as Angelica jumped in, "Why don't we head over to Jane's station, Jack—I can give you some spray over there."

As they left, Barbara's foils crunched as she sank back in her chair.

Mars?

CHAPTER 7

The next morning, the day of their on-air debut, Barbara decided to pay Jack Stone a visit. She'd gone straight to hair and makeup that morning. After being caught looking like a foiled freak she didn't want to look anything less than professional. She'd picked out a navy pinstripe suit which had just the right amount of sartorial machismo. And it offset her new "look": wavy hair with a softer tone of red sprinkled with gold, heavier eyeliner and fake lashes, and large-as-collagen-injected lips. "Viva Las Fucking Vegas," Jane had proclaimed when they were done. She and Angelica truly were magicians.

Jack hadn't seemed too friendly yesterday and yet who could blame him for not laughing at her lame "Mars" joke. Maybe he just had the new hire jitters. Be a team player, friendly, welcoming, Barbara told herself. Cal will reward you for being a go-along, get-along girl. She walked down the hallway and saw the silver slats where Jack's nameplate would soon be placed, and knocked on the door.

"It's open," came the deep voice from his office.

Barbara opened the door. "Hi Jack. I know we're on deadline, but I just wanted to say 'hello' before we make our debut together." She stayed by the door, not knowing if he'd invite her in. "Glad we got to do all those practice reads together, huh?"

Jack let out a disgusted sigh. "Please, come in." She took a few steps closer to his desk.

He didn't offer her a seat. "I must tell you that I'm pretty frosted that management thrust this schedule upon us so abruptly," he enunciated as if he was on television. And *frosted?* Jack stood up and reached into a cardboard moving box with dozens of silk ties, a rainbow of color, but heavy on the greens—no doubt to match his eyes. His starched white shirt was buttoned to the top and his black hair had an immaculate side part; he was clean shaven but by the end of the day, stubble would probably cast a dark shadow.

"I guess that's how it goes in cable, huh?" said Barbara.

"Yes, showbiz," he said, leaning on the "z" sound contemptuously. He selected a navy tie, draped it around his neck, and looked at his computer screen. He didn't want to play.

"I hear you came from that *other* cable channel," Barbara tried anyway.

"Yes. I hosted a crime show and did some anchoring as well, but when I met Cal at a business function this spring, he made me an offer my former channel simply could not match."

As he spoke, Barbara took inventory of the pictures he'd already moved onto the shelves of the bookcase in his office: Jack arm in arm with a man who looked like an older version of him; Jack barely smiling next to the same older man pointing to the front page of a newspaper; a shot of Jack in a tuxedo, shaking a U.S. senator's hand; a young Jack in a sweatsuit and goggle-topped swim cap, his arm raised in the air by a jubilant coach. And on a cabinet behind his desk, two pictures: a little girl in a fancy dress, and an 8 x 10 black-and-white profile of a beautiful woman with long, straight, dark hair. Had to be the wife. But was she an actress or something—why the head shot?

Jack got up to grab some papers from the printer in his office, dropping a few as he placed them on his desk. Barbara took another step toward him and placed the morning rundown on his desk.

"I didn't know if you'd seen this. Thought I'd drop it off. Not much of a rundown, really—it's a little helter skelter around here sometimes."

Jack sat back down and read it, as Barbara read it upside down along with him.

Guest segments:

Psychologist t.b.a.—Al Gore's body language during concession speech

Former ambassador t.b.a. on what's ahead for Yugoslavia in the new year

Entertainment segment t.b.a.—Grant Danes's top 10 movies

Inauguration preview: have your own inauguration party right at home!

Guest Information:

TALENT: Stone/King

TOPIC: Kosovo

GUEST: Former U.N. Ambassador Slovodan Msyrskiezkwyrkchek (pronounced: MEEbsheh-RISKY-kwirk-CHK)

PRE-INTERVIEW NOTES: Pre-interview to be conducted this a.m.

RESEARCH: See producer

Jack shook his head. "Is this some sort of initiation prank?"

Barbara was tempted to say, *Thank You Sir, may I have another?* but figured it would fall flat. "Um no, I'm afraid it's for real. Things will get better though when Danko starts producing our show. He's taking a few days of R & R." He was in Woodstock.

"Well," said Jack, pushing the rundown aside and inching his chair up closer to his computer, "I'll see you on the set?"

"Sure thing," she said, and walked briskly out of his office.

What a stiff. He practically kicked her out—she wasn't going to hang around and chitty-chat—she had things to do too. And *an offer they couldn't match*. They were probably paying him more than her to do the same job.

A couple of hours later, Barbara walked to the set and Jack was already there. Two chairs—of nearly barstool height—had been placed next to each other. And on either side of the chairs were two small round tables, each one equipped with a laptop. Computers aside, it looked like a set up for two cabaret singers to perform a duet.

Jack, back straight, was turned toward his computer, probably proofing copy, when Barbara ascended the steps. *8:58:00 a.m.* The morning show that preceded theirs and broadcast from a separate studio had just tossed to the two-minute commercial break. That could mean 120 seconds of awkward, off-air anchor chatter. Let him initiate it this time, Barbara thought. I tried to be nice this earlier this morning.

Jack gave Barbara a quick nod and cordial smile as she sat down next to him. Jesus, who moved the barstools so close together? But that was another thing about co-anchoring: management liked to make you sit practically on top of each other so even if you hated each other's guts, you'd at least be close, literally.

Barbara busied herself by scanning her hard copy and scrolling through a few scripts in the computer. Should she say something to him? He certainly wasn't trying to break the ice. But at least he wasn't one of these anchors who primped on the set beforehand, always asking to see their shot in the monitor and running their hands through their hair like they were a cast member of *Grease*.

Tex asked if they needed anything—some water? They both politely shook their heads no and then Jack asked, "This set is actually moving?" And then, smiling at Barbara a little, he added, "Unless that's another rite of initiation."

She laughed. "No, it's true."

"Took an ambulance call once," Tex interjected. "Some fraternity initiation. Guy had to have a beer funnel removed from his…."

JACKANDBARBARALISTENUP!

The producer who mumbled was screaming into their earpieces.

"A minute back," said Tex and he walked over to a television next to one of their cameras and hit the remote until the screen had live pictures of a car racing down a wide roadway.

THROWINGOUTTHERUNDOWNGOINGWITH THECARCHASE.

Barbara looked at Jack and said, "How 'bout I start, welcome you, and then…

"…I'll pick up wherever you leave off," he said.

Barbara leaned over to his computer and said, "If you hit that key with the lightning bolt on it, it'll bring up all the latest from the Phoenix satellite desk—not that there's going to be much."

Jack nodded and they both started scanning their computers.

HAPPENINGINLOSANGELESWILLGETYOUMOREINFO!

"Fifteen seconds," said Tex, "They wanna open on a two-shot of you guys, then take the live car pix full."

A car chase. Ratings gold. The whole newsroom would be watching their show—not because it was the first time Barbara and Jack were on air together, but because no one would turn away when the car could crash into a concrete wall, or the suspect could ditch his car and run off naked.

GOINGON7SECONDDELAY!

Viewers would be seeing their broadcast delayed by 7 seconds, so if this suspect did anything crazy (strip, scream profanities) or violent (kill himself, a bystander, or a cop), the control room would be able to cut away from the disturbing pictures before they aired.

"Five, four, three,...." said Tex, as Barbara pulled her eyes away from her computer screen, sat up straight in her barstool and crossed her legs—since there was no desk in front of them, they'd be seen head-to-toe on the two-shot. The bulletin sound-effect whooshed.

A Phoenix News Flash. Good morning, I'm Barbara King welcoming Jack Stone to our news team on a busy morning. A car chase is underway right now in Los Angeles.

Jack picked up.

Thanks, Barbara. We want to take you live to the freeway in the San Fernando valley where the driver behind the wheel of that white Ford flatbed truck is leading police on a high-speed chase.

Okay. He didn't make a big deal of his introduction, didn't try to drag out his hello to get more face-time; he called for the live shot right away. Barbara continued and they alternated lines.

We have information that the suspect is wanted for questioning in a domestic dispute.

And that's why police are going to have to proceed with extra caution in bringing this to a conclusion.

Exactly. Typically, Jack, the California Highway Patrol will try to use a pit maneuver to stop the suspect.

Yes, and they'll likely use quite a bit of manpower when this does come to an end—it might seem odd to a viewer to see so many officers trying to apprehend one suspect, but as I'm sure you know, Barbara, a suspect's adrenaline often necessitates such measures.

The car chase ended an hour-and-a-half later. The suspect ran a few red lights, crossed into the opposite lane of traffic a couple of times and yes, did need to be tackled by seven officers, but didn't perform any more lurid acts. When Barbara and Jack tossed to the first commercial break at 10:32 a.m., cheers went up in the newsroom. Tex held his hands up as if he were pushing back a crowd and said, "Alright. Calm yourselves down."

When the show was over, Barbara and Jack quietly left the set so Lois Spencer and Will Topper could begin their two hours. Barbara would swear that Lois looked annoyed that the suspect hadn't saved his run at freedom for her on-air hours. Barbara walked through the newsroom and out the door that led to their offices. She heard Jack behind her, quickening his step.

"Quite the debut," she said, slowing down so they could walk side by side down the hallway. She had to give Jack credit. Many anchors faced with a breaking story would have stumbled and stammered, or nervously adjusted their clothing for the two hours, or asked for more powder or water or information, please, please, from the control room. Others would have been mic hogs—spewing every iota of the scant information so there was nothing left for their co-anchor to say.

Jack's eyes were shining; he clearly found breaking news as exhilarating as she did. "You, Ms. King, are certainly as cool as you are fluent under fire. They can't teach you that in journalism school," he said.

He'd cut right to what she prided herself upon: the ability to think on her feet. Her training in radio had taught her to be self-reliant, to cull her own material, learn it, and then ad-lib about it, without the aid of pictures, by the way. It was nice that

Jack appreciated it, but she wasn't sure she wanted him to see her beaming.

She stopped at her office and put the key in the door, speaking into the handle. "Well, the good news, about the rundowns here? Is that most days, they get thrown out."

"The more breaking news, the better," he said, as he continued walking down the hallway to his office.

"Careful what you wish for!" she called after him.

That night at home, Barbara and Ben sat on their leather sectional couch, her legs stretched out on the couch's chaise section and Ben's head in her lap as they watched TV. Barbara made it a policy not to torment herself by watching the Phoenix prime time she so coveted; instead they watched a tape on the VCR of her favorite show, the cruelly-cancelled *Freaks and Geeks*. In this episode, the character Barbara liked best, the good student Lindsay, was coming to the sad realization that the sort of cute, burnout drummer, Nick, was not her cup of tea, romantically.

During the commercial, Barbara said, "I still don't like the idea of a co-anchor at all. Even if he's good."

"A lot of the big stars were co-anchors once...even your Barbara Walters, no?"

"That was a disaster," she said, "But you're right."

"Come on, put it out of your mind. At least he's not flatulent."

Barbara laughed at the memory of entering their college radio station studio after a certain bean-aficionado anchor had finished his shift. "As far as I can tell, this one has mastery of his bowels," she said.

"Well, give him a chance," said Ben, "you might wind up liking him more than you think."

Barbara kissed Ben's hair and they turned back to the travails of 80s high schoolers.

CHAPTER 8

A week later, the Phoenix had finally exhausted its Grant Danes coverage, and everyone was aflutter, wondering which anchor would get the big new year's eve assignment in Times Square. Barbara, of course, wanted it and hoped the new year would mean a promotion up and out of dayside. She'd been languishing in dayside for a year, but the rigors of her shift left little time for Walter Mitty–style fantasies about the day Bill "Ironsides" Hunter would wheel off the set (which not only moved, but included a retractable ramp), hand her his copy and say, *It's your time, now, Babs.*

The knock on her door at 7:16 on this particular morning was not part of her hectic routine of reading, writing, and researching to prep for interviews. Maybe it was Danko, who had looked spent when he returned from Woodstock, but had eventually shaved and started producing their new co-anchor show.

"If you're looking for Max Yasgur, he's down the road a little ways, Danko," she called through the door which was slightly ajar.

As the door opened, she saw the starched white dress shirt and realized her mistake. "Oh, hi, Jack," she said, "I thought you might be Danko."

"I just ran into Rip in the newsroom," he said, still standing in the doorway, a lock of dark hair falling onto his forehead. "He was in the middle of one of his 'challenges' if you will. Someone had a question about the Mexican volcano and that led to Rip's recitation of the world's top ten active volcanoes."

"Classic Danko," said Barbara, wondering why Jack had stopped by. She didn't like cutting into her quiet study hall time and she was dying to dive into her egg sandwich. "Would you like to come in?"

"No, I'm afraid I've digressed. Rip asked that I tell you there's going to be a meeting in the conference room at 7:30 this morning."

"Why?" asked Barbara. She looked at the digital time in the corner of her computer screen. 7:18. She wouldn't even have time to change out of her sweatshirt and jeans, let alone get any hair and makeup done before the meeting.

"I don't know," said Jack. "The scant speculation I overheard is that Cal has an announcement. I'll save you a seat," he said, closing her office door.

Maybe Cal would finally announce the Times Square assignment, thought Barbara. And as for Jack, why, he'd become right friendly since that first *frosty* encounter in his office. Was he really going to "save her a seat" or had he merely meant it like "see you there"?

When Barbara opened the door to the conference room, she immediately saw Jack at the far end of the long oval table, his arm draped casually over the empty chair next to him. She hesitated, but he caught her eye and took his arm off the chair. Barbara nodded and, still in her casual attire, sat down next to him, feeling Lois Spencer's eyes following her. Spencer, in full anchor regalia, sat at the opposite side of the table, boring a hole in the front page of the *Wall Street Journal* with her brown button eyes. Barbara remembered the first time they met they were both decked out in sweat suits.

When Barbara worked at *The Buzz,* she'd been invited to co-emcee a walkathon with local television news personality Lois Spencer. It was awkward; Barbara could tell that no one assembled in Battery Park knew who she was.

Thanks so much to all of you for coming out on this beautiful Sunday morning...It's...

Lois grabbed the mic and threw her arm around Barbara as if they were longtime gal pals. Her eyes, the whites consumed by her exceptionally large irises, had an expressionless, yet crazed gleam to them.

...a great day for a walkathon, isn't it?!! We are going to walk the walk today, aren't we?!!

Midway through her crowd-pleasing platitudes, Lois removed her arm from her dear friend, Barbara, who nodded and grinned at the audience like some village idiot who had mistakenly wandered up to the podium. Lois prowled the stage, lathering up the crowd, imploring them to beat whatever ailment it was that prevented otherwise privileged children from enjoying certain snacks. But then, during mile two of ten, just as Barbara was unwrapping an allergen-free fruit roll, she spotted Lois driving off in a limo.

Bitch bailed.

This morning, Lois was wearing a golden yellow suit with brown patches for pockets and with her thatch of dark hair and long neck, she looked like nothing so much as a giraffe. The News Giraffe: News 'R' Us. But Barbara couldn't completely hate Lois. Apparently she hadn't always been such a hard case; Angelica and Jane reported Lois had once been wildly, passionately in love with her camera man. There were even unsubstantiated rumors of "if this van's a rockin', don't go a-knockin'" ardor in the news mobile. They were about to be engaged when he was killed in an accident racing to the scene of a breaking story in the Bronx. Not long after, Lois met her agent boyfriend Arthur—even his name sounded old—at a business luncheon. Angelica termed it a business arrangement. When Barbara offered, "Maybe it's love?" Angelica said, "You seen what he looks like?"

The conference room was filling up and Barbara could hear Danko was on the call from his office. Either he had a bag of cats in there, or Neil Young was on his turntable. He had deemed "Cinnamon Girl" Barbara's new, post-makeover "theme song."

Cal joined the call from his perch on the 25th floor. "Good morning, campers!" Even though he couldn't see them through the phone, Cal's perky canteen boy salutation made everyone in the room sit up.

"I have three announcements!" Cal sounded more revved than usual. "First, congratulations are in order this morning! Can anyone guess how many homes we have now?"

Silence. Was he talking viewers—cable television had its own terminology—or was he talking the number of vacation homes he and his wife owned?

"Since you're all still sleepy, I'll tell you! 40 million homes now have access to the Phoenix News Channel. That's 4-0! Americans are telling their cable operators they want their news straight up—No Filters, No Fluff! We are on our way to making the Phoenix America's #1 news channel."

Tepid applause. It was early for a pep rally, plus, no one really believed the Phoenix could ever be number one.

"And second, as part of a new focus on dayside, I'm implementing a morning meeting and conference call—right here at 7:30—same time, same place, same channel—ho, ho!—so we can review dayside's rundowns each day."

Well, that sucks, thought Barbara. She'd have to add another race to and from the conference room to her routine.

"And last, but certainly not least, I'm excited to announce that Sloane Davis will be joining the weekday producing team, working with Lois and Will."

Sloane?! Turns out she'd been sitting, concealed from view behind large Lois, in one of the chairs against the conference room wall. Sloane leaned from side to side, waving with her little hand, then pushed the pencil further behind her ear and handed Lois a piece of paper, apparently to demonstrate just the sort of duties she'd be performing for *her* anchor.

"Alright then," Cal continued when no one clapped, "Clarence, let's start with you. What dynamic segments do we have lined up for dayside today?"

Will Topper suddenly joined the call from a windy-sounding location. "Topper here. On my way into the studio. Any big interviews in the 11?"

Lois rolled her eyes and let out a sigh that Topper could probably hear even if he was actually in some babe's bed with a fan blowing on him—any club he'd partied in would be closed by now.

"Danko," Lois jumped in, craning her long neck toward the phone in the middle of the conference table. "The entertainment guest in the 9 o'clock show is a former 1970s sitcom star. But that segment would work really well during my midday hours—it's perfect for our demographic. I've told booking to switch it to the noon hour."

Told? That segment should be mine, Barbara thought—I've seen every episode of that sitcom. The News Giraffe was eating from her guest tree!

Barbara moved to the edge of her seat, so she'd be as close to the phone as Lois. "We're counting on that guest for the 9 and...."

"But," said Lois, practically coming out of her chair, "A nostalgic segment like that would be perfect for our core audience and..."

Sloane, like a kid asking the people at the grown-up table to pass the mashed potatoes, popped out from behind Lois and waved again, interjecting, "We need the segment because it would appeal to our demographic."

"Our demo's the same!" Barbara snapped.

"Let's put the sitcom star in the noon," Danko broke in before the hoop earrings could come off. "Barb, we have a comedian booked—we'll put him in the 9."

Cal quickly adjourned the meeting, leaving Barbara with the better-known D-lister and leaving everyone still wondering who'd get the big assignment on New Year's Eve.

CHAPTER 9

Later that morning, when Barbara hustled down to hair and makeup, Angelica told her she'd just missed Spencer. "Jane had to do her today."

Lois typically had her own "people," Willy and Celia (aka Wilhelm und Grace) to do her hair and makeup. Willy was a built, butch Bavarian, who called everyone *Schatzi* and *Mausi* but gave them the follicular equivalent of a fisting by violently combing and curling and teasing their hair, then leaving them gagging in a cloud of hair spray. *Wundershon!* he'd exclaim when he was finished. And Celia had several gold teeth which she revealed when she laughed at things that weren't meant to be funny.

Celia, could I get some powder?

Ah ha ha ha ha!

Her English was a stew of languages and utterly incomprehensible, but one thing was clear, she was in love with Willy. They were a team and Lois had demanded they come with her when she was hired at the Phoenix; her local fan base expected her to have a "consistent look." One condition of their employment was to handle touch-ups on the set and sub for Jane and Angelica, who Barbara decided were *not* allowed to take days off.

"Lucky Jane," said Barbara ruefully. "She get any 411?"

"Lois was on the phone with her boyfriend, talking about New Year's," said Angelica. "But Jane couldn't tell if she was going to Times Square or not. You still have a chance."

"Yeah, no one knows. We were too busy at the morning meeting fighting over has-beens. I get to interview a comedian who wants to talk about the very serious issue of insomnia."

Angelica leaned in and whispered, "Careful—I hear he likes the hooch."

"Great. Let's just hope he doesn't finally fall asleep on the set."

It was 10:45, just 15 minutes left in the show, and Slappy Smith, who'd originally been scheduled for 9:50, was nowhere to be found.

Tex pondered the finer points of insomnia. "Once, there was this ambulance call. Had to pull a stiff out of his car. Drove it into a pole. Hadn't slept in days. Insomnia. Finally fell asleep." He gave his Fu Manchu a tug. "At the wheel."

At 10:49, the *funnyman,* as the copy had it, finally made it onto the set. Slappy was ancient. No wonder he didn't sleep—old people didn't need to, right? His jacket was worn at the wrists and speckled with dandruff at the shoulders. When Barbara noticed his shoes fastened with Velcro straps, a wave of pity welled within her.

When the comedian turned his back, Tex jerked his thumb toward him and pantomimed throwing a drink down his throat. Angelica was right.

"Hey, this thing moves!" Slappy remarked about the rotating set, not making eye contact with Barbara. And he thought he just had a case of the twirlies. "Nice studio you got here," he added, the "here" emitting a vapor of alcohol.

Tex gave the count and when the red light came on, Slappy Smith was transformed: alert and smiling a giant yellowing smile, gazing at Barbara admiringly. One of these guys who saves it all for the show.

"Nice to be with you, Red—mind if I call you Red? Not Red like Red Skelton—you're much prettier than him! You're no Clem Kadiddlehopper!" Barbara imagined the younger spectrum of their audience collectively turning off their televisions.

"Before we talk about insomnia," Barbara started, "I hear there's a DVD release of your stand-up classics from the 1960s. Do you miss those days?"

A string of spittle expanded in the corner of Slappy's mouth as he opened it to answer. "Oh, Beverly, I miss the crowds, but life on the road is hard."

"Do you think having lived that life makes it hard to settle in for a good night's sleep? Tell us about your campaign to get the word out about insomnia."

Slappy looked at her blankly.

"You know Red," he started. Okay, back to Red. "When I was on the road, I used to come home very late at night..."

She nodded sympathetically.

"... and I did everything I could not to wake the wife up. I turned the headlights off when I came in the driveway. Took my shoes off before walking up the stairs. I got undressed in the bathroom. When I got in bed I snuck under the covers..." he leaned in to her.

Gin. Definitely Gin. And mothballs.

"And the wife," he continued, "She always woke up and yelled at me for being out too late!"

Good Lord, where was he going with this?

"But I finally found a way to get the wife to stop yelling!" he continued, shimmying his shoulders a bit.

"Oh?" Better let him go on. Anyone who was still watching probably wanted to hear him say something funny.

"A friend told me the cure. Told me he stays out 'til all hours without waking up the wife and getting hollered at. He says to me: 'I come screeching into the driveway, I clomp up the steps, I turn on the lights, I plunk down on the bed, grab my wife and say, 'HOW BOUT A BLOW JOB?' And guess what? She's always sound asleep!"

A roar went up in the newsroom as Slappy slapped his knee with a dash of vaudevillian flair, wheezed, and grinned directly into the camera. Tex made a chopping motion across his neck to let Barbara know it was okay to cut to commercial. Jack, seated at a satellite news desk adjacent to the set, had his head down and his shoulders were shaking. The director cut to Barbara on a single shot. With an expression she hoped would convey *I am so terribly sorry we subjected you to that,* said, "We'll leave it there and be right back after a quick break."

Back in her office after the show, Barbara called Ben to tell him what had happened. "A lousy 3 minutes to interview him and he tells a dirty joke?" For Ben, the greater crime was that the medium didn't allow for more depth. But he laughed when she said she hoped Rory had instead been watching *Zoboomafoo.*

After she hung up, Barbara logged on to her computer and saw the instant message cue flashing. Producers, writers, overseas correspondents, even bureau chiefs—everyone was suddenly a funnyman.

The FCC's on line two for you, Red.

Hi Beverly! Hope you're able to get a good night's sleep after that interview!

Guess what? Cal's changing our slogan. No Filters, No Fluff, No Fellatio (jokes).

Clem Kaddidle-who?

From Danko:

You really bring out the beast in a geezer.

Her reply:

You should know.

From Cal:

My dear old friend Slappy just called to apologize. That scoundrel!

Phew. He wasn't angry with her for letting a dick joke be told on the air.

And then from Jack.

I have intelligence that Slappy is at the Pepperpot. If you'd like to head over there, I'd be happy to hold him down while you... er...slap him. Once again, you were grace under pressure. And you are indeed much prettier than Red Skelton.

Barbara smiled. What a flirt. But she wasn't headed to the Pepperpot; she was on her way to her agent's office to try to get that New Year's assignment before Lois outfoxed her.

CHAPTER 10

"Horsefuck!" Gene screamed as he slammed his phone down and waved Barbara over from the doorway where she stood next to his cowering male assistant.

Barbara had never cared much for Gene Cline, but as he himself would have said, he wasn't in the business to be liked. Near freakishly tall and gaunt but with a history of heart trouble, he was an agent-as-adversary. With the exception of his cowboy boots, Gene had shaken the dust off his country-western heritage and, "horsefuck" aside, had adopted the vocabulary and mien of a city slicker representative.

"Tough day, Gene?" Barbara asked, taking the very large chair opposite his desk. He seemed to like people to feel like Edith Ann when they faced him.

"Yeah and it ain't...it's not over yet," he said, shuffling some papers on his oversized oak desk. "The schmucks at your former network decide they're 'going in a different direction.' Not going to renew my client and they don't have the balls to tell him themselves."

That certainly sounded familiar. After graduating Amherst in '88, Barbara toiled in local, then Boston radio as a street reporter and anchor before landing the morning anchor job at *The Buzz* in 1992. When she was promoted to the early morning network television show in '96, she quickly realized her glamorous TV job was just more somnambulistic up-at-1-a.m. hell. Originally, her show, *Dawn,* aired at 6 a.m. But when the affiliates clamored for that time slot so they could air local news, the network ceded the time and Barbara's show was moved to 5 a.m. and renamed *Early Dawn*. The bitter staff came up with a list of alternate show titles: *Dawn of the Dead, The Dawn Dishwashing Detergent News Hour, Dawn Go Away, You're No Good for the Network,* and the one she liked best: *Middle of the Goddamned Night.*

The show did have a history of promoting its anchors to the network's wildly popular morning talk show, so Barbara hung in, and even got to read the news updates for the big show one snowy Christmas morning. But the promotion was not to be. Instead, one morning, Barbara was walking past an edit bay and waved to a producer who met her hello with a nervous nod and then shifted his body to try to hide the monitor he was using. Curious and paranoid, as *Early Dawn's* ratings had just had a lackluster week, Barbara took a step closer so she could see the screen. Frozen on it, was a promo for the local affiliates' show with a large banner announcing a new time: 5 a.m. When Barbara set about trying to confirm her show's unceremonious cancellation, she couldn't get through to anyone in network management—*Dawn* was dead and she was dead to them.

"My former network, behaving in a cowardly fashion?" she asked Gene. "Shocking."

"So how's life at the Phoenix?" he asked, twirling a toothpick in his mouth. "Chief Walks on Wheels still hanging in?"

"I was hoping you might have some intel on that, Gene. I could also use your help with Cal—maybe you could tell him that I should be the one anchoring from Times Square next week." She sat up in the big chair and added, "I've been there a year now and I haven't made any progress toward prime time."

Gene slammed his hand down on his desk. "What you need, goddamnit, is a branded show!"

For a second, she thought he'd reverted to Western slang, but by "branded" he just meant a show with a name.

"Here's what you need to do, Barbara. Call a meeting with Cal, tell him you're a player..."

"For 10 percent of the gross, Gene, can't you do it? He's not the easiest guy in the world to meet with and you guys are friends. And besides," she said, knowing this would inflame him, "Lois Spencer's already lobbying him for the New Year's gig."

"That Lois isn't half the anchor you are," he said, breathing angrily through his nose. Gene hated Lois' boyfriend. "And that old putz she sleeps with. Nose up everybody's ass." Gene snorted. "Screw them. I'll take Cal out for steaks, tell him it's high time he showcases you. Then, we'll see about getting you prime time in the new year."

Gene smiled, probably envisioning pouches of gold strapped to his saddle. "And some more money."

Barbara took the train to Bayville and drove from the station to her home, where her parents' slate-blue Buick was parked in the driveway. She opened the door and went up the stairs to find her father, Hans, eating his Wurst and drinking his warm beer. He was sitting on her leather couch, an incongruously modern setting for an old-fashioned man.

"Hallo, Barbara," he said mildly as Barbara kissed him on his balding head.

"Hello, Miss X-rated TV host!" her mother bellowed from the kitchen, hand on her hip, towering in her pink housecoat. As

Barbara walked into the kitchen, Rory came rushing down the stairs from his room; after his half day of kindergarten he'd done a quick change into the Spiderman costume Barbara wouldn't let him wear to school.

"Spidey!" Barbara cried, and Rory jumped down the last three steps and into her arms. Despite working full-time, Barbara never got the cold shoulder from her boy; he never punished her for being away by clinging to Gammy and Gampy. Barbara carried Rory into the kitchen, kissing his hair, his cheeks. "How was school?"

"Okay," said Rory. He'd never give details immediately after school. They'd trickle out over dinner or bath time.

"Don't say hello to your old mother," said Siobhan turning off the stove burner and spooning mac-and-cheese into a plastic dish. She turned her cheek to Barbara so she could kiss it. The three of them sat down at Barbara's round Formica table which Siobhan had covered with one of her own lace tablecloths so it would look "proper"; Siobhan commandeering her kitchen was the price Barbara paid for having her parents babysit in her home. Barbara and Ben also covered their expenses, since her father was retired from his job in the sand pits, and her mother had quit her job as a grocery checkout girl to watch Rory.

Rory was already plunging his spoon into the yellow vinyl, but Siobhan gently grabbed his wrist before he could bring the food to his mouth.

"Sorry, Gammy," said Rory, and the three of them bowed their heads and said a quick prayer.

Grace over, Siobhan motioned to the stove and the mac-and-cheese, "Have some, Barbara."

"Nah. Thought I might go for a run. Wanna take a walk around the track with Ror while I run?"

"Always so afraid of getting fat."

"You notice any fat women anchoring on television lately?"

Siobhan shrugged and gave a little hmmmph. "I did notice an old rummy on television. I hope he got his comeuppance!" said Siobhan.

"Did you wash his mouth out with soap, Mama?" asked Rory.

Barbara laughed and said, "Let me guess, Rory, is that what Gammy said I should do?"

"Uh-huh," he said, the cheese already falling onto his red and blue polyester costume. She'd have to wash it when he was asleep.

"I was just glad the boss wasn't upset about it," said Barbara. "I need to get him to put me on TV on New Year's Eve." Barbara rose to pace the linoleum floor as she recounted her conversation with Gene.

"Work on New Year's Eve?" said Siobhan. "I thought working overnights and holidays was for...what was it you said...'the weak links'?"

Siobhan had nearly 100 percent recall when it came to anything that had ever happened to Barbara or anything her daughter had ever said. If Barbara were to ask her mother right now who the girl was who'd broken her Thumbelina doll in kindergarten, her mother would not only recite the kid's name, rank, and serial number, but would point out that Barbara had called the girl a "hiney face" just before slapping her.

Barbara rolled her eyes. "This is an exception. Anchoring the ball drop is a big assignment."

"A more important assignment than being with your husband?" asked Siobhan, tucking a stray hair into her red beehive, a movement that signaled she felt she was winning an argument. Siobhan loved Ben, even if the man who'd married her only child wasn't Irish or Catholic. The first time Barbara had brought him home, Siobhan pulled her aside in the kitchen and said sweetly, "Ben *Malka,* what is he, Greek? Is he Orthodox?"

Not Orthodox. Sephardic. Jewish. The first time Barbara met Ben in the Spring of her senior year in college, he looked like a hulky, swarthier, ponytailed Serpico-era Pacino. It was a Sunday afternoon and Barbara had to go to the radio station to record a preview piece for a Monday morning Amherst town meeting. He was in the air studio, hosting the Sunday afternoon Jazz show, *Sunday Stylings: Miles and More.* As news director, she didn't pay much attention to weekend music programming and could have done with less Miles or any jazz artist, for that matter. But that jazz host sure was cute, she thought. After she cut her report, she headed to the front office ostensibly to check her mailbox, but really just to get another look at him. He caught her checking him out through the glass and gave a friendly wave. Barbara decided to be bold and walk into the air studio; the red light over the door was off and she was station management, after all.

A languid sax solo was underway on the studio's speakers, so Ben pushed the mic closer to the board and rose from the black swivel seat behind the large mixing board. "Ben Malka," he said. "You're the news director, right?"

She shook his hand. "Barbara Konig." She looked down at her Amherst track sweatshirt and running shorts. "Looking like a professional newscaster right about now," she said.

"Hang on a sec," said Ben and he reached into a bin behind his chair and pulled out a Chick Corea album and set it on a second turntable, preparing for a segue. Segue, thought Barbara—who'd ever be able to tell where one errant horn ended and another began?

"You don't have to break in with a news bulletin, do you?" he asked. His brown eyes slanted slightly downward in the corners; they were big, sincere eyes.

"Oh, no, no. I was cutting a voicer for tomorrow and just checking my...."

"Couldn't find the record, Benjamin." The door to the music library adjacent to the air studio opened and out walked a woman with frizzy hair bordering on a 'fro. She was wearing overalls and a tank top and her underarms were visibly hairy. "But I found your Ferlinghetti," she said, holding up a book as she walked to the other side of the board and sat on the floor in the lotus position. She pulled a notebook from a macramé bag and a pocket knife from her overalls and began sharpening a pencil.

"Barbara, this is Willow," said Ben as he cued up the Corea record. The only thing more annoying than the subsequent hand clapping in the record was this creature, who barely looked up when introduced. Why was she hanging around the studio? She pulled an apple from her bag and cut herself a slice with the knife she'd used on the pencil a second ago. At least there was no indication the knife had been used for personal grooming.

Ben held up a Miles Davis album. "You like jazz, Barbara?" he asked.

"It's the best, man," Willow offered, crunching her apple slice.

No one asked you, Yoko.

"I'm more of a rock 'n' roll girl," said Barbara. "Huge Beatles fan."

Willow grunted. Ben said, "Cool," and sat back on the swivel chair; apparently the cacophony was coming to an end and he'd have to switch his mic on soon.

On the way out of the station, Barbara heard Ben's voice on the loudspeaker and thought: He'll never make it in the business—his voice isn't very deep for such a big guy. But too bad he has a girlfriend.

Barbara saw Ben's eyes in Rory's face now as he wiped his mouth on his sleeve and ran upstairs, probably to get his Spiderman hood so he could sneak up on her and make her jump later.

"Ma, I'll head right home after midnight," Barbara told Siobhan. "I need to push harder for prime time so I can get the heck out of cable news and back to a network."

"Oh, dear girl. Always so ambitious. Always were. It wasn't enough to be a track star and get good marks, you had to be a newspaper editor too. But you're not just a career girl anymore. You have a family now. A job will never love you back. As we used to say at Bohack's, 'You're only as good as your last day at the register!'"

Barbara wasn't sure what that last part meant, but she understood her mother thought she should concentrate on her marriage and raising her son instead of raising her profile on television. But having a child hadn't just magically sapped the ambition out of Barbara. And Ben would understand. She gave her mother a wan smile.

"Ben and I can celebrate when I get home," she said.

CHAPTER 11

"I know you're in there, Rip, open up," Barbara knocked brusquely, taking care not to disturb the homage to the outgoing president affixed to his door: Danko's head superimposed on the Clinton presidential-podium-finger-wagging shot with the caption: "I *did* have sex with that woman!" New Year's Eve was in two days and there was still no word on assignments.

Rip opened the door slowly, revealing his turntable spinning *Rubber Soul*.

"While you're in here spinning records, I'm spinning out, wondering what the heck I'm doing on New Year's Eve. Why aren't you answering your phone?"

"Sorry, baby," he said, gingerly lowering himself back into his desk chair. "A bit hung- over this morning."

"Couldn't wait, huh?" she shook her head. "Have you heard anything? Let me guess, they're giving the ball drop to Ironsides so he can pop some celebratory wheelies in Times Square?"

Danko barely laughed. Barbara picked up the cup on his desk and sniffed it.

"It's coffee...mostly. But it was bourbon last night." He winced. "Had drinks with Cal in a back room of the Pepperpot."

"There's a back room?" she asked, but then remembered that Danko had known about the coatroom the night they hooked up at the *Buzz* Christmas party. "Wait, who cares! What happened?!"

"If you're nice to me, I'll tell you," said Danko, taking a sip of his *mostly* coffee. He explained that he had met the boss after Cal had shared porter house and creamed spinach with Gene at their favorite steak house. Gene had told Cal if he wanted to win the ratings race in dayside, he needed to showcase his talent, meaning Barbara, to which Cal agreed, saying something to the effect of "that gal has legs like Secretariat." The old horse traders, thought Barbara. Rip said by the time he'd met Cal at the Pepperpot, Cal was already schnockered, but the two of them managed to hammer out names for the dayside shows.

"Ours is *This Just In*. Lotta breaking news. Ton of live shots," said Danko.

"Well, that's great! A real show!" And the name wasn't bad, even if it smacked of old-time announcers cupping their hands to their ears and twitchily smoking during their broadcasts.

"Yeah," said Danko, "But you're not going to like the rest of it. He's giving the ball drop to Spencer, Topper, and Sloane...."

"Aw, come on!" Barbara shouted.

Danko winced again at her volume. "Shhhhh. It's nothing against you. He wants Sloane to cut her teeth on special event coverage. But he's looking to do something with you and Stone in the new year. Maybe D.C."

"D.C.? Really? For the inauguration?!" Cal owed her that much, as he'd shut down her request last fall to cover the 2000 non-election and its aftermath, assigning all the coverage to Ironsides, just because he'd been covering administrations since Johnson, or Hoover.

"That's all I got. Had to put him in his limo and get him home to the wife."

"I guess we should tell Jack, huh?" asked Barbara as she headed for the door.

"Yep. Sure." Danko flipped over *Rubber Soul* and leaned back in his chair. "Just turn the lights off on your way out?"

As Barbara walked down the hall to her office, she saw Jack standing outside her door. He'd been stopping by in the mornings lately, often with a helpful article or information about a police guest he knew from his days as a crime reporter.

"Morning, Ms. King. I have some reading material for you," he said as she reached him. His hair was wet; the guys on the set once compared workout notes and Jack mentioned that he liked to swim laps at his sports club before work. Wearing his anchor suit, but with the top buttons of his shirt undone and no stage makeup on yet, he looked even better than he did on television, thought Barbara. But she was, of course, only considering this aesthetically.

"And I have some news for you, too," she said. "Would you like to come in?"

"Why, thank you," he said and put his duffel down and his breakfast bag and the *New York Times* business section on her desk. "It's a column about the Phoenix—hot off the presses. It seems the Old Grey Lady has deigned to write about our scrappy little news channel." Jack pushed the newspaper toward her and she opened it up on her desk. "Page 5," he said. "May I read along with you?"

Media Column: "The Phoenix Rises?"

Stars don't make television; television makes stars. That old showbiz saw seems to be the philosophy behind Cal Carmichael's hiring blitz at the Phoenix News Channel. The cable news channel's irrepressible leader has eschewed the notion of populating his lineup with correspondents with gravitas, and instead, has placed an interesting array of obscure personalities in his galaxy, in the hopes they will shine brightly enough to propel the channel out of third place.

Carmichael established a niche in cable programming by filling his prime time with conservative chatterboxes; whether he aims to duplicate that in daytime remains to be seen. His early-morning show, the bossily titled *Wake up, America!*, stars real-life husband-and-wife team Stan Keegan and Dorie Luce, former hosts of *Stan and Dorie, Mornin' Glory!*, a country radio show whose humor made *Hee Haw* seem like a bastion of sophistication. Looking disturbingly like brother and sister, Stan and Dorie enthusiastically interview guests ranging from a grandmother who's sewing a quilt for former president Reagan, to a pig who purportedly burps the National Anthem.

Inventively, Carmichael's just hired a third banana who's not a weatherman, but a consumer reporter, who was plucked from the even greater obscurity of a Spanish-language channel. The addition of James John (formerly Jaime Juan) is no doubt aimed at silencing critics who've noted that the Phoenix is a virtual on-air Aryan nation.

To that end, another recent hire is Stacia Cabrerra, a pint-sized attorney-turned-Miami crime-reporter who tries to prove her prosecutorial chops on *Cabrerra's Case File* (why not just complete the alliteration and make it *Cabinet*?). Open the file, and you'll hear such "exclusives" as, *"I just got off the phone with a source who says a friend of the defendant believes the defendant will be proven innocent."* If spewing speculation and proffering platitudes were crimes, Cabrerra would be guilty.

Cathryn Collyns has also recently joined the "news" team. Aside from her obvious distaste for the letter "i," the former catalogue model and cable home improvement hostess has been assigned to read news briefs. To say she's flawlessly beautiful would objectify her, to say she looks like a deer in the headlights would be mean, so I'll just say this: whatever the channel's paying the teleprompter operator is not enough.

No Filters, No Fluff is the channel's boast. Catchy, but come on—every station airs fluffy segments. There's no shame in it, even if the Phoenix does seem to get a disproportionate share of bottom-feeders. As for the filters, so far the pretty people who populate the daytime anchor desks are just breaking-news disc jockeys; they don't filter the news through a conservative lens. But as the channel evolves, we'll likely find out if Carmichael will be able to resist the urge to put his hero's ideology on the daytime airwaves.

Barbara waited for Jack to finish the article. He'd pulled his chair next to hers to read and she leaned back in her chair to create a little distance between them—they sat close to each other on the set, but not this close.

When Jack finished he sighed, "Are you disappointed we didn't get a mention?" He pulled his coffee out of his bag. Guess he was staying? "At least they called us 'pretty people'."

"Speak for yourself," she said, smiling. "Anyhow, I have a few Phoenix news alerts that broke late last night...too late for the esteemed *Times* to include in their snarky column."

Jack got up and moved his chair back to its place opposite her. “Do tell!”

When Barbara finished delivering her news, they toasted coffees. “Here’s to *This Just In,”* he said, cupping his hand over his ear. “And to a sojourn south in the new year.”

Barbara checked the clock on her computer: 7:32. They’d be late to the conference room meeting. “Meeting time.”

Jack stood up as Barbara furiously punched the conference call code into her phone. “Better just dial in from here,” she said, motioning for him to sit back down.

When they joined the call, Sloane, not Cal, was speaking. “Spencer and Topper,” she commanded, “I’ll need you at the site by 8 p.m. Coverage starts at 10. We’re running a Keegan, Luce, and John 2000 *Wake Up, America!* bloopers package prior. Stone and King will do news briefs at the top and bottom of the hour starting at 7 and need to babysit the set in case the feed from the site crashes. Oh, and have the Cabrerra Case file reruns and Collyns’ “Sprucing Up Your Home in the New Year” package ready to go just in case. Questions?”

Barbara mouthed, “Babysit?” to Jack.

“Lois Spencer here!” came the next voice on the call.

Barbara pantomimed stabbing the phone and Jack stifled a laugh.

“I’ll probably be arriving at Times Square earlier,” Lois said, “to familiarize myself with the site and scope out revelers for interviews.”

Jack scribbled “suck up” on a piece of copy on Barbara’s desk.

When they hung up, Barbara said, “Can’t believe they gave the gig to Spencer. Marcia, Marcia, Marcia.”

“Cheer up, Jan,” said Jack, “Everyone watches Dick Clark anyway.”

CHAPTER 12

Barbara stood at the bottom of a grassy hill. She needed to get to the top, but as she started walking up the gentle slope, it turned to dirt and grew dramatically steeper. She'd have to dig her fingernails in and climb. She was just grabbing a fist full of black earth when Ben shook her shoulder.

"Time to wake up, honey."

Barbara rolled from her back to her side and put her hand on her pillow; the tips of her French-manicured nails were still white. "I had that dream again."

"Such a prosaic metaphor," said Ben, yawning and turning off the alarm.

"I know. But I'm never going to get to the top," she said.

Ben brushed her hair out of her face. "Stop it, Baba. You will. The ball drop's not news anyway."

"Maybe not, but I have to figure out a way to get to Cal sooner in the new year," she said, getting out of bed and walking to Rory's room. It was New Year's Eve morning and she would be away from him, at the Phoenix, all day and night.

Barbara stood in the doorway of Rory's room; it would be selfish to wake him, but she really wanted to hold him before she left. She tiptoed on the dulling blue wall-to-wall carpeting and knelt at his bedside, watching him breathe. Instead of touching his cheek, she arranged his stuffed animals—a dachshund, a bear, and a turtle—in a row against headboard. He liked his "friends" there when he slept.

Barbara worried about Rory being a lonely only child. Since she and Ben were only children, they wanted Rory to have at least one sibling, but since Barbara had been hired at the Phoenix only a year ago, another baby would ruin her planned ascent. Ben agreed they could wait another year; he knew how much her career meant to her. Even though she was 34, plenty of women were delaying childbirth into their late thirties and even forties nowadays. And this way, she could continue to focus all of her love and nurturing on Rory. She tucked the blue fleece blanket up around his chin and whispered, "My world. I love you." Better get in the shower before she started tearing up. She could call him from work to hear his sweet little voice.

The morning routine with Ben was nearly balletic. He stepped out of the shower, she stepped in, neither noticing the other's nakedness. He dressed, she toweled off. They shared the sink, spitting into their respective corners. Ben went downstairs and turned the coffee machine on while she dressed. She came downstairs to cook her breakfast while he checked e-mails and opened the door for Siobhan and Hans.

Barbara stood at the stove and spooned her eggs onto the toast she'd placed on a piece of tin foil. "I'm going to be pretty late tonight," she said.

Ben looked up from his computer screen. "How late you think?"

"Well, there's some talk about post-show drinks at the Pepperpot and I thought I might stop by for a quick one, since the station's springing for a car ride home. Figured I could get a little face-time in." That last part was disingenuous. Cal wouldn't be there; he and the missus would probably be home watching *The Lawrence Welk Show* reruns. Danko, perhaps to endure yesterday's hangover, had arranged a drinking session for *This Just In's* cast and crew. Barbara had to admit, she was intrigued at the prospect of Jack being there. Maybe she'd find out what he was like outside of work. He was certainly proving to be a competent co-anchor. And funny. And considerate. And not stingy with compliments for her. Compliments that really resonated. But Ben. She really should get home to him. Wait, what if she *made it up to him* when she got home?

"I suppose you should go," said Ben, returning to his computer.

Barbara put her sandwich in her tote bag and came up behind Ben and put her arms around him. "I don't have to..."

He patted her hand. "No, you should go. I know you want to climb the ladder there. It just sucks that it's such a stupid assignment."

"I know, I know," she said, stroking his arm. "How 'bout I wake you up for a little celebration when I come home?"

Ben turned around and smiled at her as she wriggled her eyebrows. "Sounds like a plan," he nodded.

In hair and makeup that morning, Angelica decided to give Barbara some long curls. "Party hair. You cool with that?" Angelica's own hair, a crown of cornrows, made her look regal. Her occasion was a special mass at her church.

"Sure, it's a party out of bounds here at headquarters!" said Barbara. She'd, of course, shared with Angelica her disappointment over her assignment.

Angelica twirled a strand of Barbara's hair and looked at her in the mirror. "But I don't want to make you look too sexy, drive your co-anchor crazy."

"Excuse me?"

"I hear things," said Angelica.

"What *things*?"

"One of the techies came in for a cut the other day. He says the guys sometimes watch you two on the monitors during the breaks—they think Jack has the hots for you."

Barbara sat up from her usual reclining position in Angelica's chair. "That's ridiculous. He's just being friendly. We're supposed to get along on TV, you know."

"Yeah, and on TV," said Angelica, "he sure looks happy when he's sitting next to you. Gets that dopey-ass grin."

"What's he supposed to do? Frown? Gimme a break!"

"Girl, I'm just telling you what I see. And what I hear. You know people around here love to talk."

"Well, I just want our show to do well so I can get out of dayside," she said. "Crazy," she muttered as Angelica continued curling her hair.

Angelica and Jane's cosmetic wizardry that morning not only included the saucier hairstyle, but dramatic makeup too; it was a look that said, *Yes, I look like a whore, but I'm a clever one.* And while she doubted Jack would be driven to distraction, Barbara did notice him look up when she walked onto the set that morning.

Back on the set that evening, the hours dragged. One of the techies thought it would be funny to make the set spin faster; he actually got it up to near carousel speed, but Tex put a stop to the hijinks, shouting, "Last thing I need is to be moppin' up hurl butter on New Year's!" So the crew settled in, playing cards and giving each other massages.

Jack and Barbara entertained themselves by reading Barbara's fan e-mails, with Barbara sitting in her barstool as Jack stood behind her. "First," she said, bringing up her in-box, "the leg fetishists."

Mrs. King,
God you got great legs
There incredible
Jim

Hi

Can I get an autograph pic of you, with you showing your legs? You're a good reporter too.

Thank you mame
Bill

"I suppose you have the gam-cam to thank for those," offered Jack, quickly moving his eyes off her legs and nodding toward the camera that took the wide, two-shots of the anchors when they sat in their barstool-style chairs.

Barbara scrolled through the in-box. "I'd like to write back, just to edit their copy."

"Don't."

"This next guy," she told Jack, "is so impressed with my reporting, he writes me just about every day.

Good morning!

I am such a devoted fan of yours. I admit that I am partial to women in their 30s and 40s.

I am a Christian man and struggle with my affection for you. I wish I was Jack Stone.

Mark

Hello again Barbara,
Your daring cat eyes hypnotize me.
Mark

"It's good to be Jack Stone," he said, looking into her eyes, "Catwoman."

"Forties. Son-of-a-bitch." She brought up another e-mail. "This next one actually does applaud my interviewing skills."

Dear Ms. King,

I just wanted to say that you can really keep your cool in a heated debate and you seem very sweet---though I must confess that at times I get the sense that you could easily kick a guy square in his bean bag and laugh.

Justin

Jack doubled over, pretending to protect himself. "Oooofa!"

"Oh, and then there's the Metaphor King," Barbara continued.

Today you're prettier than a duffel bag filled with crispy Ben Franklins and your eyes sparkle like hope diamonds.

Dave

"But here's my favorite," she said. "I just can't improve upon this clear, concise prose."

PLEASE BARBARA SPANK MY BARE BOTTOM!

"At least he didn't ask for something as unoriginal as an autograph," Jack laughed, as Tex signaled for him to get back in his chair. It was getting close to midnight and Lois was scheduled to interview a former mayor from her Times Square location. Danko, who'd apparently set aside his *Rolling Stone* end-of-year edition long enough to negotiate with Sloane, had arranged for Jack and Barbara to participate in the interview since the guest was, for the Phoenix, an A-lister.

"Back from commercial in 15," said Tex. "T-minus ten to midnight. Hope nobody yacks on hizzoner during the interview."

"Remember, everybody plays on this one," Danko commanded from the control room.

Barbara sat at attention. Finally, she thought, we get to sink our teeth into an interview instead of reading that stale newscast copy. She looked at the monitor and noticed Lois adjusting her earpiece, huddling next to the jowly, frozen-looking ex-mayor.

11:50. Lois started the interview and Tex gave Jack and Barbara a thumbs up to indicate their mics were hot. "Get ready to jump in," Danko told them in their earpieces. And then to Lois, "Toss to Stone and King for questions. Now."

Lois held her earpiece, and with a grimace, appeared to push it deeper in her ear. She asked the next question.

Mr. Mayor, are you satisfied with the security precautions taken here at Times Square?

While the ex-mayor was bloviating, Danko said, "Spencer, next question goes to the anchors in studio."

Barbara was shifting in her anchor chair but smiling at the camera, ready for the director to cut to her so she could jump in. Lois either had a problem hearing Rip, or she was shaking him off so she could hog the interview. She'd already gotten rid of Topper. He'd been dispatched to report from the crowd but hadn't done a hit in an hour and by now was probably in a passionate clutch with a girl from Staten Island, their silver top hats askew.

As the former mayor uttered the last syllable of his answer to Lois's question, Barbara burst in:

Mr. Mayor, Barbara King and Jack Stone here at Phoenix headquarters....we were wondering...

But Lois, arm around the mayor, shouted:

We'll head back into the studio in a moment but we have breaking news here at Times Square—I've just learned that a city sanitation crew member has been arrested for public lewdness—Mr. Mayor, I'd like your reaction.

The ex-mayor, who'd been blinking into the camera, ready to talk to Barbara and Jack, snapped his head toward Lois, her brown eyes like two magnets pulling him in. Not expecting to be fought over, or to be asked about an arrest, the hapless hizzoner fumbled through a 2-minute-long answer. When he finished, it was 11:55, time for a commercial. Lois beamed.

Mr. Mayor, thanks so much for talking with me. I'll be right back with the final countdown to the year 2001!

"We're clear," shouted Tex.

Barbara turned to Jack. "What the hell?!"

"Spencer claims she was having trouble hearing us," Danko explained from the control room.

"Bull shit!" screamed Barbara, getting out of her chair and waving her copy in the air. "She heard me start the question—she even said 'we'll go back to the studio in a moment'..."

"Cool it, Barb," Danko cut her off. "Ain't worth fightin'. Overnight crew's taking over."

Jack took Barbara's arm to guide her back into her chair and gestured for her to look at her computer. She released a loud exhale and clicked on the flashing instant message.

Stone: I'll tell the bartender at the Pepperpot to make it a double, ok?

The corners of her mouth twitched into a smile. He was going.

Stone: But seriously, don't let 'em see you sweat, as the saying goes. Spencer's the one who looked like a rabid dog...or giraffe, as you would say...on air. Keep smiling and get ready to ring in the new year properly!

Barbara gave Jack a teeth-clenched television smile and joined him and the crew as they gathered around the monitor to watch the ball drop. What did he mean by *properly*—get drunk at the Pepperpot? Make out at midnight? Most people *did* kiss when the clock struck twelve. If she and Jack *didn't* exchange a congenial co-worker buss, suspicious minds might surmise he was on to the people who thought he *had the hots* for her.

Three, two, one...Happy New Year! Lois shrieked.

Jack turned to Barbara and gave her the quickest of hugs and an air kiss—far from a sailor-versus-nurse-in-Times-Square mash, but her stomach fluttered nonetheless. "Happy New Year!" he shouted to the crew. And then he whispered to Barbara, "I'm glad I got to see it in with my television wife."

CHAPTER 13

Danko had intercepted Barbara on the way to the Pepperpot and took her arm as they walked in the cold air, his breath streaming as he sang the old Who song "21" about a couple seeing the new year in together.

She wondered if he was making a sly reference to what Jack had said to her at midnight, or just giving her a rock music quiz.

"It's from the album *Tommy*. Give me a hard one, Rip," she said, as they opened the bar's stained-glass doors.

He raised an eyebrow and steered her to a couple of empty stools at the big mahogany bar.

"Wild Turkey?"

"Very funny." Of course he'd suggest what they'd drunk the night of their tryst. "Make it a beer, I better pace myself."

"Stone coming tonight?" Rip asked, lighting a cigarette.

"Think so." She tried to sound extra casual. "He said he had to swing by his office." Probably to call the beautiful wife in the 8 x 10. Maybe she'd make him come home.

"He's a handsome guy, isn't he?"

"Well, yeah, I guess. I mean, not for nothin', he's a television anchor." Rip was starting to look slightly leathery, but still got his share. Why was he remarking on Jack's looks anyhow?

"I hear he was a real rake in his day," said Rip, blowing out smoke.

"And I hear he's a happily married man now."

"To his wife or his *TV wife?*" Damn, he had definitely listened to their midnight exchange from the control room. "I see the way he eyeballs you when he thinks no one's looking."

Better not sound too defensive. "I only have room for one 'friend with an asterisk' in this joint. Besides, you had your chance long ago, Mister."

"Don't I know it," he said, turning to face a very pretty, very young intern who was tapping him on the shoulder.

"Hi, Mr. Danko, remember me? I'm Jenny."

Barbara could tell Rip didn't. "Hello there." He took a stab. "Intern last summer?" He turned to talk to her.

With that, Tex and his crew entered the bar. One of the stagehands, who might or might not have been of legal age, bellied up to the bar and said, "Eight lemon drops, please," as if ordering from a candy store.

The beer had been a wise choice for a starter. The lemon drops *were* candy for children. Children who got very drunk. After tossing hers back, Barbara felt light-headed but perturbed; there was still no sign of Jack. Tex joined her at the bar and ordered her a beer and lit a small cigar. He'd just started telling her about a Times Square stampede he'd once witnessed in which the "vics faces were mashed to a pulp," when Jack walked into the bar.

The crew hoisted their second round of shots in his direction. "Jack Stone!" In his short time at the Phoenix, Jack was already popular among the crew. He took the blame when a mistake was made, never asked for makeup or water, and made a point of saying he was grateful to be in the studio and not riding shotgun in cop cars anymore.

Jack walked up behind Barbara and clapped Tex on the back. "Ms. King, may I order you that double now?" He must have brushed the spray out of his hair because the dark strands were falling onto his forehead and gone was the anchor makeup that hid the five o'clock shadow. Gone too was his tie, and the first button of his dress shirt was undone.

Barbara elbowed Tex and said, "We already have a shot under our respective belts—I better just stick with beer." She hoped Jack hadn't noticed her noticing him.

"Yeah, no more Nancy drinks, heh?" Tex looked at his empty shot glass. "Any more of them gumdrops and EMS'll be pumping our stomachs later."

Jack laughed and ordered a couple of scotches and another beer for Barbara and accepted Tex's offer of a smoke. Barbara picked Rip's pack of cigarettes up from the bar and helped herself to one—she didn't want to interrupt his conversation with the intern who was young enough to be his...something.

Jack wedged a barstool between Danko's and hers and said, "Ms. King, I am shocked and saddened."

She blew her smoke away from him and said, "Oh. Sorry. Old habit. Well, not really a habit, but a party habit."

"For a runner?"

"And a swimmer, fouling his lungs with cigar smoke, Mr. Stone?"

"Ah, but I'm not inhaling."

"Ha! You're working at the wrong place to use that excuse, Bubba!"

"Interesting that we both participated in sports that focus on individual achievement," mused Jack.

"Unless you count relays."

"True. Though I sometimes wonder if I'd be a stronger competitor had I chosen a contact sport such as football or lacrosse.

I could probably stand to be a little more aggressive about getting ahead at work."

"And I could probably stand to be a little less so," said Barbara. "But what would you want to be more aggressive about?"

"Oh, I suppose I wouldn't mind being sent out on assignment on occasion—not Times Square—perhaps a slightly more exotic location."

"Well, you could get your wish soon."

"Ah, yes, D.C."

"I thought you were happy not to do street anymore?"

"Oh, I am. I love the stability of the anchor schedule. And I was tired of covering the cops. Some reporters start to think they're one of them. And it is hard to be fair in one's reporting—hard not to root for the good guys—I suppose there were times when I checked my objectivity at the door, or, at the patrol car. But then," he sighed, "Cal discovered me."

"You mean, a la Charlie's Angels, he *took you away from all that*!"

"And now I work for him!" said Jack. "When he brought me to the Phoenix, he and my agent actually bandied about the idea of putting me in prime time."

"You mean Ironsides' slot?" The slot she was after?

"No, not the slot you covet. One of the shows after 8 p.m."

"Would you have wanted that? To be one of those...what was it that article called them...*conservative chatterboxes?"* Those hosts had sold their souls as far as Barbara was concerned. She ground her cigarette out on the red pepper insignia of their shared ashtray.

"Prime time is more prestigious," said Jack, following her cue and extinguishing the mini cigar. "God, that's awful," he said, looking at the flat ecru filter, "A gentleman should *not* offer a Tiparillo to anyone!"

She laughed as he continued, "The fact that I'm even associated with this channel probably has my father spinning in his grave."

"Newspaper man, right?" Barbara thought of the picture in Jack's office of father and son.

"Yes, and a true journalist. A Democrat, to be sure, but eminently fair."

"Did you have one of those demanding father/rebellious son relationships?"

"Not really. He was pleased I followed in his footsteps, until the Phoenix. He was demanding. Insisted I become a voracious reader. A scholar and an athlete, he used to say. He made damn sure I got into his alma mater, Duke."

"I went to a pseudo-Ivy, too—Amherst," said Barbara.

"Excellent institution. And my father was adamant about having perfect diction—he would not stand for any of that *suthehn* boy drawl."

That explained Jack's near robotic enunciation. "Pu-lease. Try combating the curse of the Lawn Guyland accent."

"Why, you've never been anything less than articulate."

"You've never seen me drunk."

"Perhaps I'm about to." He looked at her latest beer which was almost empty. The beers and whatever was in that Lemon Drop had landed in her knees.

"Hey, Barbara, back me up on this," said Danko, reaching around Jack's back to grab her arm. She leaned back and turned toward him.

"The song's name is 'Norwegian Wood,' right?"

"No," said one of the writers standing next to Jenny the Intern. "It's called 'This Bird Has Flown.'"

"Danko is correct," said Barbara. "`Norwegian Wood' is the title. "'This Bird Has Flown' is the parenthetical phrase after the title. First side. Second song."

"Both the Capitol and EMI releases," added Danko, exhaling smoke through his nostrils.

The writer walked away. Jenny, standing next to Rip's barstool, said, "I like the Beatles!"

Danko pulled Jenny closer to him and oozed, "We can sing a few songs later—I'll handle the words and you handle the lyrics."

Barbara leaned forward in her barstool again and, affected a serious anchorwoman tone, said, "Back to our lead story, Jack. I can't believe you were almost a shill, I mean, host."

"It also pays better than dayside," he said. "And Mrs. Stone does like to be kept in a certain amount of luxury."

Barbara wondered if Jack was about to throw his wife under the bus, a sign that he might be taking their conversation into the realm of the indisputably flirtatious. She thought of the beautiful woman in the picture: a ringer, actually for a young Ali MacGraw in *Love Story,* but not the poor girl Jenny Cavilleri she portrayed—Mrs. Stone was of the rich, preppy Oliver Barrett ilk.

"How so?"

"There's the riding. She's an equestrian. And her shopping habits now include purchasing art." He took a belt of his drink. "Some of which, to me, looks like something a child could have painted."

"Fingerpainted!" laughed Barbara. Jack probably didn't understand his wife's art anymore than she understood Ben's poetry.

Jack had mentioned that "Mrs. Stone" was a real estate broker, but apparently she didn't make enough coin to support her habits. "I understand the clothes shopping," he said. "She's starting to become involved in charity work and says she needs to present herself a certain way at all the luncheons and black-tie dinners she has to attend."

"Those sound like a drag," Barbara said, the drinks making her want to swipe another cigarette from Rip's pack. But she didn't want to smell like a chimney.

"Most certainly not my scene. She tends to go stag a lot, given the early hours I keep."

"Hey, Jack and Barbara! One more round!" From across the bar, the crew member who'd initiated the shots was holding up another couple of cloudy yellow drinks.

"No, thanks; we're okay!" Barbara said. She clinked her beer bottle with Jack's scotch and said, "Well, I'm glad prime time didn't pan out for you." Barbara hoped he wouldn't beat her out of Ironsides' chair one day, but he seemed content with his lot on dayside—heck, he hadn't even lobbied for Times Square or pushed to get their show a name.

"And I can only pray that Ironsides doesn't wheel off into the sunset anytime soon, so you abandon me." Jack raised his glass and said, "To the best damn anchor team..."

"This side of dayside."

They laughed. "Whatever that means," she said.

Barbara followed the motion of his Adam's apple as he swallowed the rest of his drink and said, "We are quite the team. Why, we're able to..."

"...finish each other's sentences?"

"Just like that."

"I think what you're trying to say is...." She paused to pretend to say it in sign language. "I. Complete. You."

He laughed again. Then he looked at her with a serious expression and leaned in. "Hold still." He took a strand of her hair that had become entangled in her earring and gently freed it. He studied her. "I have never met anyone quite so..."

"Hey, Barb!" Danko called to her from across the bar where he was helping Jenny into her fun-fur coat. "I'm gonna split." Barbara waved goodbye.

"Mr. Danko. Quite the ladies man," sighed Jack.

"Funny, he says the same about you. Says you were once quite the rake."

"Was I used for backyard cleanup in the fall?"

Barbara giggled. She felt warm and happy. *Never met anyone quite so...* What?

"I suppose I had a few lady friends," said Jack, "but I met my wife when we were teenagers."

"Is that right?" Barbara wasn't sure she wanted to talk about her anymore. It could be a buzzkill.

"Our families both had homes on a small, southern island. We spent our summers there. Our families were close friends, practically family. She and I grew up almost like cousins."

"Were you Franklin to her Eleanor?" Barbara wanted to keep the mood light.

"We are most definitely not blood-related."

"Well, that's good. And I'll bet she didn't fall off the ugly tree like old Eleanor." Barbara knew damn well she hadn't but didn't want to let on that she'd noticed his wife's picture in his office.

Jack rattled the cubes in his scotch and said, "During college we lost touch and I did a lot of traveling in my capacity as a newspaper, then television journalist—that's probably where my reputation as a lawn tool came in—but then our families had a reunion on the island and I met up with Mrs. Stone again and we started dating."

"Sounds like it was meant to be for you and *Mrs. Stone*, as you call her," Barbara hated that cliché but didn't know what else to say. And she wondered if Jack wouldn't speak his wife's name to make her less real. Or maybe she had a name that didn't match her appearance. Not Eleanor, but perhaps Zelda, Gertrude, or Agnes?

"I'm not sure how fateful it was. You see, a few weeks later, when I was still,...er...traveling, she invited me to the island for a weekend, just the two of us."

"Oh?"

"Suffice to say, she knew full well that if our relationship was consummated that weekend, there was a high probability she'd get pregnant. And she did."

"Wow, that was..."

"Manipulative? Underhanded? Evil? Yes, all of those things. But no one held a gun to my head when we had relations that weekend. So I took responsibility. I couldn't imagine the outrage among the families if I hadn't. We told them we had eloped on the island that weekend so they wouldn't think their precious granddaughter had been conceived out of wedlock." He emptied his scotch glass. "That was ten years ago. And truth be told, I can't imagine life without my Madeleine." He didn't have a problem saying his daughter's name.

"That's..." for the second time that night, Barbara was near speechless. "That's quite the story."

Jack sighed. "One last round?"

"Why not?" she said, needing another one after that story. So the beautiful Mrs. S. had stooped to getting herself knocked up to get Jack Stone to marry her. Forget manipulative. How 'bout unimaginative? But Jack must love her if he'd stayed with her for ten years. Unless it was just for the girl.

"Well, here I am prattling on about my life and times. Tell me a story about your past. About Barbara King, girl reporter. Where were you ten years ago? Before you were, you know, punching your guests in the crotch and making your viewers beg for spankings."

"Ha!" she laughed loudly. "Ten years ago. Well, working radio. Single. Toiling away on mornings before moving on to even greater anonymity on *Early Dawn.*"

Jack didn't seem to hear the details of her resume. "Imagine if we'd met then," he said.

She touched her earring, the one he'd touched. "My dreams of network stardom were crushed when they cancelled my show."

"Heard about that, Cy," said Jack.

"What did you just call me?" she said slowly.

"I had my sources check you out when I found out I was working with you."

"Reeeeaaaaally?" Of course, she had done the same.

"The reports came back clean," said Jack. "Except for one."

Right after Barbara had so humiliatingly learned her show *Dawn* was being cancelled, there was an incident in which the entire newsroom most definitely "saw her sweat." She was on the air one morning when tape after tape after tape misfired and she was left apologizing to the audience again and again and again. It was painful to watch and worse to anchor. After the show, the producer insouciantly explained, "Happens. And who gives a shit anyway? We're going under."

Barbara reportedly said, "Who gives a shit?! I give a shit! I'm up there looking like an idiot, I have nowhere to go, I'm apologizing to our audience and ad-libbing and sweating and you're in the control room...."

He interrupted her, "Come on, it was funny. Why don't you just calm down, Barbara?"

And with that, she screamed "Funny?" and picked up the nearest object, a New York City snow globe the producer kept on his desk, and hurled it across the newsroom. It shattered, and the miniature skyscraper toppled onto the newsroom carpet, sprinkling it with tiny faux flakes. The guys in the newsroom dubbed her "Cy Young."

"Some of the guys at your former network said you could really throw heat." Jack squeezed her arm. "Others," he said, "just thought it was hot."

"Last call!" shouted the bartender.

It was 1:30 in the morning. Time to go. Most of their crew had already dispersed except Tex and one of the techies who were probably engrossed in morbid conversation. Barbara told Jack she wasn't going to brave the Long Island Railroad—no side-stepping barf under the fluorescent lights for her—the Phoenix was paying for a car. Jack suggested that since they both lived on Long Island (he in horsey Brookville), it would make sense to share a ride, so he called for one of the sedans to leave the line in front of headquarters and pull up to the Pepperpot. They said their goodbyes to Tex.

"Careful, yous two," he said. "I just mean, lot a drunks on the road. Make sure that driver stays awake."

When they got into the back seat of the sedan, Jack put the armrest down between them. Was it so both their arms could rest on it, maybe brushing against each other a bit? Or maybe he was using it as a barrier, afraid he'd jump her or she'd jump him. Okay, so she was buzzed, but he sure was good-looking and sexy and witty and he looked at her with such...what was it exactly....desire?

But she couldn't betray Ben. She loved him, his intelligence, his sincerity. And Rory. Her Rory! Motherhood had blindsided her: she'd never felt anything nearly as powerful as the love she felt for her boy. Barbara couldn't put it into words, but her ob-gyn had summarized it, just moments after Rory was born: "You just met him and yet, you'd kill for him, right?" Right. And to wreck his home and relegate him to the role of the child who would never remember a time when mommy and daddy lived in the same house?

But what if Jack just kissed her? Just once. She'd get to experience that singular thrill of a first kiss from him, that acknowledgement that he was attracted to her. And they could leave it at that. There wouldn't have to be any affair, or scandal *(PHOENIX LOVEBIRDS CAUGHT CANOODLING!)* or ruined lives.

As their car pulled away from the curb, Jack's head tilted in her direction; his eyes were closed.

But he wasn't offering his lips. He had fallen asleep, his studied posture still perfect, only his head bowed.

So he'd been drunk! Wasted! On the cusp of passing out when he'd been so funny and flirty and bracingly honest and open. He probably would have treated any other woman the same way after all that scotch, ex-Casanova that he was. My God, had she really thought they were going to grope each other in the back seat of a car? She'd better get her drunken arse home to her husband.

CHAPTER 14

At home, after Barbara checked on Rory to make sure he was sound asleep, she walked into her bedroom to find Ben awake, in pajama bottoms but shirtless, standing in front of their dresser, pulling what looked like a plastic cigarette out of the top drawer.

"Hi, honey, Happy New Year," she said, taking her earrings off and placing them on the dresser.

Ben gave her a peck on the cheek. "Happy New Year. How was it?"

"Okay, not such a big party. Boring night on the set." She wanted to seem sober, serious. "Have you been up all night?" Was he holding a toy cigarette—they didn't make those chocolate or bubblegum-filled fake cigs anymore, did they? "What the heck is that?"

Ben held up the cigarette and unscrewed the tan-colored filter from a hollow white plastic tube. "I was reading some poetry. I nodded off a little. But since you said you wanted to celebrate when you got home, I thought we might ring in the new year with a little ganja." With that, he extracted a small Ziploc bag from his underwear drawer.

That was not what she had meant by *celebrate*.

"It works like a pipe," said Ben, demonstrating as if lecturing a Science class. "You stuff a little weed inside, like this, and then it looks like you're just smoking a cigarette. Sometimes I take a toke on the way to the train so I can do a little writing on the ride home." He rooted around in the drawer again and pulled out matches. "Oh, I have a new poem I want to show you."

As she had grown more ambitious at the Phoenix, Ben had become more disgruntled at work, frustrated by working with numbers all day when what he burned to do was write. She wanted to hear his poem. Well, okay, not really. But she couldn't tell him not to smoke, when she'd been drinking all night, and flirting with another man, in a bar on New Year's Eve. She needed to indulge Ben. But smoking weed in public?

"Sweetheart, even Hemingway was sober when he wrote," she tried to joke.

"Actually, just when he edited."

"But what if you get caught?" She could see *that* tabloid headline: *PHOENIX ANCHOR'S CAREER IN ASHES AFTER HUBBY CAUGHT WITH CANNABIS.*

"Come on, Barbara, I'm careful," he said taking the cigarette into the bathroom. "Care to join me?"

The last thing she needed was getting in trouble with the law, thus violating the morals clause of her contract—her dream of prime time would surely *Go up in smoke!* Still, she hated to be such a scold. And she used to smoke with Ben now and then, like on the night they met again at an Amherst homecoming.

After their initial encounter at the radio station, Barbara never ran into Ben again at the station or on campus. But five years after graduation, at their 1993 homecoming, she spotted him under a beer tent that had been set up on a campus quad. Ben's dark hair was now in a semi-sensible, lustrous shag. The beard and mustache were gone, as was some of his bulk. In his jacket, crisp white shirt, and rock star-ish scarf, he looked great.

Barbara was working at *The Buzz* at the time and hadn't met anyone she'd liked enough to break her 5 p.m. weekday curfew. And there was no sign of Yoko in a yoga pose next to the keg. Barbara approached just as Ben was just pouring some of the foam off the top of his beer. He looked at her and smiled. "The news director! Barbara, something with a...K?"

"Konig. Well, it's King now." She quickly added, "I changed it for radio." She didn't want him to think she was married. Why hadn't she worn something prettier than her jeans and Amherst Alum sweatshirt? "And you're Ben Malka."

"Good memory," he said. "So you made a career of it?" he asked, grabbing a second red plastic cup of beer from the table next to the keg and passing it to her.

"Thanks," Barbara said, taking a sip. "I did. I'm working at a station in New York." She didn't want to give the call letters and brag and say it was a network flagship station. He was probably more the NPR type anyway. "I take it you didn't pursue a radio career?"

"No, that was just for kicks. Working for a hedge fund, sadly," he said, rubbing his chin where the Serpico beard had once been. "Would you believe I was a poetry major?"

She would. "I was a double major—English and History," she said. "I have to admit, I avoided the poetry classes. Over my head. But I did take Lindner's comp lit class."

"He was one of my poetry profs," said Ben, becoming more animated at the memory.

A group of jocks looking sweaty, despite the cool evening, approached the keg, perverting the lyrics of a nostalgic 1980s Cyndi Lauper number; the girls in the song no longer wanting to "have fun," but instead wanting to "get done."

"I remember liking his reading selections," Barbara told Ben. "Had us read *The Color Purple,"* she continued, trying to ignore the out-of-tune sing-a-long.

"Great book. That passage about God's presence reflected in the beauty of nature always stuck with me," said Ben.

"Me too!" Barbara was about to elaborate but she was distracted by the jocks who'd moved closer; she could swear one of them had farted. And wait a second, was that the shot putter from the track team she'd made out with at a frat party? To Ben, she continued, "But spiritual themes aside, I suppose the book was really about female empowerment."

The smell was dissipating but the jocks were now fracturing the lyrics to the Thompson Twins ballad, "Hold Me Now."

Blow me now

Suck my cock...

Ben didn't seem to notice them gyrating their hips and—just in case someone had failed to understand their revised lyrics—pointing to their crotches. "Yeah, Willow was big into that."

Oh no. Was he still with her and maybe she'd just skipped the kegger to scream in a gallery?

"She's living with her girlfriend now," he quickly added. Barbara wanted to say, "Thank you, Alice Walker!" but didn't want to flirt with him; she didn't want to seem like a slut.

"Hey, hot legs!" the shot putter now had his arm around one of the hip-thrusting singers and raised his beer to her, spilling some of it on his friend. The friend swatted the cup out of the shot putter's hand. This could deteriorate into a brawl, or at least, enough excitement to produce more anal acoustics, thought Barbara.

"Would you like to take a walk?" asked Ben. He produced a joint from his pocket. "I'm not a big keg guy," he said. And she wasn't a big weed girl, but why not?

They strolled around campus and toked and talked, delving into deep discussion (they were both only children and agreed it was no fun being doted on your whole life), debate (who truly precipitated the fall of the Wall, Reagan or Gorbachev?) and dilemma (he wanted to write poetry but didn't want to starve, she loved her work but hated the hours.)

Ben walked Barbara back to the dorm where she was staying, and kissed her quickly good night. "I really like you Barbara. Can we go out when we get back to New York?" So guileless. The shot putter would have had her staring at the dorm room's cinderblock ceiling by now.

"I would love that, Ben."

They were back in Amherst a year later; they eloped and got married in the campus chapel. A year later, her career seemingly stagnant in radio, they decided to try for a baby and got pregnant with Rory on the first try. That's when she stopped being Ben's partner in misdemeanor marijuana crime.

Barbara heard Ben now opening the bathroom window, striking a match. She could only hope a police car wouldn't be driving down their street at the exact moment Ben was exhaling out the window.

"I think I'll pass," she said and went downstairs to fetch a glass of wine. Barbara wasn't giving up on her interpretation of "celebration," so she changed into a lacy nightgown before crawling into bed. A la Annie Hall, weed usually put Ben in the mood. When Ben joined her, his eyes decidedly bloodshot, he kissed her on the cheek, but then got out of bed again and rummaged through the satchel that lay next to the bed. He crawled under the covers and moved closer to her. To show her his new poem.

"It's modeled after Philip Levine's 'What Work Is,'" Ben explained.

I stand on the train platform
waiting at Penn Station. For work.
The sleep in my eyes blurs
my vision
Better not to see another day ahead
More numbers
The man
saying buy, sell
Another day
Knowing
You've sold out.

She got it: Ben, and this Levine guy, hated work. But was the poem any good? It just sounded like a lot of complaining with capricious capitalization. "I'm glad you're finding the time to write," she said, rubbing his arm.

"One day, Barbara, I would love to just quit. Get a '49 Hudson. Drive cross-country..."

"That'll be all, Mr. Kerouac," Barbara interrupted, downing her wine to level the playing field. "I mean, I can't exactly trade in my Phoenix-issue pumps for Birkenstocks," she said and wrapped one of her legs around Ben and kissed him on the lips.

"I'm starving," said Ben, putting his notebook on his night table. "Want something to eat?"

The munchies. Go ahead and eat the whole damn pound cake on the kitchen counter, she thought. And while you're at it, wash it down with some granola or bean sprouts, man. So much for alleviating her guilt about bantering—that's all it really amounted to, anyway—with Jack at the Pepperpot by having passionate sex with her husband. Come to think of it, Ben hadn't really initiated sex with her much anymore. And so much for the *Annie Hall* analogy. Though there was that other scene in which both Alvy and Annie report to their analysts the same frequency of sex per week—he characterizes it as "hardly ever," she, as "constantly." Was she the Alvy in their relationship?

"I'm good," she said as Ben headed to the kitchen. Barbara chugged the rest of her wine, changed into a *Buzz Newsradio* T-shirt, turned off the light and fell asleep.

At work the following Monday morning, Jack knocked on her door, just before morning conference room meeting time. He put his lunch bag and a lone pink rose on her desk. "I stole it from the bouquet at reception."

"Okay?" She laughed. "It's lovely. But what's the occasion?"

"It's the least I could do after we *slept* together."

"For the record, I was wide awake."

"I'm going to blame the scotch for the fact that I wasn't much of a conversationalist on the ride home—my lapsing into unconsciousness certainly was no reflection on your company. I had a great time."

Barbara grabbed an empty coffee mug, poured some of the water from her bottled water into it and put the rose in it. She could dry it and press it later.

"Me too," she said.

January 2001

CHAPTER 15

Barbara had decided 2001 would be the year she channeled her inner hurdler and made the leap to prime time. But so far she hadn't been able to spring over old Ironsides, as his ten-feet tall image—a publicity shot that dated back to the 1960s—was plastered on billboards all over New York City. Smiling a youthful smile against the red, white, and blue billboard backdrops, he taunted not only Barbara, but the competition. Cal had the posters strategically plastered onto buildings directly opposite the other cable channels' headquarters.

It was a week before the presidential inauguration and Barbara still didn't know if she was going to Washington. She'd started to think that Cal had stolen a page from her school district's playbook: don't give grade school kids their classroom assignment until a few days before school starts, so parents will have less time to complain about their teachers and classmates.

Nonetheless, Barbara had an inauguration preview interview that morning, and when she tried to print out her research, the printer jammed and she was soon on her hands and knees in the hallway in front of her office. She was trying to extract the accordion-folded paper without losing a hand, when Jack happened by.

"May I be of assistance, young lady?" he asked, stopping before her.

Barbara kept her eyes on the paper bin, afraid that if she turned toward Jack, her eyes would be at groin level. "I was trying to fix it myself so I wouldn't have to call one of those imperious computer nerds."

"Better get up," Jack said, looking at her legs. "Any rug burns on those pantyhose could give people the wrong idea." Jack was revealing himself to have quite the randy sense of humor, a sign of a healthy libido? In a million years, Ben wouldn't have made a crack like that.

Just as Jack was offering his hand to Barbara to help her up, Rip walked by.

"Printer trouble!" Barbara blurted.

"I can see," said Danko, watching as Barbara let go of Jack's hand. "Want me to bring you a copy of the rundown?"

"I can fix the printer for her," said Jack.

"Sure, whatever floats your boat," said Danko, sauntering off.

Jack tended to the printer and Barbara went back into her office. "I'm going to dial in to the meeting," she called out to him, just as the printer started chugging. "May I offer you a seat in exchange for sparing me the condescension of the geek squad?"

She needn't have made the quid-pro-quo invitation—their morning breakfasts had become routine. They agreed that they didn't have to attend the meetings in person. Cal, who was in his office, couldn't see who was in the conference room, so only the real bootlickers like Lois and Sloane attended in person. And just as it was getting close to meeting time, Jack always had a reason to drop by her office (cold medicine on a day when she had the sniffles, a question about the rundown, a piece of gossip). So now, they typically ate together before joining the call.

"This just in," Jack said as he followed Barbara into her office. "I have our lead story this morning."

"Spill, brother."

Jack sat and removed a cup from his breakfast bag and in undoing its lid, spilled some of his coffee on her desk, right where she kept a picture of Ben holding Rory on his lap. "Not literally!" she laughed.

Jack picked up the picture and said, "Sorry about that. I'm such a klutz." Barbara had noticed that when she sat down next to Jack on the set he sometimes dropped his copy or a pen. She didn't make him nervous, did she? Then again, when he came to her office in the morning, he was often sporting a Band-Aid that covered some household injury. It was hard to believe that Jack would be anything but agile; he certainly had a sleek, athletic build. Aesthetically speaking, of course.

Barbara took the picture from him and wiped it with her napkin before coffee could seep under the glass. "My boys," she said, the napkin lingering on Rory's cheek.

"Mr. King certainly is swarthily handsome."

"Oh. Yeah. Thanks." Although they had shared pictures and stories about their children—Jack lit up whenever he talked about his 10-year old daughter Madeleine—the spouses who'd helped produce them were never conversation material.

"So, you were about to deliver a headline?" Barbara took her foil-wrapped egg sandwich out of her tote bag.

"Yes. I had lunch with Sloane Davis yesterday."

"Excuse me?" Barbara stopped unwrapping the sandwich.

"She wants us to anchor our show from D.C. on inauguration day and the day before as well."

They were going to D.C.—fantastic!—but lunch? Barbara thought that their eye-rolling antics whenever Sloane hogged the conference call meant that Jack didn't like Sloane either. "You had to go to lunch with her to find out?"

"What could I do but accept her invitation?" He put down his coffee. "I thought you'd be delighted. This will certainly raise your profile...a lovely one at that...here at the Phoenix." Then Jack explained that in addition to telling him about D.C., Sloane also wanted to "get the big picture" of dayside and since he was their "lead anchorman," she wanted to "pick his brain."

"Big picture. She's on her way," said Barbara, staring at her uneaten sandwich. Sloane had risen from weekend, to weekday producer, to special coverage producer, in no time. She had to be gunning for executive producer, just one management layer beneath Cal.

"Oh, I think it's no secret she has her eye on the prize. And if you have aspirations for prime time, Ms. King, sorry as I'd be to see you go, it might behoove you to befriend her," said Jack.

"She's obviously more interested in befriending you," said Barbara. Wench was probably grooming Jack instead of her for Ironsides' chair.

"Barbara, you know I have no aspirations to anchor prime time." He took a bite of his muffin and chewed happily. "She did, by the way, ask me if I enjoy working with you."

"Great!" Barbara was getting flushed. "She probably wanted you to say you hate me so she could replace me with one of those ding-dongs they hired last year!"

"That's ridiculous. I told her you were an outstanding anchor, exceptionally fast on your feet."

"Great, so now she thinks I'm what—a lively dancer?" asked Barbara.

"I think she recognizes your talent, even if you've clashed in the past. She is asking us to anchor, as a team, in Washington."

"Then why didn't she invite us 'as a team' to lunch?"

"I don't know, Barbara, maybe she's intimidated by you. Maybe she senses you don't care for her. It was a spur of the moment invitation when I happened to bump into her in the newsroom. Although, I must admit, she was a bit...how shall I say it...forward, which made me think there's the possibility she...fancies me."

"'Fancy' you?" What was he, a Jane Austen character? "Fancies you, like, wants to take you to the ball, Lady Stone, or..."

Jack seemed delighted that Barbara become undone. "Enjoys my work on television! How dare you suggest I am nothing more to our future Phoenix president than a slab of meat?" he laughed. "And need I point out that she, or Cal, has chosen you, not your archenemy Lois, for this prestigious assignment."

Barbara smiled. "So, we're going to D.C."

"Yes, that is the lede."

"Alright, then." Barbara picked up her sandwich. "But you are a slut."

"Cal loves her bony little ass," said Angelica after Barbara told her she was going to D.C. and that Sloane was producing the inauguration coverage. "But I hear he won't make her E.P. just yet—doesn't wanna piss off the old-schoolers."

Angelica snapped a black cape around Barbara's neck and started misting her hair. Angelica's hair was straight today, pulled into a tight ponytail high atop her head, making her look like a "sexy Genie," as one of the horny young bookers said when he "needed" to drop off some guest information for Barbara. Angelica's husband, the much older pastor of her church, had died of a heart attack 5 years ago, leaving her to raise their then two-year-old son. Of her young admirers at work, Angelica said simply, "Ain't got time for that."

Angelica also would have nothing to do with the styling of Sloane's hair, which had gotten shorter and darker, making the pigment-free tuft above her forehead more pronounced. "But Pepé Le Pew will be running the place one day," said Barbara. Barbara agreed that Cal placed great faith in Sloane because he recognized her raw ambition and not because he saw a younger version of himself. Unlike Cal, Sloane didn't believe in any political philosophy; she wanted only to exploit her *viewers'* beliefs to get ratings, to win.

Angelica laughed. "That hair works for her. Heard she's dating some good-looking guy."

"Oooo, let's hear it," said Barbara.

"Well, Lois and her gentleman friend Arthur had their engagement party over the weekend and Willy and Celia were there." Willy and Celia had already announced with great fanfare that they were going to be doing the bride's hair and makeup on her wedding day. And Lois had asked Sloane to be her maid of honor, a shameless political move. "Willy," Angelica said, rolling her eyes, "says Sloane was there with a real fox.'"

"A fox!" Barbara howled. Of course he would notice.

"Yeah," Angelica laughed. "Said he's a hockey player or something."

"Another jock," said Barbara. She'd told Angelica about Sloane's Amherst boyfriend who'd reportedly married her but then divorced her for a preppy blonde.

"I don't know what she's got," said Angelica. She grabbed her curlers and started setting Barbara's hair. "Mother was a hairdresser, did you know that?"

"I would have guessed she was from money." Barbara had pegged her for one of those rich girls who dressed shabbily as a way of declaring their independence from their family's wealth.

"Raised her to get ahead," Angelica continued. "She told Jane once that as soon as she started making money here, she set them up in a nicer apartment in the city. Jane also heard her on the phone once in the greenroom. Thought she was talking to a girlfriend, but no, Sloane was chatting with her mom."

"That's nice she takes care of her mother. Does it mean I can't hate her?"

"You can," Angelica said, making a giant circle with her elegant arm as she sprayed Barbara's curlers. "But try to be smart? And watch your step in Washington, and not just with her."

Barbara gave Angelica a dirty look, knowing "not just with her" was a reference to Jack.

Angelica pursed her lips. "I'm not sayin', I'm just sayin'."

CHAPTER 16

At the Phoenix Washington, D.C., bureau, the day before the inauguration, Barbara and Jack anchored several hours of preview coverage, with a cranky Danko in the control room, constantly being "fucked with" by Sloane.

Jack had been wrong about Barbara being chosen over Lois to go to D.C. Spencer had Marcia-ed her yet again, co-anchoring the 7 o'clock Ironsides news hour from Washington, with Bill Hunter at headquarters in New York. Hunter wasn't traveling because he was reportedly on the mend from the flu. Angelica's intelligence, however, suggested he'd been on a bender with an equally liver-spotted former co-anchor. In any event, the 6 o'clock was Barbara and Jack's last hour of the day, and a young protester already staked out at the parade route was Barbara's last interview of the hour. During the commercial preceding it, Danko got in her ear.

"This kid's from Sarah Lawrence College. He plans on holding up signs at the parade. Things like 'Shame' and 'Not my president!' Might hold 'em up during your interview, too." Danko stopped. "Check your computer for more info."

Barbara wondered if Danko was sending her information that the young man had some physical defect she should know about so she wouldn't be startled when he came up on the live shot. She clicked onto the flashing computer message.

Danko: *The Special Coverage Nazi called from the newsroom and wants you to fight with the guest. Hammer him.*

King: *You know that's not my shtick.*

Danko: *Her quote was "Make him look like a pussy."*

King: *@#$%^&*(!*

Danko: *Exactly. She's driving me to drink.*

The station's core viewership, the pork-rind-chewing crowd, would already hate the college student for attending a liberal East Coast institution instead of doing an honest day's work with his hands. They'd hate him for protesting against the president and trying to ruin his long-awaited victory lap. She didn't need to make him look like anything. And it was her job to let the kid say his piece, let him argue why the election was illegitimate. She would play devil's advocate by pointing out that the Supreme Court had ruled on the election and that many Americans felt it was time to move on. But give the student a fair shake, as her high school English teacher Mr. Martels would say.

Blake Martels was the reason Barbara had pursued journalism. With his mutton chops and lazy eye, he instilled terror in the wisecracking staff of the *Truman Times* on their trips to the printing press because he had no depth perception and was therefore always on the verge of ramming his stick-shift VW van into the vehicle in front of him. In their high school's publication room, Martels moderated spirited discussions about ethics and fair journalistic practices. When the class president, a football player elected on the "I'm popular" ballot, got into a brawl with a stoner and, in an exceedingly unmanly act, bit him, Mr. Martels pointed out that it had never been proven that the teeth marks on the stoner's chest matched the class president's dental records. Martels invited the class president for an interview by *The Times* editors to tell his side. After answering only a few questions, the class president exploded, "Fuckin' burnout had it coming!" That led to another staff debate about whether a swear word could be printed (it could not). When she graduated, Barbara got a book on journalism ethics from Mr. Martels with the inscription "Always give everyone a fair shake. Mr. M."

Barbara watched the college student protester in the preview monitor. He seemed like a good sort, smiling at the audio person who was hooking up his microphone, then taking a bandanna out of a back pocket and wiping his brow. He knew he was in for a bitch-slapping on the conservative network but still had the guts to go on live television to make his case.

While they were still in the break, Barbara looked up at the teleprompter and read the introduction to the college student. On the line of type beneath the words *He joins us now live,* was the word, *QUESTIONS.*

The instant message arrow flashed again.

Danko: *Crazy bitch hacked into the script. Whatever you do, I'll back you up.*

Barbara had the teleprompter operator scroll through the questions so she could read them before they came back from break.

Jordan, you and some friends are trying to disrupt a celebration in our nation's capital—doesn't that strike you as being un-American?

Coming from a liberal East Coast campus, did it ever occur to you that you might be out of touch with Middle America and the fact that they're ready to embrace our new president?

Are you concerned at all about backlash—that your protest might spur retaliation among the assembled crowd?

Barbara gave the teleprompter guy a thumbs up, signaling him to return the script to the introduction. Barbara's red camera light flashed on.

"Jordan, you're planning on protesting along the inaugural parade route—why?" Barbara began her interview. Screw you, Sloane.

Jack had seen the questions in prompter and winked at her as Jordan nervously stammered through his first answer. When the interview was over, Barbara had another message awaiting.

Danko: *Want me to tell Sloane the prompter went down?*

King: *No. Tell her the questions were there and you told me about them.*

Barbara had a hunch who would message her next.

Davis: *Is there any reason why you blew off my suggested questions?*

King: *Yes.*

Barbara decided to leave it, cryptically, at that. Sloane should have the sense not to engage in an electronic fight with an anchor while she was on the air. Barbara didn't read the rest of Sloane's angry messages until she was in the last commercial break before the end of the show.

Davis: *Can you please tell me why?*

Davis: *Don't you understand our audience hates this kid?*

Davis: *Can you please call me during the next break?*

Davis: *I will meet you in the greenroom after the show.*

Just before they left the set, Barbara showed the messages to Jack and he raised an eyebrow. "I have to run to the hotel before cocktail hour, meaning I will not be able to restrain you in the greenroom. Show me your hands."

Barbara splayed her palms to prove to Jack her fists were not clenched, but by the time she got to the greenroom, she was tensing up. She should probably linger on the set a bit to cool down, then have a calm, sensible discussion with Sloane tomorrow. But no, Barbara wanted to confront her. How dare Sloane try to tell her what to say? She was nobody's puppet. Dayside was the remaining redoubt of unfiltered (*No Filters!*) news. It would have been wrong to *hammer* that kid—not a fair fight at all!—and unethical to present only the side of the president's supporters. Barbara felt a wave of anger and wasn't sure if she could ride it out.

She walked determinedly into the greenroom where Sloane was waiting, tapping her fingers on her hip, looking like an angry cartoon skunk. "Why weren't you answering my top-lines?" she demanded.

Barbara imagined socking Sloane, sending a circle of twittering birds swirling around her head. "I didn't want to be distracted from the show."

Sloane exhaled and tried a different tack. "Why didn't you use the questions I put in the prompter?"

"I had my own questions." Answer quietly, slowly, Barbara told herself.

"I specifically told Danko to tell you to hammer him."

"He told me."

"Okay," said a clearly exasperated Sloane. "Let me ask you again, why didn't you use my questions?"

Barbara met her eyes. "Because they weren't fair."

"Fair? Oh, that's rich!" Sloane laughed.

Using the word "rich" in a context other than money or food—Sloane had really gone too far.

"Yes, Sloane, there are people, good Americans, who think the election results are bullshit and in a democracy they're actually allowed to voice their point of view without being accused of being unpatriotic." Barbara's voice was rising. "Your suggestion that our guest's protest might be a legitimate catalyst for a backlash? What are you trying to do, incite a riot?"

"I am trying to keep our audience watching is what I'm trying to do!" Sloane shouted.

"The only way we can keep them is by asking questions that sympathize with their views and then beating up on the guests who don't share them?" The writers and producers in the adjacent D.C. newsroom could probably hear them.

"Don't you get it? Our audience loves to hate a kid like that."

"Yes, I get that. But why does the anchor have to act like she hates him? We're supposed to ask the questions—neutral questions!—and let people hang themselves with their own answers if they're going to. And as for that student, surely some of our coveted middle-American audience have kids that age. Maybe their children even go to college so they can have a better life than they did."

"I know all about that, Barbara. But I don't particularly care. Our audience likes to know that our anchors are on their side. The right side."

"I think you're confusing daytime programming with prime time."

"And I think you're confusing the future of the Phoenix with its past."

In the cartoon, the anvil would have come down on Sloane's head. But instead, Sloane spun on her tiny heel and marched out of the greenroom. Barbara stormed into the bathroom and for lack of a better physical outlet for her anger, took off one of her black leather pumps and beat the plastic garbage can with it.

CHAPTER 17

Barbara's heels clomped angrily as she walked the few blocks to the hotel where she and Jack and Rip were all staying overnight ahead of tomorrow morning's coverage. They'd agreed to meet in the hotel's pub-style restaurant after the show. None of them had any business drinking, seeing as they had to be on the parade route by 6 a.m. to do hits for *Wake Up America!* and field fawningly worded questions about the new Republican administration from morning hosts Stan and Dorie, who were now sporting identical brunette pixie haircuts. But Barbara needed a tall one after her near brawl with Sloane.

Jack and Rip were already in a booth and as she walked over, Jack immediately slid farther into his seat so she could sit next to him. "I've taken the liberty of ordering you what Danko and I are drinking," he said, "a fine 18-year-old scotch."

Barbara took a belt as Danko toasted, "To scotch that's older than our interns."

"You, Mr. Danko, would be the one to know about that," said Jack, winking at Barbara, who was still out of breath from her angry walk.

Rip lighted a cigarette and flashed the pack at her. "You and Sloane slug it out?"

Barbara shook her head "no" to the cigarette; she craved one, but didn't want to share an intimacy with Rip in front of Jack. She let the scotch scorch her throat instead and recounted her argument with Sloane. "Sounds like dayside's days as the bastion of unfiltered news are numbered," she finished. "I felt like hitting her."

Jack patted Barbara's hand. "There, there, Ms. King. Spare your elegant, manicured hands. Sloane has not been inaugurated yet."

Danko looked at their hands touching and took a deep drag. "Before the year's out, though. And if today's any indication, when she's in office, she'll make sure the fourth estate becomes the fourth *branch*."

"Not necessarily," said Jack, swirling the scotch in his glass. "Inauguration coverage tends to be flattering for the branches of government—Democrat or Republican."

Barbara's eyes darted from Jack to Rip and back, as if she were following a tennis match. She'd wondered how these two might get along when one wasn't on the set and the other in the control room. "Wait a second, Danko, you said 'end of the year.' You mean Sloane could be the new Cal by then? What do you know?'"

Danko leaned back in the booth. "Nothin'. We all know she'll be E.P. soon and then from there, there'll be no stopping her."

"Bullshit," said Barbara. "You know more."

"True dat. I have a Phoenix news flash," said Rip, leaning into Jack and Barbara in the booth so their three heads were nearly touching. "Topper's out," he whispered.

"What?!" Barbara and Jack exclaimed in unison.

Danko signaled for the waitress to bring them another round. "Seems young Will and a couple of the production assistants, and even an intern, I think, had a gambling ring going. They were betting on how many mistakes happened during his show—you know, anchor stumble, technical glitch, typo in the copy. Someone snitched on him to Sloane. Topper swore up and down," Danko laughed, releasing a puff of smoke, "that it wasn't like the Black Sox—that they never threw a show."

"So Lois gets her own show?" Barbara had already made the political calculation. With Lois anchoring solo, would she be a stronger candidate to replace Ironsides? Barbara drank more of the scotch. Smooth.

"Hold on, what is to become of Shoeless Will Topper?" asked Jack.

"Did he sign a confession with an 'X'?" Barbara elbowed Jack, despite her growing discomfort with Lois's imminent elevation. The scotch really was excellent.

"Cal's putting him on weekends, maybe doing something on *Cabrerra's Case File,* or reading news briefs like the luscious Cathryn Collyns. And Spencer's show's being renamed, *New Day with Lois Spencer.*"

"New day? She starts at 11 a.m." Barbara noted.

"New president," said Danko. "Get it?"

"And a new president at the Phoenix, too, Danko?" asked Barbara. "Cal's your deep throat on all this, isn't he?"

"I'd go to prison before revealing my sources," said Danko, finishing his scotch in one big gulp. He put out his cigarette and rose. "I'm gonna call it a night and leave the hard drinking to you youngsters," he said.

"Oh come on, Danko, where's that legendary hollow leg of yours?" Barbara didn't want to let him leave so easily, didn't want him to think she wanted to be alone with Jack.

"Nah. I had a rough night last night. I'm heading out to the site early to case the joint." He kissed Barbara on the cheek. "See you in the morning," he said. Then, to Jack, "Don't do anything I wouldn't do."

Barbara felt warm and relaxed thanks to the scotch and Jack had made her feel better about Lois getting her own show. "She's not half the anchor you are, Ms. King. She lacks your warmth and personality, for starters."

What a sweet thing to say. When she'd gotten back to the hotel room and called Ben and told him all the evening's news, he said, "Do you really want to fight for prime time at a channel that's becoming so obnoxiously political?" She couldn't weigh her station's ethics right now; she wanted to enjoy her buzz.

Barbara settled into a comfortable nightshirt and leaned against the headboard of her hotel room bed. She and Jack had debated a third round but decided discretion was the better part of valor, or at least vanity was the better part of sensibility: they had to be up at 4:30 a.m. Barbara and Jack's rooms were next to each other and just as they were saying an awkward good night in the hallway, his room phone rang. It was probably "Mrs. Stone," in a 200-dollar negligee, calling from a bed with 600-thread count un-rumpled sheets. Jack quickly promised to meet Barbara in the lobby the next morning.

Eleven o'clock and Barbara felt restless. She cycled through the hotel TV channels and decided a movie was in order—if she watched the Phoenix, she'd never get to sleep. She happened upon *A Walk on the Moon,* a Diane Lane vehicle in which a woman approaching middle-age embarks on a torrid affair with Viggo Mortenson's character, a handsome hippie who sells blouses out of a van. Chick movie. Perfect.

Barbara got under the sheets and propped a second pillow against the headboard. Suddenly she felt a knock on the wall behind her headboard. *Bum-bum-bum-bum-bum....*

"Can you hear me, Ms. King?" Jack's voice, muffled by the sheetrock, was coming from the next room.

She answered with two beats. *Bum bum.* He rang her room.

Barbara picked up, and watching the tangle of arms and legs on her television, said, "Should have gotten a doggie bag filled with Scotch."

"I should have made a more persuasive case for that third round," he said.

"Burning the midnight oil, studying?" she asked.

"Well, truth be told, I never managed to compile any prep for tomorrow—I'm wondering if you perhaps had some materials I could peruse?"

"You're in luck. I have a research pack. I even highlighted it," she said.

"May I knock on your door to borrow it?"

Barbara gulped and wondered if he was maybe just using the research as an excuse to come to her room and then *into* her room. If he made a move, she wasn't sure if she'd have the strength to say no. She quickly rooted through her overnight bag to throw on some pants under her nightshirt but Jack was already knocking and besides, the minis she wore on set were shorter.

He was in sweatpants and a white undershirt; she realized she'd never seen his bare arms before. She leaned against her open room door so she wouldn't lock herself out, and handed him the research. "Lots of factoids in there too. Temperatures of past inauguration days. Top hat trivia and such."

"Well, I won't be able to sleep, so maybe this will keep me occupied," he said.

"Oh, yeah, good..." she trailed off. *Occupied?*

"Excellent. I appreciate it," he said, looking at the stack of papers and then at her.

Barbara jumped in, "I'm trying to take my mind off politics with a movie." She gestured through the open door toward the television and Jack peered in. Another love scene was in progress.

"Pay channel?"

She laughed and then they both said, at the same time, "So..."

Someone had to say good night. "If you don't see me in the lobby at 5 a.m., please give me a wake-up call?" said Barbara.

"You'll do the same?"

"Of course."

"Well, good night then, Ms. King."

"Mr. Stone," she said closing her door. He'd sure looked good out of his anchor clothes, not at all the way presidential candidates looked when they campaigned in chest-high Dockers and windbreakers. She thought of him being just a wall away and wondered if he might knock again.

Barbara watched the rest of the movie, in which the Diane Lane character is contemplating leaving her family for her long-haired lover, a dilemma her teenage daughter distills to a simple equation: "So you love the blouse man more than all of us?"

March 2001

CHAPTER 18

Back at headquarters, the ratings during February sweeps proved to be a disappointment, or as Danko put it, "definitely *not* all that and a bag of chips." He told Barbara on the sly that Cal might be up to something in the spring, but when she pressed Danko for details, he said, "Dunno. You and your boyfriend are just going to have to wait to find out."

Her boyfriend. Barbara thought of the defense she would have used in high school when someone suggested one of the male hurdlers she hung out with by the bleachers was her boyfriend. "He's a boy. He's a friend. Doesn't make him my boyfriend." And so it was with Jack. They were friends. Nothing had happened in D.C. She'd beat up on herself for even wondering what it would have been like to sleep with him. She'd "prayed on it," as Angelica might say, in church, asking God not to lead her into temptation. She hadn't given in to her attraction to him, and if her co-workers noticed her and Jack hanging around the bleachers (newsroom) after the show, so be it. And the betting ring bust had at least silenced some of their accusers. Angelica reported that just before they'd been caught, Topper and company had started to lay bets on how many times Barbara and Jack flirted on the set.

One Friday morning, as Barbara and Jack were having breakfast, the phone rang. Cal's extension. Barbara told his assistant that there was no need to conference Jack on the call, as he happened to be in her office.

"I've been wanting to tell you two that you look marvelous together. Smashing!" Cal bellowed. "If I didn't know better I'd think you were an off-screen couple as well—what chemistry—ho ho!"

Barbara released a guffaw, to echo Cal's; it was loud and hung in the air.

"But that's not why I called," said Cal. "As you might have heard from Clarence, the ratings haven't been spectacular—no fault of yours, of course, slow news cycle and all. So I thought I might shake things up a bit. I'm sending Sloane to D.C. so she can become familiar with the inner workings of the bureau, and she suggested that the dayside shows could broadcast out of D.C., as a way to boost the numbers. We're assigning Lois a new dayside producer and working on new graphics and a new set for her here at headquarters, so I naturally thought my dynamic duo could head down to Washington to anchor for a time."

Barbara scrawled "What the ???!!!" on a piece of copy and pushed it toward Jack. But she was excited. Even if it was because Lois was unavailable, Cal was choosing her for an assignment.

"That is certainly an intriguing offer, Cal," said Jack. "When you say 'for a time' what do you mean?"

"Good question. Perhaps a month. Maybe two." Two months?! That would be a long time away from home. Too long.

Jack smiled broadly and raised his eyebrows. Barbara just stared at the phone.

Cal continued, "I thought you, Jack, might be able to use some of your contacts from your crime reporter days so we could give our favorite congressman more air play. He does rate for us." A congressman who was rumored to be bisexual was the favorite target of the Phoenix's Washington bureau reporting lately. Not necessarily because he was a Democrat, but because his young male aide and presumed lover had disappeared on the way to a Pilates class in D.C.

"Now, you don't have to answer right away," said Cal. "And Barbara, I know you have babies at home so if this doesn't suit you, I will certainly understand and we can always have you co-anchor from headquarters."

"Actually, I just have one child and he's...," said Barbara.

"Take the weekend," said Cal before she could finish correcting. "Let my gal know on Monday what you've decided so she can make the arrangements."

The next morning, Barbara was awake at 6 in the morning even though it was a Saturday—she couldn't stop thinking about Cal's offer. She hadn't even called Gene; she knew what he would say: "Go, for Crissakes!" Jack was going; he said he'd enjoy a little reporting again and that D.C. "certainly was lovely in the spring." He didn't give her a hard sell, maybe noticing the anguished expression on her face. "I shall support whatever decision you make, Ms. King, she of whelping babies," he'd teased.

She couldn't leave her baby, Rory, or Ben all week long and see them only on weekends. When Ben came home from work late last night and crawled into bed, she told him about the offer and he acted as if she had already declined. "Nice of Cal to think of you," he said. Nice just to be nominated.

Rory was still asleep this morning, done in from a rigorous week of kindergarten. Ben was awake, reading e.e. cummings. Barbara moved closer to him. Maybe if they had some raunchy sex, her decision would be made once and for all and she'd stop fantasizing about being in D.C., being in the same hotel five nights a week with Jack.

"Whatcha readin'," she asked, stroking Ben's arm.

"Cool poem called 'it is at moments after i have dreamed.'" He held the book open before her and continued to read.

She didn't want to read along with him.

"So, whatcha doin'?" she ran a finger down his chest.

He smiled and put the book down. She kissed him on the lips and was just starting to let her hand drift when Rory ran into the room.

"Mama, can I have a playdate with...Hey! Are you kissing?" he asked.

"Rory! Come here, little man!" Ben shouted a little too delightedly as Rory nestled between them.

"Wanna watch some TV downstairs, buddy?" asked Barbara.

"Better yet, Ror, why don't you get a book and we can read together," said Ben.

As Rory obeyed and went to his room to get a book, Barbara crossed her arms and said, "I was hoping *we* could have a playdate, if you know what I mean." She felt pathetic having to spell it out for him. "I'm sorry, I'm just happy to get to spend some time with Rory," he said, putting his arm around her.

Barbara turned her back to Ben. "Maybe I should just go to Washington," she said.

Ben took her arm and gently turned her back toward him. "Barbara, that's not fair. Look, I didn't even get to see him last night. And you can't be serious about going to Washington."

"It would be a feather in my cap for prime time. And for the networks. They always give their anchors the White House beat for a while."

"But this isn't the White House," Ben shot back. "It's to cover that Congressman, who's not even a suspect and who the Phoenix is trashing before they even know if..."

"It's more than that!" she protested. "Cal wants to showcase me finally! Raise the profile of our show."

"But that kind of reporting, Barb," he said, "It's not your style. You've always been so ethical. What about the convenience store?"

As news director of her college radio station, Barbara had refused to broadcast the names of two students who had been killed in a college town convenience store hold up. It was the biggest story to hit the sleepy hippie town in ages and everyone in the newsroom was hot to go on air with the scoop of the girls' names, having gotten a tip from a station disc jockeys who'd dated one of them. But Barbara slapped an embargo on the IDs until police had notified the families. It wouldn't be right if the girls' next-of-kin found out from us, she'd instructed, to the collective eye-rolling of the budding journalists who desperately wanted the story on their resume reels.

"That was...different," Barbara said, realizing that it really wasn't. Both cases boiled down to how journalists treat the people they cover, and whether they had the right to ruin them in the interest of ratings.

"To thine own self be true," quoted Ben. "Isn't that what you told them when they asked why you were being so stubborn?"

Just then, Rory raced into the room, holding, of all titles, *When Mama Comes Home Tonight,* and waving a piece of green construction paper. A few of the dried macaronis glitter-glued to the paper in the shape of a shamrock for St. Patrick's Day fell onto the sheets. "Mama, look what I made you!" he said, bouncing on the bed before snuggling between them. Barbara grabbed Rory and took his face between her hands and kissed each of his cheeks several times. "Sit down. Mama wants to read with you."

The next Friday morning, when Jack came to Barbara's office he was carrying more than his usual swim duffel and breakfast bag: he had a large black suitcase and, under his arm, a box wrapped in shiny lavender (her favorite color, she was pretty sure she'd once mentioned) wrapping paper.

"Running away from home?" she asked, as he put the suitcase down.

"Ha. They'd hardly notice," he said, taking his usual seat opposite her.

"Oh?" Barbara fished, taking a sip of her coffee.

"Well, my Madeleine gave me a weepy goodbye hug this morning," he said. Was that to say Mrs. Stone hadn't shed a tear? Jack placed the lavender box on Barbara's desk and grinning, said, "I have something special for you today." He seemed sure that whatever was inside the box would please her very much.

"A gift? For me?"

"So it would appear."

"Is it my own telestrator to jazz up my end of the show?" Barbara asked. Lois, as part of her new show, had been given a telestrator so she could draw circles on the map of Washington when describing the route the Congressman's aide would have taken to the Pilates studio. During off hours, the crew roundly abused the telestrator as a way of venting their hatred of Lois, who'd become a diva within days of starting *New Day*. Just yesterday, Tex groused about having to erase the telestrator after someone had drawn a stick figure Lois with a giant penis in her mouth.

"Ah, the blameless telestrator," Jack laughed. "No, it's nothing quite so practical."

Barbara untied the white satin ribbon, knowing she'd save it, and tore at the wrapping paper, revealing a shoe box containing a pair of black patent leather Jimmy Choos with stiletto heels.

"Jack," she gasped, hand over her mouth. "What in the world? Why are you doing this?" A gift, first of all. And such a personal one at that. "They're...I don't know what to say. These are....beautiful. May I....pet them?" She took one of the stilettos out of the box.

Jack sprayed a little of his coffee, laughing. "Yes, you may. But you are not allowed to use them to assault any innocent trash cans, okay?" He leaned back in his chair, contentedly. "If you debut them today, I shall alert Tex to fire up the gam cam."

"Jack, why did you do this?" she asked, putting the shoe back in the box and carefully refolding the tissue paper.

"A parting gift. I know you wanted to go but I understand it would be impossible. I have the advantage of having an older child who's busy every day after school with the myriad activities her mother chooses for her," he said, frowning. "And I know how much you want prime time here, but honestly, this is not the story that's going to elevate anyone..."

"Anyone except Sloane," Barbara interrupted. "She probably knew I wouldn't be able to do it, when she suggested us as the anchor team. Remember, it's you she *fancies.*"

Jack held up his hand. "Hold it right there. I am not the one who wants prime time, the one who daydreams of dispatching old Ironsides Richard Widmark style. I am perfectly happy anchoring dayside. With you."

"Hmmm," said Barbara. She believed him. But she didn't trust Sloane. After her stint in D.C., she'd likely be anointed executive producer, the final step before succeeding Cal. Then she'd have the power to replace Ironsides with Jack or Lois. "She didn't want me to go. Five bucks says she was the one who told Cal I had a litter of babies."

Jack shook his head, smiling. "The show will look great and you'll be here in New York to fill in." Ironsides had started taking more vacation and all the news fillies were neighing in the barn, restless and hopeful they'd be trotted out in prime time. Stacia's weekend legal show had been getting good ratings and she was starting to imagine herself a star, audaciously bringing her Louis Vuitton–encased Chihuahua along with her to hair and makeup. Jane hated the dog ("licks his naughty bits, then licks her face!") and after Angelica discovered Stacia's real age, she nicknamed her "Abuela." As for Cathryn, she'd won accolades for her coverage of the Inaugural ball fashion. And she'd picked up a tip from the entertainment reporters she'd met in D.C. for the event. Seated on the set before reading her news briefs, she now applied shimmery lotion to her legs.

"I just hope he doesn't give any of the substitution to Stacia or Cathryn."

"I don't think they're any threat to you. Cal likes his women good-looking *and* smart," said Jack.

So seductive, always with the perfect compliment, thought Barbara. But Ben understood the deeper reasons for her not going. And maybe with Jack away for a couple of months, Barbara would stop daydreaming, not just of wheeling Ironsides down a staircase, but of being with Jack. It was getting too hot; they were getting too close. He was picking out sexy heels for her, for crying out loud!

"Say, how'd you know my size anyway?" she asked.

"Child's play. One morning you got up to retrieve copy from the printer and I opened your closet. You already have quite the impressive selection."

"But no Jimmy Choos!" She rose and put the shoes in her closet. Before she sat down again to dial in to the conference call, she touched Jack on the shoulder. "Really, Jack, thanks."

He rose and faced her and gave her a chaste hug. "Best we say goodbye now. Tongues might wag were we to embrace on the set." So he'd also heard they were the source of gossip.

"It's not going to be much fun around here," she said, slowly breaking away and sitting back down behind her desk.

"Nor in our nation's capital." Jack sat back down too; he looked sad. She thought of that night in D.C. when a mere hotel wall separated them, as her desk did now. Barbara slowly punched the numbers in to join the conference call.

May 2001

CHAPTER 19

Jack was returning from Washington because May sweeps were ending and the Congressman story was over. After finding the aide's dirt-encrusted, trampled leotard in a D.C. park, police quickly closed in on the parolee who had killed him for his MP-3 player. And the Congressman was left posing the query of the falsely accused: "Where do I go to get my reputation back?"

Barbara had a severe case of ants in her pants; she could barely sit still in Angelica's barber chair. Jack had e-mailed her to tell her he would have to miss their "reunion breakfast," as he was flying in on the Shuttle that morning and making a quick stop at home before coming to work.

"You sure look happy," noted Angelica.

"Who? Me?" asked Barbara, and just as Angelica put her hand on her hip, Cathryn Collyns, who was now a New York bureau correspondent, appeared behind Barbara.

Cathryn looked at herself in the mirror as she asked, "Is it real?"

Barbara thought maybe Cathryn was wondering if becoming a correspondent with so little effort was all just a happy dream! But Angelica answered, smugly, "It's all real, all hers," and ran her fingers through Barbara's long red locks.

Cathryn, with her cornflower blue eyes which didn't look real, took another long look at Barbara's head and said she'd come back later.

"What'd she think, I wear a wig, like some hooker?" asked Barbara.

"Nah. She just jealous." Angelica opened her console drawer, revealing a cache of blonde hair extensions. "She uses these."

"Hey, those remind me of my Barbie with Growing Pretty Hair! Remember? The doll with the hole in her head?"

"Anyway...." Angelica closed the curtain to her station and gave Barbara's hair a little tug. "You happy he's back?"

"Sure. Whatever. It's always nicer to work with someone when they're in the studio, versus them being on satellite."

Angelica stopped setting Barbara's hair. "You are working my last nerve."

Barbara heard footsteps and her eyes widened. She looked at Angelica in the mirror as they heard Jane say, "Glad you're finally back. Messy bunch in Washington. Never gave you enough fucking powder!" Barbara's face reddened immediately and Angelica held up a curler, shrugging. Half of Barbara's hair was already set, there was no going back.

Angelica's curtain pulled back and there he was. All 6'3" of him. Hair falling onto his forehead. Dress shirt opened at the top. Green tie draped around his neck. Her insides contracted. She wasn't even hearing the perfunctory welcome-backs and how-was-D.C.s? Barbara knew how it was anyway—they'd e-mailed each other long, carefully-crafted letters every few days. Gossip was the premise: Sloane being anointed executive producer; Sloane at the bureau, showing off her ex-jock TV sports anchor boyfriend; Barbara filling in for Ironsides but being bored without all the breaking news dayside provided; Cal announcing a bump in the ratings making the Phoenix the number-two cable news station.

She read the e-mails over and over, telling herself at least she wasn't *seeing* him every day if you didn't count TV. And she had tried to focus on her marriage; she had initiated more date-nights, romance, sex. Ben was receptive, but also distracted—he'd grown to hate his hedge fund job and mused more and more about quitting and leading the Bohemian lifestyle. Such talk bored her because it was so unrealistic—she only made cable money and they needed Ben's salary. And not once, during their "together time" had her stomach flipped at the sight of Ben. Barbara stared in the mirror at Jack, speechless.

"I'm afraid I am the bearer of bad news," said Jack. "We are doing your least favorite segment today, Barbara. Phone calls."

The Phoenix had moved on to another salacious story. Not too far from Sin City, a first-grader had "gone missing," while his parents—purported swingers and apparent students of the movie *The Ice Storm*—attended a neighborhood key party. The school pictures of the boy in his scout uniform, front teeth missing, hands clasped angelically at his desk, pulled at Barbara. Rory was just about the same age. Not that Siobhan and Hans would ever host anything more than a *Kaffeeklatsch,* but Barbara nonetheless asked them to lock the doors, so Rory couldn't wander outside and be intercepted by a pervert in a curtained van.

"Yeah, calls," said Barbara. They made her uneasy too—the technology didn't always work and even when it did, the anchors were often hung out to dry in other ways. "I hope we don't get any crime buffs."

"Ah yes," said Jack, directing his response to Angelica. "The viewers who follow the case obsessively and expect us to know every scintilla of information and, while we're at it, solve the crime."

"Exactly," said Barbara, "I mean, do I look like Matlock?"

Angelica finished setting Barbara's hair and then stepped up on her tip toes to comb Jack's hair back and spray it.

"Actually," he said, closing his eyes, "More like one of Charlie's...or shall I say Cal's Angels."

Barbara patted her curlers and gave an ironic laugh, as Jack ducked back behind the curtain and called, "See you on the set, Ms. King."

Angelica rested her hairspray on the counter, next to her Bible. "Just like old times, *Angel.*"

On the set that morning, Jack and Barbara braced themselves for the dreaded call-in segment on the Swingers.

"Jeff from Alabama, you're on the air. Go ahead."

(Extended dial tone)

"Okay, let's try Janet from Arkansas. You're on the Phoenix, live."

"Am I on?"

"Yes, go ahead."

"I just want to say I enjoy watching y'all."

"Thanks, Janet, do you have a comment on the case?"

"No, ma'am."

"Joe from New York, you're next."

"I'm a criminal defense attorney and have been studying this case and have reached the conclusion that BABABOOEY is innocent!"

Jack was the one to field the Matlock call.

"Bob from Pennsylvania, you're on."

"I've been following this case very closely and feel there's overwhelming evidence against the so-called 'person of interest' in the case. I have a detailed scenario of exactly how he committed the crime and think you'll agree that he should be charged. Firstly..."

During a commercial break, Tex explained that if the boy had been dead for a while, his body was probably already decomposing, "That smell. You never get it out of your throat." For her part, Barbara choked on the hair spray Willy had just fired at her head. Celia touched her up with powder, saying, "Smile, Mami! Ah ha ha ha ha!" Tex shooed them off the set.

Back with more of your calls on the Phoenix. Denise from New Jersey is next.

"I understand that boy's parents were so-called swingers. If so, their neglect and reckless behavior should be punished! Are they likely to face charges?"

Back in her office after the show, Barbara looked at the picture of Rory on her desk and quickly collected her belongings to go home. *Neglect.* She wasn't *neglecting* Rory by working, and he was extremely well cared-for, doted on, by her parents, his flesh and blood. Still, if she bolted now, she could greet his bus and take him to the park after school.

"You look like a woman on a mission," said Jack as he poked his head in her office, jangling his car keys. She could have asked him if he was on his way to a key party, but there was nothing funny about the story they'd just covered.

"Just want to get home to Rory," she said, slinging her tote over her shoulder.

"I feel the same," he said, "but my Madeleine is booked this afternoon. A vegan cooking class, I believe." He held his keys up. "I drove in. Can I drop you at home?"

And despite her protestations that it was out of his way (it wasn't exactly—Bayville was closer to the city than his Brookville, Long Island destination), Jack drove her home in his, what else, sleek black Mercedes. As they pulled away from Jack's spot in the New York Press parking zone, Danko, out on the plaza for a smoke, lowered his shades and nodded to them.

CHAPTER 20

In the weeks that followed, Barbara and Jack didn't establish a carpool routine, although it occurred to her that they *could* drive in to work together, now that she was no longer commuting with Ben. His hedge fund needed him to be up to speed on European markets and so he took an earlier train to work. When he got home, he was exhausted from waking up at 4:30 a.m. and since no one empathized with early rising more than Barbara, she didn't complain when he turned in early. She could tell he still harbored dreams of the poet's life, but he kept it to himself, only releasing the occasional sigh when reading a particularly stirring sonnet.

With Ben having less time for Rory and school out for summer, Barbara wanted to get home earlier and sometimes ran for the train directly from the set. But there were times when Sloane asked Barbara and Jack to stay after the show to cut a promo—"Coming up tomorrow on *This Just In!*"—and on those days, they left work together, either sharing a cab to Penn Station or driving back home to Long Island in Jack's car. On warm days he put the top down. Letting the wind blow the spray out of her hair and turning her face up to the sun, Barbara imagined they were movie stars, off to a tryst in a hotel with a four-poster bed and French doors wide open to a view of the Riviera, white curtains blowing in the breeze. Basking in Barbara's joy, Jack smiled and said it was nice to make use of the convertible. "Mrs. Stone rather prefers the top up."

On one windy, rainy day in early July, Barbara was taking the train home and Jack was headed uptown for an appointment, but he insisted they share his umbrella for the walk from the Phoenix plaza to Seventh Avenue to hail their respective taxis. Halfway there, Barbara noticed a man approaching them. He was bald but for a few cotton-candy tufts of white hair, wearing a denim jacket adorned with embroidered patches (a cluster of grapes, Mickey Mouse, an American flag), zebra-print pants of the fashion favored by football players and rappers a decade prior, and a bow tie. Within seconds, he'd caught up to Barbara and waved a small spiral notebook in front of her.

"Can I have your autograph?"

Barbara and Jack exchanged incredulous looks and kept walking.

"We can only hope it's not one of your e-mailers," Jack whispered in her ear, as he put his arm around her shoulder protectively.

"Please, just sign it?" The autograph seeker jumped in front of them, flapping his notebook like a windshield wiper.

Barbara noticed masking tape precariously holding together the man's eyeglasses at the bridge, and she was just about to feel sorry for him, when he started pulling a shiny object from his breast pocket. Was it a knife, a canister of mace....a harmonica? Barbara could certainly understand why eyewitness testimony was so unreliable; things really did happen so fast! But Jack wasn't pondering the state of the judicial system. He slammed the tip of the umbrella on the ground, snapped it shut, and, gripping it like a pole, thrust it against the guy's throat. As the man walked backward being shoved by Jack, Barbara brought up the rear of the conga line by clattering behind them in tiny steps, the only moves her heels and pencil skirt would allow.

"Go get security," said Jack once he had the man up against the grey marble of the Phoenix's façade.

As Barbara redirected her dainty dance steps toward the revolving doors of the Phoenix, she saw a man in a suit wearing an earpiece running past her and over to the autograph seeker, who was still pinned to the wall, shiny silver pen in hand, flapping his arms, making bird noises.

Ka-kaw, Ka-kaw, Ka-kaw!

When the man in the suit reached them, Jack slowly lowered the umbrella and took a step back. As he was freed, the autograph seeker let out a joyous *Ka-kaaaaaaaaaaw!*

"Shut the hell up," said the man in the suit, grabbing the bird man by the arm. "I told you you can't hang around here."

"Tony, thank you," said Jack. "Barbara, this is Anthony Miletto, head of Phoenix security." The former detective she'd interviewed the morning of the Grant Danes plane crash. Miletto's pockmarked complexion and menacing expression belied a gentle voice, though Barbara imagined it could be used to great effect when dealing with perps.

"No problem, Jack, Miss King. I was just leaving the building for lunch when I saw our friend here."

Ka-kaw!

Miletto squeezed the bird man's arm. "One more time and I'm gonna kick your crazy bird ass." To Jack and Barbara, he explained, "He's living on the streets, trying to get autographs to sell."

"I wasn't going to sell Miss Spencer's!" the bird man protested, apparently too busy squawking to absorb the introductions.

"Sorry for the trouble," said Miletto, as he turned the bird man toward the avenue, like a nurse escorting a patient after an unauthorized romp in the asylum solarium.

"Ka-kaw! Ka-kaw!"

Jack unfurled the umbrella and as they ducked underneath it, he put his arm around Barbara.

"I know this isn't the headline," she said, "but *Miss SPENCER?!!!"*

They had a good long laugh recapping the events, but the rain started coming down sideways, so Jack hailed her a cab. As Barbara slid into the backseat, she noticed his eyes drift down her legs.

"I guess I'll just see you in the morning," he said.

Just? As opposed to what—come with her? He sure looked like he didn't want to say goodbye. And she had to admit, she was completely turned-on by the way he'd reacted. It was so brave, so barbaric, so...*hot.* She thought of his hands wrapped around that umbrella. She'd never seen them used for anything but pecking at a keyboard, but watching those hands put to such manly use! And they were practically mitt-sized—how had she missed that? She let herself imagine what they would feel like against her wet legs, feverishly hitching up her skirt in the back of the cab. In the Lifetime movie now playing in her head, Jack would command the driver to take them to his pied-à-terre where he'd throw open the door, push her up against a wall, and, in a tasteful montage set to Kenny G....

Kill the sax. What the hell was she doing? She was supposed to forget about Jack when he was in D.C., but she was more attracted to him than ever. And now, in addition to having breakfast and being next to each other on the set for two hours, they'd found a way to squeeze another drop out of the workday by leaving the building together.

But...Ben. In that Lifetime movie, would he have been blithely tie-dying T-shirts while she and Jack made violent love? Today was Ben's birthday. How could she be so depraved as to have a lurid, detailed sex fantasy about her co-anchor when she was supposed to be looking ahead to a night out with her husband, her best friend of 8 years, the father of the boy she loved more than life.

Barbara looked up at Jack as he leaned against the cab door. "You're a good friend, Jack Stone. Thanks for keeping me safe," she said. Jack gave her a little salute, his fingers releasing a raindrop from his forehead. Still watching her from under his umbrella, he stepped away from the cab.

CHAPTER 21

That night, Siobhan, who had recently remarked that Barbara had a "dreamy look" about her, offered to take Rory overnight so Barbara and Ben could "have their privacy." It was gross to think that her mother was pimping her off to give Ben birthday sex, but after the bird man incident, Barbara figured it was probably the right course. Plus, Ben had been working so hard, he deserved a night out and a morning after to sleep in.

So Barbara and Ben went to the movies and then to their favorite chalet-style restaurant. When Ben gave the hostess their name for the reservation—*King*, only because it was a easier to spell than *Malka*—the hostess said sorry, she didn't see it, it would be a 20-minute wait, unless they wanted to eat at the bar. Barbara had hoped the young woman would recognize her name, but no, Barbara was an anonymous daytime cable anchor. No *"we have your special table for two Ms. Walters right this way!"* for her. Oh well. The hostess wasn't a scowling x-ray and Barbara didn't want to spoil the night, so she and Ben took a seat at the dark wood bar where the bartender brought them menus and a wine list. Ben ordered a pricey bottle of Cabernet.

"Sorry, Barbara," he said, pulling his barstool close to hers so their legs were touching. He'd held her hand in the movies too.

"It's fine—it's not like we're going to have to eat military rations," she said, referring to *Pearl Harbor,* the movie they'd just seen, only because the art house film Ben would have preferred was being shown at inconvenient times.

"True," he said, nodding as the bartender showed them the bottle and swiftly uncorked it, pouring a sample for Ben who unpretentiously took a small sip. "That's great, thanks." When both their glasses were full, Barbara held hers up for a toast. "Happy Birthday, to the best husband a girl could ask for."

They clinked glasses. "To you, Barbara, the love of my life."

"Oh, honey, that's so sweet," she said, truly touched. "And here's to the other love of our lives, our Rory." She was determined to focus on Ben and her life with him and not let any thoughts of the Phoenix and Jack Stone creep into their night out. "Mediocre movie, huh?" she said, and then, rubbing her chin and modulating her voice as if she was a movie critic, "I found Affleck's searing portrayal of a Southie ruffian more convincing than his depiction of a wartime cuckold."

"What movie was that?" asked Ben, smiling because he knew she was trying to be funny.

"Good Will Hunting?"

"Oh, right." Returning to *Pearl Harbor,* Ben said, "I always think our generation's so spoiled. Can you imagine, coming back to the States after having seen combat overseas, trying to readjust to society." He held up his wine. "It might be hard to indulge in the finer things in life again."

"Or, you might be ravenous, desperate to enjoy them again," she added, remembering how much she enjoyed their serious conversations. So what if he didn't get her silly movie references.

"I think I might prefer to savor them," Ben said thoughtfully, inhaling his wine for a brief moment before taking another sip.

When they got home that night, Barbara and Ben, buzzed from the wine, walked hand-in-hand up the steps to the first floor of their split-level. Rory's dirty little light-up sneakers and catcher's mitt were strewn on the living room floor and, seeing those dear personal effects, she felt an overpowering urge to hold him. He'd looked so cute in his flannel pajamas when they'd dropped him off at Siobhan's that she'd run back over to the chair where he was sitting on Hans' lap to give him a second round of goodbye kisses. "My Rory," she said. "My mama," he answered. Barbara bent down to pick up the mitt and held it lovingly, but Ben took it from her, rested it on a table and kissed her, passionately. "You look pretty tonight," he said, helping her out of her coat.

Barbara had barely put on any makeup that evening, nothing compared to what she wore on television. "I'm not even done up," she said, as they proceeded up the next short flight of steps to their bedroom.

"I always think you're more beautiful this way," Ben said, his hand on her back.

"Well, don't expect me to start wearing overalls anytime soon," she joked and this time he laughed.

Barbara pulled a short, low-cut nightgown from the bottom of one of her dresser drawers and changed in the bathroom. When she emerged, Ben was sitting up in bed, leaning against the headboard, wearing nothing but....a pipe? A book was open on his night stand.

Oh, come on. Wasn't the wine enough? Why did he need his Annie Hall weed? And would it serve as a relaxant, an aphrodisiac, or would it just inspire him to whip out his Whitman instead?

"Really?" she asked, hand on hip.

"I got this pipe at that little head shop in Amherst—remember that place?" he said, separating the seeds from the straggly brown leaves; he'd made a small pile on the bed sheet that covered his lap.

She didn't. Barbara pulled the sheet back on her side of the bed, careful not to disrupt his little mountain of ganja, moved next to him and stroked his chest. "Ben, do you really want to get high and discuss poetry?"

"I just thought a little toke would be fun," he said, tamping the weed down into the pipe's golden bowl and setting it on his night table. He puts his arms around her. "Why don't you join me?"

It had been so many years since she'd smoked weed, she didn't know how she'd react. But she wanted to be agreeable. "I guess one little hit wouldn't hurt," she said, looking at the sheet where the reefer had been.

"That's right," he said, putting his hand under the top of her nightgown and on her breast. He kissed her, then removed his hand and reached over to the night table for the pipe and put it in her mouth. She held the green metallic stem of the pipe as he flicked a lighter with a retro flower power design. She took a deep inhale and held it in before releasing it slowly, tipping her head back.

"Take another one," he said, getting out of bed to open the armoire where they kept a mini stereo system and CD player. "Want some Beatles?"

He was being nice. And he did seem to want to get some. "That's okay, jazz is probably more appropriate, seeing as we're smoking dope. Or wait, if we listen to Jazz, shouldn't we switch to heroin?" She took another hit and instantly felt altered.

Ben got back in bed, not bothering to cover himself with the sheet, and moved up against her, taking the pipe from her hand. "Hope Coltrane's okay," he said, kissing her before taking a pull. "This is 'Stardust.'" He closed his eyes to the music.

Wait. Was he talking about the pot? It was Stardust? Like Angel dust? "What?" she said slowly. She was high.

"The song," he said, taking a big hit, making the seeds in the pipe bowl burn a bright orange.

The seeds were mesmerizing. Like little stars. Stardust. So that's what they were smoking? No, it was name of the song, the song. The melody sounded familiar. Barbara's eyes followed Ben's arm as he put the pipe into the ashtray he'd set on his night table. He turned off the lamp and came back to her.

Barbara listened to the music and closed her eyes and they kissed deeply. Ben took his time: he'd always been deliberate, cautious almost, in bed. Barbara's mind wandered back to the song; it sounded so sad, like a soundtrack in a movie, a war movie, like the one they just saw, where a soldier's going off to war, leaving his love behind. She opened her eyes and it was Jack who looked back at her, with the same expression on his face as he had that rainy morning when he'd saved her from the autograph seeker and clearly didn't want to say goodbye.

Barbara didn't quite gasp but broke off the kiss and said, "Can we turn the lights on?" She needed to see him. Ben.

September 2001

CHAPTER 22

Barbara was swimming in a long, rectangular pool. It was nighttime. The water had a neon-blue sheen to it and waves which shattered into sparks of white as they crashed. Nimble, lithe, she dove underwater and broke through the surface and into Jack Stone's arms.

BUZZ NEWSTIME 5:20. Her clock radio alarm blared: *TIME FOR SPORTS ON AN EARLY TUESDAY MORNING*. She didn't want to get up; she wanted to stay in bed, stay in the water.

Ben was already dressed and racing for the bedroom door—she blew him a kiss and mumbled "Love you": a compensatory display of affection, even though he couldn't read her mind or see her dreams. She knew this dream would come back to her in erotic waves during the day and more vividly at night during that limbo between consciousness and sleep.

Sitting on the toilet, Barbara shook her head in disappointment: no period. What if she was pregnant, her womb home to a tadpole squirming in its own water-logged world, while she committed subconscious aquatic adultery?

She counted. It was the 11th, nearly two months since Ben's birthday sex. After the vision of Jack, she hadn't wanted to interrupt Ben again to put in her diaphragm. Could she be pregnant?

Her cycle had always been erratic and lately she'd been running longer distances, trying to run away from herself and her feelings for Jack. So maybe she'd just skipped like she did during her track days. But what if she was? A pregnancy would be a career killer—she'd carry the stigma of the Woman Who Puts Family before Career. She'd have to tell Cal there would soon be yet another baby at home. While on maternity leave, Ironsides would finally keel over and Miss Big Shot Solo Anchor Spencer would get Ironsides' coveted time slot.

Unless. She could become the modern-day equivalent of the woman who lies down in the field, gives birth, and then straps the plough harness back on—she could be back in the anchor chair within a couple of weeks! She and Ben did want to have another child, eventually, a future companion for Rory. And they could afford it. The upside to Ben's expanded role at the hedge fund was that he was making more money.

Rory appeared in the upstairs hallway. He'd been waking up earlier since first grade started last week; his best buddy was in his class and he looked forward to more than just recess now. Barbara wrapped her arms around him. "You don't have to get up for another hour, little man, why don't you go back to sleep?"

"I'm not tired," he said. His plaid pajama bottoms and soccer jersey looked dirty; she could have sworn they were clean when he put them on last evening.

"I'm going to miss you so much today!" Barbara said, taking his face in her hands and kissing him on both cheeks. "I love you."

"I know," he said, patting her back with his little hand.

"I know? Is that all I get?"

"I love you, too, Mama," he giggled, and her eyes welled. It really wouldn't be the worst thing in the world to have another precious person to love. Barbara took Rory by the hand and they walked downstairs, just as the doorbell rang. Not even 6 o'clock in the morning yet, and Siobhan was in her pressed blue jeans and a floral-print blouse, her red hair swept up into its impeccable beehive. She reported straight to the kitchen, Hans, to the living room to turn on the Phoenix, so he could wait for his daughter to "come on the television."

Barbara and Rory joined Siobhan in the kitchen where Siobhan kissed Rory. "Good morning, my little prince."

"Listen, I'm catching the first train home today," said Barbara, packing her sandwich and thermos in her tote bag.

"Glad you're not filling in for that cripple tonight. Bad enough Ben has to work so hard," said Siobhan.

"Ma!" Calling him Ironsides was one thing. But the distinction would be lost on her mother. "Looks like a gorgeous day," said Barbara. "I'll take Rory to the track with me after school."

In the Phoenix bathroom, Barbara was disappointed for a second time. She remembered being pregnant when she worked at *The Buzz:* being even more exhausted when she woke up in the middle of the night, waddling around the radio station and having to endure strangers patting her belly, asking "What have you got in there, a watermelon?", and living in fear of going into labor behind the microphone. If it happened at the Phoenix, Tex would have to mop up her amniotic fluid as it cascaded down the steps of the set. And then, when she came back two weeks later, she'd have to pump milk in her office. If news broke, she'd have to rip the humming suction device off her nipples, sending milk spraying all over her silk blouse—the camera would then surely magnify the stains. But before she got to the set, she'd have to creep by Jack's office to put her lacteal harvest in the fridge down the hall. Well, at least the breastfeeding would help her lose the baby weight quickly so she wouldn't look lumpy and doughy on television. And if she had another vaginal birth as she had with Rory, she could probably start running again within a month to sweat off any remaining tonnage.

"You're late," Jack said, as he stood in front of her office now, breakfast bag in hand, a tiny piece of toilet paper adhered to an apparent shaving cut on his chin.

Barbara gulped but quickly realized he wasn't any sort of menstrual Kreskin. It was past 7:20.

"Sorry, a little disorganized this morning," she said. If she was pregnant, she'd have to tell Jack, and then he'd know that she and Ben were still doing it. Would he feel jealous? Would the baby look like him because she'd pictured him when she was in bed with her husband? Okay, she needed to get a grip.

Jack came around to her side of the desk and tapped on a computer key, bringing up a memo from Cal.

Remember campers—we are not, repeat, not in the late summer doldrums. The recent shark attack segments have gotten impressive ratings and brought some of our daytime hours close to beating the competition. Go make some great TV!

"Former investigative reporter that I am," said Jack, "I would surmise that if Cal's missives are now appearing in the computer, he is no longer leading our morning meetings."

"And this could mean the Reign of Terror is imminent," said Barbara. And if Sloane's the new Cal when I'm preggers, she thought, the little she-devil will surely try to find a way to shit-can me.

"I think we'd best work our sources," said Jack.

"Copy that."

Hair and makeup confirmed that Cal was looking to retire soon—the words "Boca" and "Raton" had been overheard—but they were still trying to nail down the departure date. Angelica and Jane had also overheard Sloane talking to her mother about her ex-jock boyfriend having "commitment issues." After doing Barbara and Jack's makeup, the girls promised to meet them in the greenroom for a touch-up, as Willy and Celia were vacationing, together. At 8:48, Jack and Barbara were getting their mic packs hooked up in the greenroom because the set was too crowded. They watched *Wake Up, America!* on the greenroom television: Stan and Dorie were interviewing a Girl Scout troop and their leader about the new Scout fitness campaign. James John, whom the troop leader kept calling "John," was doing push-ups, while Stan and Dorie talked to a scout whose sash was stretched tight over her ample abdomen. Barbara wondered if soon she'd be bursting out of her saucy suits, her heft compressing her stiletto heels.

The morning show went to commercial but was coming right back: "With a look at a new fashion line of surf-wear, designed by a shark attack survivor. That's tomorrow, on *Wake Up!*" Angelica and Jane walked into the greenroom to give Jack and Barbara a final spray and powder before they walked to the set. Barbara was shielding her eyes from the spray and Jane was pecking at Jack with her puff—"You're certainly the shiny bugger today"—when Danko burst into the room. As long as she'd known him, Barbara had never seen Rip move that fast. He had his headset around his neck and a pack of cigarettes in his hand.

"Get on the set right now. Hurry. We're busting out of the break."

CHAPTER 23

We do not remember days, we remember moments. Barbara wasn't one to quote verse, but had always felt those words were true. And while no one would forget that day, its moments were indelible.

When Barbara and Jack took their seats at the anchor desk and looked at the monitor of the first smoking tower, Tex gave them the count: "Five, four, wasn't no accident."

They were on a live shot of the towers when the second plane flew in. For a moment, it seemed they were replaying the video of the first plane hitting, but Danko told them in their headsets: "This is not tape. It happened again."

Cal was in the control room with Rip, telling Barbara and Jack that the Pentagon had been hit and that "War has been declared."

Lois and Sloane were among the first newspeople to arrive downtown. In the middle of one update, Lois gasped and reported that people were jumping from the buildings. "We will not show you those pictures," she said on air, near tears.

Cathryn began her first live shot from lower Manhattan with a description of the difficulty she'd had getting to the scene. In the middle of one of her sentences, Danko hit the bulletin sounder and cut to the live pictures of an enormous grey cloud pulling down the first tower.

Stacia was rushed into the newsroom to await any remarks by the president. She had to report instead that a plane had crashed in a field in Pennsylvania.

Angelica and Jane came into the newsroom arm in arm. Barbara could see out of the corner of her eye that Angelica had changed into her running shoes.

Barbara and Jack were finally replaced at the anchor desk that evening by Ironsides and Spencer, who'd changed and cleaned up. With the tunnels and bridges open again, Jack hailed a gypsy cab prowling the deserted streets outside the Phoenix's midtown headquarters. If it had been the day before, Barbara would have questioned the driver's credentials and wondered why his sedan's grey upholstery was so filthy. She sank into the dirty seat and Jack got in next to her, without putting the arm rest down; his beard stubble was visible through his stage makeup and his eyes looked glassy.

He took her hand and held it. Barbara thought of the jumpers and the reports that some had jumped together. She squeezed Jack's hand. "They couldn't take that away from us," she said.

They entered the midtown tunnel and the car grew dark. Jack put his arm around her. She wondered if the tunnel could be the next target. She put her head on Jack's shoulder. "Do you think it's over?"

"I..." He paused. "I do. I can't imagine they would have the resources or sophistication to execute a second wave."

Barbara picked her head up and said, "Are you just saying that or do you really believe it?"

"I really believe it," he said, tenderly pushing a strand of hair off her face. And just before the car got to the end of the tunnel, Jack kissed her. It was quick, but it was on the lips. She nestled into his arm.

As the cab neared her house, Barbara separated from Jack and leaned forward in her seat to look out the window. She saw Hans standing in front of her front door, arms folded, silently waiting, just as he did all those times she came home from an odd-hour broadcast internship. The door swung open and Rory ran outside, onto the flagstone path from the front door to the driveway. Rory waved happily to Barbara as if she was just coming home from a trip to the grocery store. Her throat tightened. She barely glanced at Jack as she grabbed the greasy car door handle and mumbled, "I'm gonna go…I'll…" She threw open the door and ran toward Rory, tears already forming in her eyes. It was like that day in first grade when a boy whipped a tetherball's chain too hard and knocked her to the ground with the ball; she'd picked herself up without shedding a tear and even launched a fist full of playground dirt at the kid. But when she came off the bus that day and saw her mother, she started sobbing.

Siobhan came outside as did Ben, who'd gotten through to the Phoenix to tell Barbara he'd made it home. As she reached them, Barbara pulled Rory to her; she couldn't hold him tight enough. Barbara didn't look at the car as it pulled away. She wept, as her husband and parents formed a circle around her.

November 2001

CHAPTER 24

Cal's persistent prediction, widely dismissed as fatuous, had come true: The Phoenix was America's number-one cable news channel. No one did patriotism better than the Phoenix: the entire day of programming was set to Sousa snares and graphics featuring Old Glory. Cal was still in charge and the rise of his Phoenix had stalled Sloane's ascent to the channel's presidency. Aside from coordinating coverage in the now month-old war, Cal wanted to make sure his own troops were safe, so he brought former Detective Tony Miletto into the conference room one morning to talk terror.

"If some terrorist decides to bomb Times Square, we're sitting ducks," Miletto predicted, looking uncomfortable holding a pointer instead of a billy club as he gestured toward a large map of Manhattan posted on a bulletin board.

"This," he tapped at the red circle drawn around midtown and the you-are-here arrow pointed at the Phoenix's Broadway headquarters, "could be the new ground zero."

Barbara put her hand under the neckline of her blouse to make sure her cross pendant was there. She'd clung to her faith since 9/11, even if it had meant some arguments with Ben. On her first day off after it happened, Barbara, who felt crampy but relieved after learning that she was not pregnant, had gone with Ben and Rory to a beach playground where she'd played as a child. Watching Rory propel himself from the swing, then land in the sand and run over to her and Ben so they could kiss him and tickle him, Barbara had thought of the Celtic saying her mother often quoted: *Heaven and earth are only three feet apart, but in the thin places, that distance is even smaller.* In that thin place, where the veil that separates heaven and earth is lifted, you get a glimpse of the glory of God. She felt she was in that thin place.

"I'm scared. I don't want anything to take this away," she'd said, watching Rory tackle the monkey bars. Barbara and Ben had tried to explain to him what had happened but he didn't grasp it—who could? Rory had struggled to quote Gammy, who had said "the good ol' U.S. of A." was going to "blow those camel jockeys to smithereens."

"I highly doubt Bayville's on their hit list," Ben had said.

"So you think they have a list?" she'd asked.

"Barb, I don't know. They might. And who knows what bombing them will incite."

Did he have to be so practical? Could *the end* be coming? Might she soon be returning to the start—ashes to ashes—here at her childhood beach?

"I keep thinking, Ben, about what the priest said at that vigil: 'God is the light. God is the way. And God will have the last word.'"

"I'm not sure you can cast this as good versus evil, God versus the bad guys.".

"I can and I will," she'd said, standing up to receive Rory as he jumped from the bars. "God's not going to let the terrorists win."

In the conference room, Miletto continued, "So if things go kaboom around here, the best thing would be to hightail it, that is, evacuate the building."

Lois Spencer, reading glasses perched on her nose, stopped taking notes, and raised her hand. "Detective, if midtown is hit and an evacuation is ordered, is there a location here in the building from which we'd still be able to broadcast?" Spencer had been briefly humanized in the first few days after, filing truly poignant reports about what she'd witnessed downtown. But then her show was renamed *Lois Spencer's America Rises* (which, if you paused after "America" made it sound like the country was hers) and she was back to her old self.

"You mean, like a bunker?" Miletto sneered.

"No, I mean a studio from which," Lois slowly repeated her words, as if for the benefit of the hearing-impaired, "we would still be able to broadcast."

Jack, who was sitting next to Barbara in the conference room, kicked her under the table. Barbara held her newspaper up so only Jack could see her cross her eyes. They had never discussed The Kiss and Barbara hadn't figured out what had even really happened on their ride home on 9/11. Was it the culmination of months of sexual tension and mutual physical attraction? Or were they just two comrades, trapped in a fox hole that day, reaching out to each other physically when no words would do? Either way, it was a chaste kiss (no tongue) so it certainly didn't count as cheating.

Miletto continued, "Well, Miss Spencer, if it's a bad enough attack that the NYPD orders an evacuation, you wouldn't want to stick around..."

Precisely. Barbara didn't want to hang around now; she and Jack had a show to anchor and then she had to prep for the special report she was doing on the Ironsides show. Perhaps as a reward for her steady performance on 9/11, Cal had given Barbara a greater presence in prime time, assigning her occasional stories on the Ironsides news hour.

"Wouldn't we just broadcast out of D.C.?" Cathyrn Collyns, in a fit of lucidity, raised one hand to ask her question, and with the other continued twirling a faux flaxen strand. She'd recently asked Barbara how to wear her American flag pin. "Which side does it go on?" Barbara couldn't tell her that no one would notice the tiny flag amid the cleavage, so she said instead, "On your left. Where you'd put your hand if you were saying the pledge."

Miletto called on Cathryn. "Yes, miss, D.C. would probably be the broadcast site if New York went down."

"Do you have any intelligence on a specific plan to target Times Square for attack?" asked Stan Keegan as he held Dorie's hand. They'd always looked more like siblings than spouses, and now, with their coordinating red, white, and blue wardrobe, they looked like Donny and Marie, getting ready to host a *Little Bit Country, Little Bit Rock 'n' Roll* 9/11 variety show. Their actual show, *Wake Up America!,* had retained its name even though America clearly had been awoken. But Stan and Dorie and "J.J." (everyone had given up on figuring out whether his name was James John or John James) had been reinvented as wartime journalists, with military men and terror experts replacing their retinue of corn pone guests.

Miletto answered, "No specific intel. Look, we're in the crossroads of the world, as they say. Wouldn't even have to be Al-Qaeda—could be any lunatic with a bomb—I'm just supposed to tell you how to get out if Times Square gets hit."

Barbara prayed it would never happen. She hadn't become blasé about the possibility of another attack, just inured to the fear. The past months had been a haze of horrible stories, each one telegraphed by a funereal-sounding bulletin chime that seemed to say "Listen up, because you're all going to die!"

A Phoenix news flash: *A source based in Yemen is saying the mastermind of the attack is likely alive and in hiding and planning more attacks, probably in New York City...*

A Phoenix news flash: *Another airport has been shut down this morning after the discovery of an unattended package. Bomb-sniffing dogs and military personnel are on scene...*

A Phoenix news flash: *Deadly anthrax has been discovered in a package sent to our own headquarters here at the Phoenix News Channel....*

Oh, for those carefree days when Detective Miletto was manhandling autograph seekers.

Miletto wrapped up his presentation by providing a blueprint of their building's stairway locations and a reminder to pick up a Phoenix-issued survival fanny packs, which contained Band-Aids, water, and a flashlight, but none of the potassium iodide everyone was trying to score. Barbara grabbed a pack and headed for Rip's office to start her long day.

CHAPTER 25

Barbara knocked on Danko's door and had to laugh when she saw the picture taped to it: ZZ Top, its bearded guitarists in bejeweled 10-gallon hats, flanking Osama Bin Laden, arms raised, sticks crossed, on drums.

"You ready for me to voice the package for tonight?" Barbara asked as she sat down opposite Danko.

"Just about," he said. "And Sloane wants to tag it with some Q&A."

Buffalo Springfield's "For What It's Worth" was spinning on Rip's turntable. The last step in Sloane's climb to the Phoenix president was overseeing prime time, which meant she'd likely be in the control room, trying to play puppeteer for Barbara's special report.

Danko reached into his desk and grabbed a cigarette, apparently just to fondle it; he was trying to quit. "Coming to the end of sweeps. She wants to go after Congressman Quagmire." In questioning the war in Afghanistan, a congressman who was a decorated Vietnam war veteran had evoked the dreaded term used to describe the war in which he'd fought.

"What'd you tell her?" asked Barbara.

Danko tapped a key on his computer and took off his wire-rimmed glasses and moved closer to the screen. "I told her we would be *No Filters, No Fluff,* as always."

"What'd she say to that?"

"Called me an asshole," said Rip, reading the script they'd worked on together. "She didn't fuck with the copy for our package, but beware, Ironsides has really been....ahem....going off the reservation lately...asking his live reporters really biased questions. Can't tell if the old son-of-a-bitch is losing it, or if Sloane's pulling the strings. In any event, careful out there."

As Barbara left his office, she heard Danko singing about battle lines being drawn.

Indeed.

That evening, during a commercial break in the 7 o'clock news hour, Barbara ascended the steps to the set and sat in a chair next to Ironsides. There were no duet-ready barstools for his show—the stage hands would have had to prop him up FDR-style for that to work, so instead, he sat in his wheelchair, behind a news desk. His hair and mustache were dyed shoe-polish black, a look that said "Robert Goulet" more than Raymond Burr. It was a holdover from Hunter's heyday as a local news anchor in the 1970s, when he and his gravel-voiced co-anchor wore matching chartreuse suits and knocked back martinis before show time. As Barbara sat down, a makeup artist flew up to the set and dabbed another layer of spackle into the deep grooves underneath Ironsides' eyes, then gave the stage manager a shrug as if to say "I can only do so much."

Barbara caught a glimpse of Bill Hunter's useless legs, which looked like they could belong to a ventriloquist's dummy. She felt a pang of self-loathing for coveting his job, for wanting to fold him back into his box for good.

"Nice to see you, Bill, thanks for having me on the show," she said, extending her hand. She wondered if he might member meeting her once at a Phoenix function.

"Pleased to meet you, Lois," he said, his speckled hand, perhaps in compensation for his floppy lower extremities, nearly cutting off the blood supply to hers. "You news anchors keep getting younger. I have ties older than you."

Lois! She laughed at his tie joke but needed to correct him, lest he call her "Lois" on air.

"I'm Barbara King, Bill. I know there are a lot of new faces at the Phoenix these days." There weren't really. She sat down.

"It looks like we'll have a little time for Q&A after your report, Barbara." What Rip warned her about. And so old school, the way he didn't acknowledge calling her Lois: never admit a mistake on or off air.

"Sure thing," she said. What was that weird smell about him? Something antiseptic. All that hair dye? But no, it smelled slightly sweet.

"Where are we?" Ironsides blurted, looking around the studio.

The stage manager, perhaps noticing Barbara's eyes widen, jumped in. "Ten seconds back from break, then the King intro and her toss to her package, Q&A, then you wrap, Bill, and toss to break." Thank goodness he just needed to know "where they were" in the show. But man, this stage manager really had to hold Ironsides' wee-wee, thought Barbara. Her eyes involuntarily flickered toward Ironsides' lap; she wondered what function remained.

After her prerecorded report aired, Barbara tagged it live, turning from her camera to face Hunter on the set.

So Bill, the Congressman says he's essentially just trying to open a discussion about how long the war in Afghanistan might last.

Ironsides jolted in his chair and Barbara wondered if he had awoken from a nap or if Sloane had put her hand up his back. He put his hand to his chin, striking a prosecutorial pose.

Yes, but Barbara, is it really appropriate for the Congressman to suggest that the war could be a quagmire, a la Vietnam—it's unpatriotic, isn't it?

What does this codger want me to do, be a pundit all of a sudden?

Well, Bill, the Congressman is a decorated war veteran who says he's merely wondering if the United States might have to stay in Afghanistan beyond the day Osama Bin Laden is killed or captured.

Barbara gave a little "back to you" nod, hoping that would end it, but Hunter was casting a bloodshot eye toward his computer.

But Barbara, given that our nation was so viciously attacked just two months ago, wouldn't it be fair to say that this is not the time to be questioning a war aimed at bringing those terrorists, those monsters, to justice?

Well, when you put it *that* way. Barbara certainly wanted the terrorists to pay for what they did, plus, she wanted to make sure her little family was safe from another attack. She didn't know how to answer.

"NEED TO WRAP. ANSWER HIM YES!"

Sloane. So she was playing the ventriloquist to Hunter's dummy. As Barbara hesitated to speak, Hunter tried again.

So, in conclusion, Barbara, this Congressman's patriotism's certainly could be called into question, couldn't it?

The stage manager was making frantic circular motions with his finger in the air. They had 5 seconds to wrap and get to the computer-generated commercial, which would cut them off regardless. Sloane screamed.

"GOTTA GO! SAY IT. SAY YES."

Yes, Bill, it could....

Barbara King, thanks. Back after a break.

Barbara got up from her chair quickly; her hand was shaking as she unclipped her mic. They made her say it. She didn't want to. They cornered her. But the words had come out of her own mouth. *Yes.*

Hunter sighed and turned his back to her, reaching for the *Washington Times*. Barbara left the set and before leaving for the evening, checked her office computer where a top-line from Sloane was awaiting.

Davis: *Now that wasn't so hard, was it?*

Damn ventriloquist. Sloane was probably in the control room, gargling with water as she threw her voice into the next dummy on the set. Barbara wanted to march down there and have it out with her once and for all. But Sloane was going to be number one soon and Barbara had recently realized that her own contract with the Phoenix was up in just a matter of weeks, at the end of December. How could she negotiate with someone she'd wrestled to the ground in the control room? Barbara typed various hostile responses, deleted them all, then finally hit "send."

King: *Yes, it was.*

CHAPTER 26

Another good reason for not brawling with Sloane was that Barbara had to leave the station quickly to attend her parents' anniversary celebration that night. It was their fortieth, but given the somber mood of the nation, they'd decided to hold a scaled-down party, not in a seaside restaurant, but in Siobhan and Hans' neat grey box of a house, where red, white, and blue balloons fluttered along with the flag on their porch.

Barbara's parents' small living room was packed with friends who'd respectfully left their construction boots, nurse's clogs, or teacher's loafers on the clear rubber runner in the entranceway. Their police officer friend had come from a funeral and checked his bagpipe there, next to the oversized umbrella belonging to the priest who had waxed so eloquent about good versus evil in the days after 9/11.

Hans held court from his tweed recliner with the well-worn arm rest covers, and drank a warm beer as friends congratulated him. Siobhan was a Technicolor dream: rhinestone pins glittering in her red hair, its color overpowered only by her purple polyester wrap dress; she worked the room and fussed over the deli trays Barbara had purchased from Siobhan's old grocery store. Barbara collected dishes at the door from the ladies in their polyester slacks and hair styled into blue clouds. Ben tended to Rory, in khakis and a blue oxford, pressed to perfection by Gammy. The crowd of people Barbara had known all her life filled their dinner plates with casseroles (macaroni and tuna, lasagna, chicken a la king) and Father Kieran sipped a glass of clear liquid Barbara was fairly certain wasn't water.

She was on her way into the crowded kitchen to get a beer for one of the checkout girls, when she spotted Mr. Martels, her high school English teacher and admired acquaintance of her parents. His wavy brown hair was grey-tinged and he'd lost the mutton chops, but he still wore a short-sleeved dress shirt with a pen handily tucked into the front pocket. All these years and it was still hard to know if focusing on the stationary eye was proper etiquette.

"Barbara Konig, I mean King!" he said.

"Mr. Martels! How's the good ol' *Truman Times?*"

"Same as ever. Sort of. I'm trying to get the kids interested in new media—like cable news! I'm usually in school when you're on, but I've caught you a few times on the evening news—like tonight. You do a fine job."

"Thanks, Mr. M." She hoped he had missed the Ironsides "No Filters" Q&A.

"You can call me Blake."

"No, I really can't." They laughed.

"What's it like working there?" As he said "there," his lazy eye meandered in the direction of a deli tray, but she knew he didn't mean the former Bohack's.

"The Phoenix? It's busy. Certainly these days. But it's good. Mostly."

He took a sip of his Coke and asked, "So, do you have writers or do you write it all yourself?"

"Well, we ad-lib a lot because there's so much breaking news. Writers handle the scripts but we're the 'editors of last resort.'"

"So if something sounded like propaganda, you could change it."

"Gee, I guess my channel's reputation precedes it." For someone who didn't watch that much, Mr. Martels seemed to have a well-formed opinion of the Phoenix.

"The famous Mr. Martels!" Ben was suddenly next to them, without Rory, who was on Siobhan's lap grimacing as a neighbor pinched his cheeks.

"Ben, right?" said Mr. Martels. "I'm afraid I was just asking your wife tedious questions about her job."

"And I was just about to explain to Mr. Martels that I'm still trying to *give everyone a fair shake*!" said Barbara, hoping his old catch phrase would warm him to her.

"Harder to do," said Ben, stroking his chin, "when your prime-time anchorman calls a war hero unpatriotic!"

Thanks, husband, thought Barbara.

"Yeah, caught that," said Martels, shaking his head in disgust. "A decorated veteran being criticized for exercising his first amendment right to free speech, just because he questioned the possible length of a war which is being fought to preserve our freedoms, the precise thing the terrorists hate, and, I think, envy so much about our society."

"The guy was in 'Nam, man!" said Ben, as if he too had once navigated that jungle hell.

"Well, my piece on the congressman was fair, Mr. M," said Barbara, not even bothering to try to redeem herself with her husband.

"Yeah, but that Hunter dude with his questions," Ben interjected. "Your channel doesn't want anyone to criticize the government. Tell that to the kids who died protesting 'Nam!"

Shut it, Mr. Kent State, thought Barbara. "I really was trying to avoid those questions calling the congressman's patriotism into question, but, you see," she stammered, "we were up against a hard break, um, meaning, we were going to commercial and..." She realized she was just making things worse. Not only had she not been able to defend the congressman on air as eloquently and succinctly as Mr. M just had, but now she was trying to justify her actions by explaining that she had to end the interview so her police-state station could make money from a commercial.

"Barbara, you're still the most famous person to come out of Truman High," Mr. Martels interrupted, as if separating a jock and a burnout in the high school hallway. "And our best editor ever. I'm sure you'll make every effort to keep it, what's your slogan, 'No Filters, No Fluff'?"

Barbara was 17 again. "I definitely will, Mr. M.," she said, as one of her mother's neighbors grabbed her arm. She smiled at Mr. Martels and, as she turned away, shot Ben a filthy look.

When they got home from the party, Barbara carried Rory from their minivan to his bed; he felt warm. She left him in his party clothes, now stained with casserole, but woke him up so she could dose him with Tylenol, then sat with him for a while, stroking his damp forehead. After arranging his stuffed animals at his headboard and covering him lightly with his favorite blanket, she walked into her own bedroom, nearly tripping over the laundry basket in the doorway. Apparently Ben's liberal beliefs didn't extend to being a house husband and picking up the goddamn clothes. She'd barely grunted to him on the way home from the party and now he was sound asleep, on his back, poetry anthology resting on his chest.

Barbara was just about to pull a night shirt out from under her pillow, when Rory let out a whimper. She sat on the bed and poked Ben.

"Huh?"

She moved in closer to him. Maybe he'd snuck a toke at the party? She sniffed. Nothing. "Rory has a slight fever," she said.

"Want me to get him?" he asked, still half asleep.

"Never mind," she said. You sleep your sleep and dream your dream of a world where television news anchors all report the news fairly.

Rory was crying, complaining he was hot. Barbara got a washcloth and ran cool water over it and gently pressed it to his forehead. Poor little guy, she would have taken the sickness for him if she could. She crawled into his narrow bed next to him, holding the compress in place.

When Barbara woke up and looked at the red digits glowing from the clock in Rory's room, it was 1:46 a.m. Her sweater was moist with his sweat; his fever must have broken. She hoisted herself out of his bed as quietly as possible and walked into her bedroom where Ben was sleeping in the exact same position as before.

She sighed loudly and plunked down onto the bed, unzipping her skirt violently and letting her pumps drop to the floor. Ben didn't stir. She finally took his arm and shook it. "Thanks for leaving me there!"

"What?" he mumbled, finally turning on his side to face her.

"Weren't you wondering why I hadn't come to bed?"

Ben rolled back away from her. "I was sleeping."

Could she really pick a fight in the middle of the night? Yes. Yes she could. "You know, it would be really nice, if just once, you could have my back."

"What are you talking about?" he asked, picking his head up and squinting at the alarm clock on his night table. "What time is it?"

"You didn't help with Rory tonight. You almost Dick Van Dyked-me, leaving the laundry basket for me to trip over. I worked today too. I'm tired, even if I spent my day quashing freedom... in the interest of preserving freedom!"

Ben turned on his night table lamp and wiped his eyes. "Dick Van What? What are you talking about?" He sat up. "Wait, so you're angry about that conversation?"

"Damn right I am. I can't believe you shit all over the Phoenix...and me!....in front of Martels. What was that about? Couldn't you back me up? Do you know how horrible I felt about that stupid Q&A?!"

"Barbara," he said, in the calmest of voices. "No one had a gun to your head to make you say what you said."

"You don't understand, I was up against the clock," she shrieked.

"But shouldn't people be allowed to question the war?"

"Shouldn't we be bombing the motherfuckers who brought down the towers?"

"That's not the point."

"Okay, but in my report I did not question the guy's patriotism!"

"But the anchor did and you didn't argue," said Ben, calmer with each volley.

"I couldn't! Sloane was in my ear screaming at me to wrap. If I had more time, I would have played devil's advocate and defended the guy, but we were up against...."

"A commercial. Right. And your metaphor doesn't work," said Ben, sitting up straighter in bed. "That congressman is not the devil. But maybe your station is."

Barbara stood up. "Okay, Mr. Liberal 'Nam Protester, trying to act all cool in front of Mr. Martels—you don't mind when the *devil* helps pay the bills and throws the parties where you can team up against your crazy, warmongering wife, huh?"

"Barbara, please." Ben gently took her arm to make her sit. "Look honey, I don't blame you. I know you try. And it's a scary world since it happened. I know you just want us to be safe and for God to punish the terrorists. But this situation is more nuanced."

Nuanced? As if she was some dingbat who didn't understand the intricacies of a civil liberties debate!

"Let's try to settle in. I'm going to read a little," said Ben and picked his poetry anthology up from his night table.

She sat on the bed, breathing through her nose.

"Barbara," he said, patting her arm. "I'm not judging you. I work at a hedge fund for God's sakes. I know your job is great in a lot of ways. I've also resigned myself to, well...the road not taken." Ben opened his book.

Quoting poetry. That was it. Barbara leapt up from the bed, ripped the book from Ben's hands and, winding up like a pitcher, hurled it across the room, hitting the laundry basket. The folded towels and T-shirts shuddered. But she wasn't satisfied; she wanted to throw a lamp or at least kick the basket around the room, even if it meant having to refold the laundry later.

But Ben threw himself out of bed and gave her such a pitying look that she couldn't perpetrate any more low-scale violence. "I'm going to sleep in Rory's room," he said.

"Good, have fun," she said, "while I sleep in this nice king size bed, paid for, *BY THE DEVIL!"*

CHAPTER 27

It was the last day of November and a subdued holiday season had arrived. Angelica had attended a prayer service last night; on her console next to her mousse lay a fan, a cardboard cutout of Jesus affixed to an oversized Popsicle stick. The thought of sugared ice made Barbara's stomach turn. She leaned back in the barber chair and hoped she hadn't picked up the stomach bug Rory brought home from the kid who barfed during computer lab. "He had pink Trix yogurt for lunch!" Rory had reported.

Jane called from next door, telling them to pick up: Barbara's agent was on the line. Angelica gave her a look that said *Oooooooooooooo,* and with nails painted red with sprays of tiny black lines that looked like whiskers, started setting Barbara's hair.

Barbara heard Gene screaming "Horsefuck," probably to his assistant, as she picked up.

"Top of the morning to you, too, Gene."

"Damn networks. Listen, ran into Cal last night. I gently reminded him your contract is up in a month. Told him we could hammer out a new one over steaks."

Barbara couldn't imagine Gene doing anything *gently.* "Great. Did you gently remind him that I've been making appearances on prime time and those shows have been getting good numbers?"

"Yeah, sure I did." He probably didn't. "But he said he wants me to meet this Sloane David."

"Davis," Barbara corrected. "Meaning what? She's not doing deals yet, is she?"

"Nah. But make sure to kiss her ass. I hear she's one tough bitch."

After Barbara relayed Gene's end of the conversation, Angelica asked, "How's the family?" Barbara knew what she was getting at: the big fight with Ben.

"We're good." Some marijuana-free makeup sex had helped them get over their spat. "I'm not sure he really gets it. But at least he's trying to help around the house a little more. Putting away his laundry, et cetera." Barbara heard footsteps and the velvet curtain opened and Jack appeared. He handed Barbara a cup of coffee. "You left this on your desk," he said. "I thought you might also like a copy of the rundown." He gave a slight bow. "Good morning, Angelica."

Angelica nodded, and Barbara said, "Oh, thank you Jack," wishing she didn't have a head full of curlers. "No Q&A with any aged anchors today I hope?" she asked.

Jack smiled knowingly. "I believe it's time to remove your hairshirt, Ms. King. You had no control over what questions came out of his drooling mouth, nor could you prevent the computer-generated commercial from preventing a defense of the congressman, who really might have been wiser not to use that particular term so soon after September."

"Thanks," she said softly, blushing. Angelica pretended to organize her brushes.

"I'll catch you on the set," Jack said, and then poked his head through the curtain one more time. "That's a cute look."

When he was gone, Angelica took the Jesus fan and handed it to Barbara. "You're flushed," she said. The crew still gossiped about Barbara and Jack. Angelica had reported just last week that one of the crew guys had referred to them as "the lovebirds." She asked Barbara, "You going tonight?" Jack and his wife were having a holiday party and Barbara and Ben were attending.

Barbara was dying to see Jack's home and meet Mrs. Stone. "Come hell or high water." Barbara immediately regretted the expression, seeing as she was fanning herself with Jesus. "Do you think you could give me a 'do' later?"

"You got it," said Angelica. "But I'll be needing a full report Monday morning."

Her hair in a messy updo, Barbara drove with Ben from Bayville to Brookville that night. They walked up the steps to the elaborately-carved mahogany door of the Stones' magnificent Tudor and Ben grabbed one of the two large wrought iron rings.

"What knockers!" said Barbara, referencing *Young Frankenstein* strictly for her own amusement. A maid in a black uniform and white apron answered the door and took their coats, and they stood for a moment in the black and white marble foyer graced by a huge, perfectly symmetrical Douglas fir. Barbara wondered how a woman with a child avoided hanging the Styrofoam Santa or a hand-stitched felt snowman on a tree. This one was awash in silver, gold, and crystal, and hundreds of tiny white lights.

Barbara and Ben entered the living room which was exquisitely furnished in coordinating fabrics—staid stripes blending with friendly florals. The tabletops and mantels were bedecked in crimson velvet runners with fringes of forest green, the same shade as the walls. The walls were adorned with family photos. Framed in frosted white birch branches, the portraits were sepia-toned and seasonally themed: Jack's daughter, Madeleine, as a toddler, tossing a handful of snow in the air; her parents' silhouettes set against a darkening winter sky. Barbara thought of the inexpensive Christmas adornments in her parents' home, including a ceramic holy family which Hans had mistaken for a *Schnapps* decanter. Barbara remembered him quietly cursing when he couldn't screw off Joseph's head.

"Let's find the bar," said Ben, and Barbara nodded enthusiastically. He looked great tonight; clean shaven, his hair slicked back. She'd teased him that he looked like a real Wall Street guy and he teased back that she looked like a real Phoenix news anchor. She asked him if, by that, he meant militaristic, and he kissed her and said, "No, just beautiful."

Barbara looked for the host as she and Ben walked through the living room, but instead, spotted *her*. Mrs. Stone. She was posed, crystal champagne flute in hand, at the bottom of a curving staircase, the railing of which was decorated in real pine garland. Wearing a below-the-knee black velvet skirt, silver satin crew neck blouse, and very large diamond stud earrings (no way were those c.z.'s), Mrs. Stone was a holiday portrait herself. She was conversing with a white-haired gentleman wearing either a turtleneck or, more likely, a dickey, and red suede blazer. She looked in Barbara's direction but continued her conversation.

Barbara and Ben were almost at the bar, when Jack bounded over to them, cocktail in hand and an expression that indicated the drink wasn't his first. She was happy to see him and relieved he wasn't wearing a monogrammed smoking jacket, monocle, or ascot. He was, however, in a stylish black velvet blazer, chosen, no doubt, to coordinate with his wife. He shook Ben's hand and gave Barbara an air kiss. "You just missed Cal," he said.

"Oh, no, you're kidding?" She could have had a little schmooze time with the boss.

"He and his wife were the first to arrive," said Jack. "I was barely out of the shower." Barbara took a moment to picture that. "And the first to leave. They wanted to turn in early."

Barbara tried to include Ben, "You remember me telling you he could be retiring any time now."

Ben nodded, his eyes drifting over to the bar.

"I have to confess something to your wife, Ben," said Jack.

Ben, who hadn't said a word, just cocked his head. It would be nice if he pitched in a little in the conversation department.

Jack took another sip of his drink and announced: "We invited Sloane this evening."

"Oh no!" said Barbara. "Seriously?" Sloane would be loaded for bear after the Ironsides Q&A.

"Barbara's favorite producer," Ben finally put in.

"Why'd you invite *her*?" asked Barbara.

"'Tis the season to be kind," said Jack. "And Mrs. Stone," he added, scanning the room for her, "correctly pointed out that Sloane will soon be our boss and it would be bad form to exclude her."

What the hell did Agatha or Mildred or whatever Mrs. Stone's first name was, know about it? "You could have sent her a fruitcake."

Jack laughed. "Come on, Barbara, it could be interesting. She's coming with a guest." He raised his eyebrows suggestively.

Before Barbara could make another snide remark, a preppy-looking man whose red velvet vest matched his red-splotched complexion slapped Jack on the back. "Jackson! Merry Christmas, old man!"

Jackson? Old man? What was this world Jack lived in? She and Ben took it as their cue to continue their trip to the bar. And even the bartender was perfect, clearly just subsidizing his modeling career. Mrs. Stone apparently hadn't worried about scaling down their holiday party in light of recent events, thought Barbara, as she and Ben journeyed to the bounteous shrimp bar.

Barbara was wiping a glob of cocktail sauce from the side of her mouth when Mrs. Stone, who'd been instructing a waiter to replenish the ice around the prawns, finally turned to them and said, without enthusiasm, "Hello, Barbara. Cynthia Stone. Happy Holidays."

Cynthia!

Barbara wiped her mouth with her napkin and accidentally flicked the cocktail sauce on the rug.

Cynthia extended a slender hand.

"My husband, Ben Malka," said Barbara, pulling up her plunging neckline; she suddenly felt like cheap goods. "Your home is exquisite." Even if your fine oriental rug is now stained.

"Thank you. You're so kind," she said, barely smiling. "The waitstaff is just about to bring out the fillets. I hope you enjoy the evening." And she pirouetted toward another guest who was reaching for her arm. They had been dismissed. Didn't she have any curiosity about her husband's co-anchor? Had Jack never talked about Barbara at home? Or maybe he did mention her—too often—and Mrs. Stone was icing her because she was jealous?

Barbara whispered to Ben, "Oughta have the waitstaff take that stick out of her ass!"

"Come on, Barb, she has a lot of people to tend to."

"She sure is pretty though," said Barbara.

"Yeah, so?" said Ben.

"So, nothing, I've never seen her in person and I just wondered what she looked like is all."

Ben looked at her quizzically. "Come on, let's get another drink," he said and they did a few laps around the party, making small talk with the Stones' neighbors at the buffet. They found a couple of chairs and Barbara ate, picking at her food.

Her stomach was starting to churn; maybe the shrimp wasn't agreeing with her? She tried not to think about what that Trix yogurt looked like the second time 'round.

Ben wiped his mouth with his monogrammed napkin and said, "Whatta ya say we go outside for a little after-dinner smoke."

"Oh jeez, Ben, I don't want to..." No way was she getting high. What if he got caught by one of *Cynthia's* pals from dressage?

Jack came up behind them, and with a hand on the backs of their chairs, asked, "Enjoying the fare?" She could smell the scotch on his breath. His wife was probably still nursing her first flute of Veuve Clicquot.

"Everything's delish," Barbara said, glancing at her empty plate. "We were just telling your wife how beautiful your home is—a regular winter wonderland."

"Would the Kings like the 5-cent tour?" asked Jack.

Barbara saw the opportunity to take advantage of Ben's drug habit to steal a little alone time with Jack. "Ben was just heading to the...men's room," she gave Ben a meaningful look.

"Yeah, that's right," said Ben. "I'll catch up."

Jack walked Barbara through the kitchen past the "staff" and down half a level of steps to a small study with a fireplace, decorated in masculine prints that evoked aged scotch and tales of the day's hunt.

"I feel like I'm at Sagamore Hill," said Barbara.

"Sorry, I haven't bagged anything to hang over the mantle," Jack said, walking behind a desk that would have done T.R. proud. "Since we have a moment alone, I thought I'd present you with an early Christmas gift." Jack pulled out a gift box from the top desk drawer. He looked at the small bow on Barbara's burgundy velvet dress. "You look like a present yourself tonight, by the way."

She blushed. "You want me to open this now?" She looked at the door, afraid Ben or Mrs. Stone would walk in.

"Please do."

Merry Christmas! Love, Jack, read the small note card tied to the ribbon. Well, that could be incriminating. As could the gift: a bottle of Chanel No. 5.

"Did I get it right?" Jack asked, leaning against the desk, unbuttoning his jacket.

She felt warm too. "This is the perfume I wear. How did you know that?" First the Jimmy Choos. And now another personal gift she'd have to keep stashed away so she wouldn't have to explain to Ben that her co-anchor was keeping her in heels and perfume, as if she were his *goomah.*

"I am nothing if not a paid observer, Ms. King."

"Well, yeah, but you never observed me putting it on." He knew her scent.

"No. I went to a department store and sampled various fragrances before arriving upon this one. The saleswoman helped me, in so far as eliminating the trendy selections and helping me chose among the more 'classic perfumes.'"

"I don't know what to say," she sputtered.

Jack beamed. "Just say,..."

"Excuse me, Mr. Stone?" A waiter appeared at the door of the study. "Mrs. Stone was in the kitchen looking for you."

Barbara found Ben back in the living room, his dark eyes now just slits in his head. He was talking with Rip Danko.

"Hey, Barb," said Rip. "I was lucky enough to run into your husband just as he was going outside to *get something he left in the car,*" he laughed. Good, they'd gotten high together and wouldn't notice how red her face was.

Jack approached again. For someone who had a house full of people, he sure was spending a lot of time with them.

"Danko, glad you could make it!" he said.

"Thanks for having the likes of me," Rip responded, his eyes feasting on a busty young woman passing a silver platter of hors d'oeuvres.

"I should talk to you about Afghanistan at some point this evening, Rip," said Jack. "Although Mrs. Stone would tell me it's impolite to talk shop."

"Afghanistan?" said Barbara. "Please tell me you're not thinking about going there." Jack had mentioned over breakfast a few days ago that Sloane had called him, suggesting he consider reporting from there. Barbara was angry that, once again, Sloane had picked Jack, to "showcase," even if Jack had explained it was just Sloane just stroking his ego.

"I think there might be an opportunity to go next week," said Danko.

"Why in the world would you want to go to that hellhole, Jack?" Barbara's stomach was starting to hurt and she felt a bead of perspiration form on her upper lip. "It's the most dangerous place in the world right now!" She should probably shut up—even if he was stoned, Ben might notice her concern for Jack.

Cynthia appeared, not a long black hair out of place. "Jack, some more of your television friends are here." More show-people, Jack. More carnival folk.

Barbara looked at the front door and Sloane Davis was taking off her coat to hand it to the maid. Not helping her out of it was a broad-shouldered, blonde young man who looked dressed for a sports awards dinner: white shirt, navy blazer, khakis. Sloane, in heavy makeup and a tight-fitting red dress and heels, smiled adoringly at him and took his arm. Jack escorted them to the Phoenix group.

"Everyone, this is Bruce Hanson," Sloane announced and Bruce tapped his forehead in a little salute. Sloane made the rounds of introductions and Jack took drink orders. Hanson must be the guy Sloane had brought to Lois' engagement party, the one gay Willy had deemed a "fox." The girls in hair and makeup said he was an ex-hockey player, then a sports announcer in Canada who migrated south to do sports for the Phoenix's cable rival. After 9/11, sports was cut and he was assigned to general news, anchoring overnights. Sloane had stumbled upon him while channel surfing and decided to steal him from the competition.

Danko squinted at Hanson and said, "Vancouver's Bruce Hanson?"

Hanson, thrilled, said, "Oh, eh, guilty as charged!" He did look vaguely familiar.

Jack returned with a beer for Bruce and a club soda for Sloane. The guys had closed their circle around Hanson, and that, unfortunately, left Barbara and Sloane to talk to each other.

"Bruce is going to be working at the Phoenix soon," said Sloane matter-of-factly.

"Oh, really?" Barbara was nursing her wine; her stomach really hurt. "Reading scores?" She couldn't help get in a little dig.

"No. I'm not going to pigeonhole him." Sloane snapped. "He's had enough seasoning over the past couple of months—the competition trained him for us. He'll be doing freelance reporting and some anchoring too."

Jack must have observed the uncomfortable body language between them, because he broke away from the Hanson conversation cluster and put his arm around Barbara and toasted, "Happy Holidays, ladies! And continued success for the Phoenix in the new year!"

Barbara smiled up at Jack. She felt victorious that he'd put his arm around her and not Sloane.

Sloane raised her glass, "Here's to staying number one. Which should be easy with the war continuing." She glared at Barbara. "I just hope everyone's on board."

"On board with what?" asked Barbara. She was starting to feel queasy. Maybe if she went in the bathroom and took off her shape-wear she'd feel better.

"Supporting the war," Sloane sighed.

Jack took a sip of scotch and gave Sloane one of his television smiles. "Why, we're all on board with reporting..."

"Jack." Sloane cut him off. "I'm talking about people who don't like to take direction when we're shining the light on representatives who are critical of our administration in a time of national crisis."

"I can't imagine who you're talking about Sloane." Barbara figured Sloane was pissed about the Q&A, but was she really picking a fight at Jack's party?

"Oh, I think we know who I'm talking about," said Sloane, spearing her club soda's lime with her straw.

Barbara mustered her strength. "Are we talking about someone who wants to, God forbid, give voice to dissent and balk at taking direction as if she were a marionette?" Barbara pulled a tissue from her purse and wiped her brow.

Jack took her arm. "No need to relive that, ladies....

"We were up against a goddamned hard break. You forced me into calling a war hero unpatriotic!" Barbara shouted. It was loud enough that Hanson paused for a moment in his animated telling of a hockey story, as the two stoners, Rip and Ben, remained rapt.

"Really, Barbara," said Sloane. The little matador indignant at the goaded bull. "Calm down!"

When would people learn that telling her to calm down only made her crazier? Barbara was ready to charge.

"You know, Sloane...." Barbara stopped. She suddenly felt that unmistakable pre-hurl abdominal heave and dryness in the throat. She put her hand to her mouth and race-walked to the Stones' foyer bathroom, where she emptied herself into Mrs. Stone's hand-painted porcelain sink, spraying the petit-point-stitched linen towels and brass rings where they hung.

CHAPTER 28

On Monday morning, Barbara was lying on her living room couch, flipping around the television channels, trying to avoid the inevitable: watching the Phoenix to see if her sub would say *In for Barbara King,* or, just pretend it was hers, all hers. Cathryn Collyns had gotten the call, despite the fact that Stacia Cabrerra had more experience anchoring. Who knew—maybe Stacia had dressed her Chihuahua in fatigues and tried to bring it onto the set and Tex kicked them off. Cathryn seemed confident, comfortable.

Siobhan, who had come over to tend to Barbara and retrieve Rory from the school bus, took her apron off and sat at the edge of the couch as Jack and Cathryn anchored another bomb threat.

A Phoenix News Flash...I'm Jack Stone...

That's where Cathryn was supposed to come in, but didn't. Jack continued.

Along with Cathryn Collyns, and we've just gotten word...

"Christ Collyns, you can jump in any day now. Help him out!" Barbara sat up in her sick bed and shook the remote at the television.

Siobhan frowned. "Why don't you turn on a soap opera instead?"

"I can tell Jack's irritated by her."

"Oh you know him so well, do you now," said Siobhan as Barbara sank back in the couch and pointed the remote at the television to change the channel. She better keep her mouth shut; she was weak and might slip and incriminate herself. Her mother had a creepy telepathy when it came to her and guys. In high school, if Barbara had been mashing with some lacrosse player at a keg party, she'd come home to find her mother waiting up for her in the living room, cigarette ember glowing in the dark. "Hope you saved a kiss for me," she'd say. Barbara's face probably had given her away when she watched Jack. Well, hell, he was her co-anchor and she didn't appreciate anyone else sitting next to him.

When Barbara woke up from the nap Siobhan had prescribed, she brought her laptop over to the couch and sent Jack an e-mail.

Re: Happy F'n' Holidays!

Dear Jack,

> *Please forgive me for spewing in your well-appointed bathroom, but letting loose on Sloane's girls' department shoes in the middle of your party might have dampened the festive spirit.*
>
> *You needn't have your bathroom fumigated—I had the presence of mind to clean up and nothing got on the art work. Oh, and I took your elegant towels home to be laundered. I didn't want you to think another guest had lifted them along with a few of those charming wreath-shaped soaps.*
>
> *I need to learn not to fight with Sloane. I watched* Rudolph the Red Nose Reindeer *with Rory over the weekend, and aside from crying during the affecting Island of Misfit Toys number and wondering what defect actually plagued a Dolly for Sue (aside from*

her bangs, which could have been a little longer), I was struck by the obstructionist elf who wanted to be a dentist. I am that elf! Why can't I just go along and get along? I will try harder in the new year.

In the meantime, I'll be enjoying your gift. It was so very thoughtful.

Barbara

Ps: What up with Sloane and the highlighted hockeyist?

It couldn't have been more than 5 minutes after *This Just In* ended, when Barbara found Jack's response.

Re: And a Happy F'n' New Year!

Dear Barbara,

I could see you weren't feeling well, prior to driving the porcelain bus in my bathroom. Thank you for avoiding the "art" work but had your aim been worse, I'm not sure the "painting" would have looked different. I would have tended to you, but Mr. King was already on the way, and I was summoned by Mrs. Stone for a different brewing crisis: the bartender had to leave because of an early morning modeling shoot.

I look forward to your return. This morning, I was tempted to tell your sub, Cathryn Collyns: "I served with Barbara King. I knew Barbara King. Barbara King was a friend of mine. Catherine, you're no Barbara King." But, of course, I would have been channeling a political figure from the opposing party and might have gotten in trouble.

Catherine (I think we can safely assume that's how her given name was spelled) has a penchant for working *the words **I, Me** and **Mine** (your favorite Beatle, George, right?) into her news stories. A story about a freeway oil spill turned into a story about her California vacation. "**I** did not have a good experience driving there either!"*

*That was followed by a political interview in which she read a question, no doubt scripted, from the teleprompter. The question began: "A congressman told **me...**" and lasted nearly a minute, longer than the answer!*

*And her crowning achievement: A segment with the wife of a soldier who had sold her hair to earn money. Catherine: "As for **ME, I** grew **MINE** long once and cut it for a makeover and fundraiser event in Greenwich."*

Off-air, I asked Catherine if the soldier had perhaps purchased a brush or comb for his wife for Christmas and she said, "Why would he, like, get her something so lame?"

I agree with your theory that Sloane likes perky yet empty blondes (I can't speak to the nature of her relationship with Hanson) and that Catherine resembles Mandy Pepperidge from Animal House, or, to quote you, "The finest film ever made." While I liked your recent suggestion of mowing her down in midtown with the Death Mobile, I think it might be better to keep her alive so you two can have a pillow fight on the set.

And. Not. To. Mention. Her. Delivery. She pauses in. The oddest of. Places? I think it's meant to sound breathless, but I find it very constipated sounding. I'm sure our viewers already miss your sultry tones.

One last thing—and please don't let this spoil your viewing of the wildly inferior "Rudolph's Shiny New

Year"—but Sloane did announce later at the party that she would indeed be taking the reins from Cal this week...

Breathe.

We knew this was happening. And fear not, together we can achieve ratings success, which is all that matters to her anyway. I will be glad to handle any interviews which might tempt you to beat her with her tiny shoes.

Yours,

Jack

Barbara read the e-mail again. *Yours.* She wondered what the shiny new year would bring.

December 2001

CHAPTER 29

On the morning of Sloane's first State of the Phoenix address, Jack had a special treat for Barbara when he knocked on her door for breakfast: chocolate croissants and cappuccinos.

"Those look sinful," said Barbara, rising to greet him and closing her office door so they could gossip.

"I thought they might help us endure the State of the Union, I mean, Phoenix, speech," said Jack. Sloane had issued a memo ordering all Phoenix personnel to assemble in the newsroom at 8 a.m. for an address to kick off her term as president. Cal would stay to help with the transition, still serving as adviser and "closer" on contract negotiations with talent. Barbara was praying he'd stick around through the end of the month when her deal was up, but realized Sloane would probably be settled into the oval office by then.

Barbara removed the croissant from its wax paper and tapped Jack's with hers, as if toasting. "Hail to the chief, Sloane Davis."

Jack ate half the croissant in one bite, dripping chocolate onto the copy on her desk. "Yes. And I believe she'll have a special announcement this morning."

Barbara dabbed at the chocolate with her finger and brought it to her mouth. "Really? What?"

"I'm afraid the announcement is embargoed until the meeting," Jack ran his fingers in a zipping motion across his mouth.

"You can't tease a story and not deliver it!" Barbara knew he wouldn't have mentioned it if he wasn't going to let her pull it out of him. But just then, her office phone rang, displaying a 516 area code. It was Rory's school, the call she'd been waiting for from his first-grade teacher. An obnoxious classmate had been picking on Rory, telling him the picture he'd drawn of Spiderman "sucked" and that his beloved web slinger was "a freak." At Barbara and Ben's urging, Rory took the first few encounters with the young art critic in stride. But after the kid pushed him in the cafeteria, Rory hauled off and hit him. Rory had told them the story at dinner last night, clenching his fists and closing his eyes in joyous re-enactment. "It felt sooooooo good." Barbara and Ben told him that hitting someone wasn't the way to solve a problem, to which Rory responded, "But Gammy said a bloody nose might shut his pie hole."

"This is about Rory. I have to take it, Jack," Barbara said, and he quickly rose. As she picked up the phone, she motioned for him to stay but he'd already picked up his cappuccino. "See you in the newsroom," he said, giving her a little salute as he closed the door.

After the call from the teacher, who implied Rory's tormentor had it coming, Barbara punched in Jack's extension but he didn't pick up. She grabbed her suit jacket and research and ran down to hair and makeup, where Angelica was standing next to the barber chair, Barbara's cape in hand—she knew it would be tight this morning.

"I got some 411," said Angelica, picking up the curling iron. "Heard the old man's contract is up."

"Bill Hunter? You're kidding! Where'd you hear that?" Barbara asked.

"One of the evening stylists heard him on the phone. He was talking to Cal, saying something like, 'My agent will call to set up a lunch.'"

"Well, they could be talking about anything, don't you think?" asked Barbara, her mind racing.

"You know Cal's been laying low since 9/11. He's paranoid. Thinks the terrorists are after him. He wouldn't be having lunch out in public unless it was important. And that Hunter's looking tired. Time to go."

This was probably the announcement Jack had teased: Ironsides was finally retiring! Sloane would announce it at the meeting and then Barbara and Jack could pitch *This Just In* to prime time.

Jane ripped open the velvet curtain and started working on Barbara's face, rushing and grumbling as she peered down from her cat glasses. "Couldn't Sloane have issued a memo? Needs to assemble the whole House of bloody Commons."

Angelica looked at Barbara sternly and said, "Make sure you move fast." And before Barbara left for Sloane's speech, she scheduled an appointment with Cal for the next day. Live, in person, in his office.

In the newsroom, in a bit of Sloane-engineered stagecraft, everyone from talent, to crew, to producers, to the sales staff gathered around the presidential podium.

Barbara watched as Lois headed straight for one of the spots that would be directly in Sloane's line of sight. She needn't have, given her ungainly height.

The early-morning team hurried into the newsroom. Stan and Dorie Keegan had taken the morning off from their show to attend the address and had probably just rushed over from another book-signing event. Capitalizing on their strong war ratings, they'd co-"written" *What Time Do **You** Have to Wake Up?,* a compilation of others' thoughts on working early-morning shifts.

Angelica walked into the newsroom and heads turned. Those who didn't know her probably thought she was a new anchor. Angelica had likely guessed Sloane might introduce her whole new team, including the new station style maven, a blowsy blonde who could barely move her mouth because of whatever had been injected into her cheeks. Her mandate was to make the channel's women look "fresher," which had translated to sleeveless cocktail dresses with open-toe sandals, perfect for reporting on war and terror.

The room quieted as Sloane walked toward the podium, chin forward, her hair short and dark, in stark contrast to the lock of white above her forehead. Following her was a mostly bald man with the kind, pudgy face of a trusted bartender. Ron Kavanagh, a former presidential campaign adviser, worked mostly behind the scenes, but had been exposed as the mastermind of a whispering campaign in which he'd outed an up-and-coming Democrat as having been a chronic bed- wetter in his youth.

Jack, looking particularly handsome in a navy suit and aquamarine tie, strode through the newsroom next, the seas parting for him so he could stand behind Barbara.

Barbara looked over her shoulder, smirking. "Tardy, Mr. Stone."

"I don't feel tardy," he whispered, pinching the back of her arm.

"You never delivered the story you teased," she whispered back.

Sloane began: "I'm here to tell you this morning that the state of the Phoenix is strong!" There was laughter and applause in the newsroom; the channel was a solid number one thanks to its patriotic fervor and scary graphics of hirsute perpetrators of horror. Once the Bearded One was quickly captured and the war won, the station could gear up for the 2002 mid-term elections.

"As we begin, I'd like to introduce you to some new faces and some familiar ones. The gentleman on my left is Mr. Ron Kavanagh, who'll be a big part of future campaign coverage."

Sloane then gave the prime-time people their props, and Ironsides, his rheumy eyes nearly consumed by the bags underneath them, nodded from his wheelchair. Don't let the door hit you in your biased ass, thought Barbara, as she clapped and gave him an admiring smile. But then Sloane didn't announce he was retiring—maybe she was saving that for last?

"Having started here as a news reader," Sloane continued, "but proving her mettle as a correspondent, Cathryn Collyns is going to be hosting her own weekend show." Applause mixed with a few whistles, as Cathryn held her hand in the air like a beauty queen in a Chevy convertible. She's probably wondering why Sloane's talking about, like, heavy metal?

Cathryn's competition, Stacia Cabrerra, held her head high, frowning. Next, Sloane, smiling broadly, introduced her boy, the new New York bureau correspondent Bruce Hanson.

"Prishyate it, prishyate it," Bruce touched his hand to his heart, as if waiting for the national anthem and the puck to drop. Big applause.

Sloane paused for a moment and then put her little hand on her forehead, scanning the audience. She pointed in Barbara's direction. "And now, I have a special announcement regarding a veteran dayside anchor!"

She couldn't possibly be announcing a promotion this way, could she? And she did say "anchor" not "anchors"?

"Jack Stone is leaving for Afghanistan today to report on our brave troops. For the next week, he'll be reporting directly from the war zone!"

"Woo hoos" and applause filled the room and Barbara turned to face Jack, who was smiling, but met her eye with the expression of someone about to duck a punch.

Barbara stared at him, clapping her hands, mouthing, "What the fuck?" Then, co-anchor smile frozen on her face, she started walking out of the newsroom, tapping at her watch as if she was hurrying to get ready for her show.

Once she was in the hallway leading to her office, she heard footsteps. She broke into a trot, but just as she put her hand on her office door, Jack caught her other arm. She elbowed him to push him off, jabbing him in the torso, but then, Jack put his hand over the one she had on the doorknob and opened the door. Pressing himself against her back, he pushed them both into the office and kicked the door shut. Barbara pulled herself out of his grip and spun around to face him. He took a step toward her, but she took a step back and grabbed a framed publicity shot of the two of them off her office wall. She was raising it to smash it onto her desk when he grabbed her arms again.

"Oh, no, you don't," he said, pulling the frame from her hands.

"How could you not tell me?"

"Barbara, take it easy," he said.

"You take it easy."

"I was going to tell you this morning but you," he pointed to her phone, "had to tend to your family."

"When did you find out about this?" They must have hatched this plan when she was on her sick bed after his party. Another reason never to give up your anchor chair for even a day. "How could you keep it from me?!"

"The plan developed in an exceedingly rapid fashion. Just yesterday, in fact, and I was sworn to secrecy, Barbara." He exhaled and loosened the knot of his tie. "You shouldn't be angry. This will certainly raise the profile of the show."

"I want to raise *my* profile, as you've often pointed out to me. And I'm not the one who's going to be the star war correspondent, you are!"

"I wanted us to go together. I lobbied quite ardently for that, I'll have you know, despite having qualms about whether you'd even be willing to leave your family to travel to a warzone. But they could only send one of us and Cal—you know how old-fashioned he is—didn't think it would be right for a woman, a mother, to go. I was afraid you might be upset about this. But Sloane insisted and I couldn't very well tell her I wouldn't accept a key reporting assignment because I couldn't stand to be separated from my co-anchor!"

Jack tried to put a hand on her arm but Barbara knocked his hand away. "You could have told me. It was bad enough when they sent you to D.C."

Jack exhaled loudly. "I believe you opted not to go that time."

"They've wanted to showcase you and not me from day one." She walked around Jack and opened her office door. "Please leave. I need to prepare for our lowly broadcasts from headquarters once again while you're off gallivanting overseas."

Fifteen minutes later, Barbara and Jack were on the set together and news was breaking in Afghanistan. Danko, who'd probably noticed their body language from the control room, said in their headsets, "Have a great show, kids." Tex, ever the Cassandra, gave them the count. "Gonna be a lot of blood in the streets of that shithole...five, four, three...."

Jack, air strikes continue today in Kandahar....

The city, Barbara, where a Taliban leader is believed to be holed up...

They traded lines and performed seamlessly. Barbara reckoned that if her beloved Beatles could stop their strife long enough to create *Abbey Road,* the least she could do was make it through her two-hour show in a professional manner. But that didn't mean she had to talk to Jack during commercials or answer his computer messages.

Stone: *You would have said "yes" too*

Stone: *It'll be good for the ratings*

Stone: *I'm only going for a week*

Stone: *Think of the press we'll get*

Stone: *Is this any way to send a soldier off to war?*

Barbara kept her back to him and edited copy on her computer, so her typing would trick him, make him think she was going to answer his messages. Tex asked her if everything was okay and when she gave him a clipped "yup," he shrugged at Jack as if to say, "Broads."

When the show was over, Barbara rose, ripped her microphone off, and quickly gathered her papers.

"I'm leaving in a few minutes, Barbara," Jack said, undoing his mic clip. "Why don't we grab a quick coffee?"

The set was silent. Tex and the rest of the crew seemed to be watching her mouth to see what words would form. Even Lois, who was getting her microphone hooked up on the side of the set, was staring with those big button eyes of hers.

"Jack!" Sloane shouted from the newsroom, as she hurried toward the set. "Need you to make a press statement before you go!"

Barbara turned away from Jack and descended the steps of the set, overhearing a techie whisper into his headset, "Honeymoon's over."

CHAPTER 30

"That thing's jiggling," Angelica said suspiciously, pointing with her teasing comb at the BlackBerry Barbara had placed on her console. At the end of her self-congratulatory address, Sloane had announced she was supplying the staff with "electronic leashes."

"To add insult to injury, I get to co-anchor with Hanson while Jack's in Afghanistan." Barbara pecked at the device with her thumbs, an awkward business. "Guy thinks he's my new best friend, sending me e-mails, even giving me a nickname, 'Bobby K.'"

Barbara placed the BlackBerry back on the counter. "So I'm going straight to Cal's office after the show, can you do that thing?" On special days, Angelica gave Barbara an updated Farrah look with long locks and soft curls.

Angelica checked her curling iron with a moistened finger. "What are you gonna say?"

"I'm going to tell him if the 7 o'clock news is opening up, I'm ready for prime time. I have a proven track record and can deliver good ratings." Barbara wasn't going to pitch her and Jack as a team anymore.

"*You're* ready. What about Jack?" asked Angelica. "Word is you two had a fight before he left."

"Jack who?"

Angelica put her hand on her hip. "What was he supposed to do? Not go because he's in love with you?"

"Angelica!!"

Angelica continued to look at Barbara in the mirror, holding a lock of hair in the iron until it practically sizzled.

"He should have told me he was going. And I don't much appreciate Sloane making him the big star war correspondent."

Angelica released the red lock from the iron.

Barbara continued. "Okay, I guess I'm also worried about him being over there. And I miss him. As a co-anchor." She hated him for going to Afghanistan, envied him, and yet she couldn't help but notice how handsome he looked on TV in his flak jacket.

Angelica worked her long fingernails through Barbara's hair, pulling at the tight curls she'd created.

"Maybe as more than that, alright? I sometimes feel...I mean... if I'd known him before, you know...but I would never...I can't... .I mean...I don't even think he would necessarily want to...you know....I just...we just..."

Angelica sprayed Barbara's hair.

"I miss him, okay already, I miss him...I do."

Great reporters know that when they pose a difficult question to a subject, the best thing to do is shut up. Let the interviewee stop and start. Do not interrupt them. Do not finish a sentence for them. Let them speak. And the truth shall be freed, or, revealed through all the stuttering and stammering.

Barbara rose from Angelica's chair. "Regular Mike Wallace, you," she said.

As she sat on a chenille couch in Cal's cozy office, Barbara's hair was bouncing and behaving and she wore a short, fitted green dress with stilettos. But when Cal walked in and Barbara rose from the couch, she immediately regretted the heels. Even with his white pompadour, and quite possibly, lifts, he couldn't have been more than 5' 4". She must have seemed like an emerald giantess to this elfin man.

"Barbara King. So good to see you again," he said, taking her hand in both of his. She wasn't about to tell him that him that they'd never actually met. Cal adjusted his raffish neckerchief and gestured for her to sit back down. "And if I may—you look more beautiful than ever."

"Thank you, Cal, that's so sweet of you to say." He might be short but he'd probably gotten plenty during his soap days.

Cal took a wing chair opposite the couch. "Speaking of sweets—may I tempt you?" He pointed at the glass jar of caramels resting on a doily on the coffee table between them.

Barbara had no desire for candy. "Why not? Thank you."

"They're how I got my name, you know," said Cal. Barbara tried to chew as delicately as possible as he continued. "Was working on the set of a soap and got a small part, but the director didn't like my name so he said, 'Cal, we're going to give you a name folks will remember.' Went through a few names—Smith, Jones, et cetera, et cetera. But then he noticed I had a pack of caramels in my hand and he looked at them and said, 'Eureka!'" And I said, 'Well, I don't think *Eureka* has much of a ring to it.'"

Barbara, who'd manage to wedge the caramel into a molar, laughed along with Cal, whose eyes were twinkling as if he was telling the story for the very first time.

"And then the director said, 'No! Cal Caramel. Carmichael. Cal Carmichael!"

"Ah!" said Barbara, hoping his sharing of the anecdote meant he liked her. "That's a great story. King's not my real name either."

"That so?"

"It's actually Konig. It means 'king' in German. Got it in radio."

"I would have pegged you for an Irish lass," he said looking at her hair.

"Oh, my mom's Irish. My father's German."

"Good combination. You know," he mused, "it's so important to hire the right people in television. Do you realize what an intimate medium television is? I mean, if a fan sees a movie star like Brad Pitt or Julia Roberts on the street, how do you suppose they address them?"

Barbara shook her head, running her tongue over the caramel in her molar.

"They say, '*Mr.* Pitt' or '*Miss* Roberts.' But if they see you, they say 'Why, hello, *Barbara.*' They're on a first-name basis because you've been telling them the news, you've been in their living rooms every day. They think of you as a friend."

Or they want their asses slapped. Where was this kindly gentleman going with this story? Barbara wondered.

"What I'm getting at Barbara is, I made a good choice when I hired you. You've been a consistent performer, you know your lines, your 'q' rating's terrific, and you and your co-star, co-anchor, that is, have marvelous chemistry. That's another thing that keeps 'em watching, a compelling couple—like Luke and Laura!"

Last she checked, Jack had not raped her to a Herb Alpert soundtrack, but it was a nice compliment. Even if Jack was on her shit list.

"Thank you, Cal." Time to make her speech. "I think you know that since I came here, I've been hoping to raise my profile, and with the success of my show, I thought it was time to take my act, so to speak, to prime time." She hoped her showbiz phrasing would appeal to him. "I could deliver good numbers in the 7 o'clock slot."

Cal leaned back in his wing chair, his feet barely scraping the floor. "Ah, so you're also hoping for the show."

Also? "Yes, Cal," she said, "I am."

"Barbara, I'm afraid I'll have to tell you the same thing I told another dayside anchor who's had her sights set on that slot." Spencer! Of course her agent fiancé would have heard Ironsides' contract was up. Or maybe it was Jack. Maybe that was another conversation he'd neglected to tell her about! "The position is not opening up."

Barbara's face fell. "It's not?"

Cal gave her an avuncular smile as if to say, "There, there." He gestured to the caramel jar and she shook her head no. Don't try to buy me off with a candy, little man.

"Let me explain," he said, leaning forward in his chair. "I understand that dayside anchors come to the channel hoping to move to prime time and then move on, or in your case, back, to the networks to become bona fide television stars. But I believe my people are stars in their own right. Our viewership is more loyal than any other audience in television. And that's what it's about, Barbara, loyalty. As one of my final acts here, I am re-signing Bill *Ironsides* Hunter—naughty newsroom, ho ho—for another two years. We've already shaken hands on the deal."

It was breathtaking. Cal knew everything right down to the nickname.

"I hope you're not too disappointed, Barbara. Just because that slot isn't opening up any time soon, doesn't mean you don't have a bright future here at the Phoenix. Sloane will be developing new shows and who knows, perhaps one of them will be your ticket to even greater fame and fortune."

Doomed to dayside. And what would happen to her when her contract was up at the end of the month and Sloane likely held her fate in her tiny, fisted hands?

"I'm not so sure about that," Barbara grumbled.

Cal reached across the table and patted her hand. "Now, Barbara, I know Sloane can be tough. I've been getting an earful from my old pal, Clarence—he and Sloane have had their go-rounds. I realize she can be a bit, shall we say, high-strung."

Barbara wanted to provide a few other choice adjectives, but she felt beaten, and Sloane was Cal's chosen heir. "I just hope," she said, trying to retain her dignity, "that you communicate to Sloane how committed I am to making the Phoenix a continued success."

Cal studied her, smiling, but didn't seem to be listening. "You've always reminded me of a lovely gal I worked with... she played a feisty flame-haired nurse. Great gal, yes, yes." He helped himself to one of his caramels and said, "I still have a little say around here. I'll make sure your position is secure and that Sloane is aware of your ambitions."

CHAPTER 31

The next morning, Barbara watched sullenly as Bruce Hanson, his hair intentionally moussed into disarray, belly-bumped an audio guy on the way up to the rotating set. During commercials, Bruce had "T" (Tex) fire up the telestrator so Big-B (himself) could draw circles and arrows to illustrate hockey stories, each one ending in a sports platitude. *All that matters is the 'W'!*

The show went smoothly. Whenever there was a Phoenix News Flash to be performed, Bruce didn't even try to contribute—he just looked on with great interest, smiling, as Barbara read the bulletins. "Bobby K—that's why you're one of the people who built this house!" he said as soon as their mics were dead. His boyish exuberance made her feel as if she were the calico-skirted granny, who, from her post in the back of a wagon, could reminisce about the days when the Phoenix was just wide open space.

There were just 60 seconds left before their toss to the last commercial break of the hour before *Lois Spencer's America. Rises*. They were ending on a light-hearted note, with Bruce finishing up a read over pictures of a water-skiing squirrel, when Danko spoke into Barbara's earpiece.

"Barbara. Tease this to break: Just in. Explosion in Afghanistan. Several injured. Our troops. And a journalist. All U.S. We have this. Not on wires."

Bruce ended his voice-over with a little banter.

That's one squirrely little fella, wouldn't you say, Barbara? Oh dear. Danko probably hadn't wanted to throw Bruce off by talking into his ear while he was reading the squirrel story, so Bruce had no idea she was about to deliver a doom-and-gloom tease.

He sure is, Bruce. We'll see you again tomorrow morning. She used those sentences to buy her a little time and change the expression on her face from one of amusement to one of grave concern. She had 20 seconds to fill.

Before we go to break we want to let you know that the Phoenix News Channel has just learned of an explosion in Afghanistan. There are apparently several casualties—among them, American troops and an American journalist.

Why did the Phoenix have the information but the wires didn't? Barbara suddenly had a terrible thought. *Again, this just in...*

Casualties? That could mean anything from a scrape to.... No, it couldn't be him. She gulped. *Lois Spencer will have more at the top of the hour, right here on the Phoenix News Channel.*

As soon as they were in commercial, Barbara ripped off her microphone herself and ran toward the control room. Danko opened the door, ready to intercept her, and Barbara caught a glimpse of Sloane sitting in his chair in the control room. Rip closed the door and put his arm around Barbara and walked her toward the greenroom.

"Oh my God. It is him. That's how we had it!" she said.

"Look, baby, we don't know how serious it is. Sloane's getting the info from Jack's producer, who was in a different convoy. Some kind of explosion. Jack was taken away in an ambulance but the scene's still chaos. No one knows anything else."

When they got to the greenroom, Barbara and Rip stood in front of the television monitor, arms crossed, watching Lois. Angelica and Jane joined them.

We are learning more from our producer on the ground in Afghanistan about the explosion on the road from Kabul to Kandahar. Apparently the Phoenix's own anchorman, This Just In's *Jack Stone, is among the injured. We have no information about his condition. Our producer is describing the explosion as "massive" so it's unclear at this point if anyone in the midst of the blast could have survived.*

Barbara gasped loudly and covered her mouth with her hand as Angelica stood behind her and whispered in her ear, "Try to hold it together."

Rip yanked the phone from the sofa table and punched in the control room extension. "You've gotta get in Spencer's ear and tell her not to fucking speculate. His wife could be watching!"

Barbara's mascara started running down her cheeks. *His wife.* Angelica elbowed Jane and she fetched a box of tissues from her station. Rip paced. A couple of minutes later, the greenroom door swung open and Sloane rushed in, BlackBerry in hand.

"Danko. I need you in the control room. I need to do interviews with the other media once they get a hold of this. And for your information, there could be a high death toll!"

Rip took his headset from around his neck and headed for the door, muttering, "Eat me."

Sloane shot him a dirty look, then turned back to her BlackBerry. "Good. The wires still don't have it," she said, eyes gleaming. She looked up at Barbara who was staring at the television, wiping her cheeks. Sloane smirked. "Hello? Barbara?"

Barbara turned slowly to face her.

"Obviously you're very concerned about your...co-anchor... but if you could pull yourself together, you might need to give a statement..."

Sloane put her BlackBerry to her ear. "Sloane Davis here! Yes, I'd be happy to, let me just find a quiet spot..." And she walked out of the greenroom.

Barbara was grateful for her BlackBerry on the way home, but staring at the device for the entire ride couldn't make it produce a bulletin saying Jack was alive.

When she got home, she took the steps up to her living room two at a time to get to the television. Siobhan was watching a *Golden Girls* rerun when Barbara grabbed the remote and flipped it to the Phoenix. "There was a big explosion in Afghanistan. Jack was there. We don't know what happened to him."

"Sweet mother of God!" When Barbara sat down and filled her in on the little she knew, Siobhan asked, "Why we didn't just drop the big one on that whole Godforsaken..."

"Shhhhhh," said Barbara, as she stood up and watched the television screen fill with the frightening *Phoenix News Flash* graphic.

I'm Lois Spencer with a Phoenix news flash. There's new information about the television journalist...the Phoenix's own Jack Stone...who has become a casualty of the war on terror in Afghanistan.

"A casualty? Does that mean he's been killed?" cried Siobhan.

"Shhhhh," Barbara said, more viciously this time. And then to Lois, "Say it. Say it!"

Stone, a dayside anchor and correspondent for the Phoenix News Channel, was at the scene when a bomb exploded on the road to Kandahar.

"Christ, Lois, we know. What's the news flash?!" Barbara gesticulated wildly at the television. Siobhan watched her daughter instead of the television.

Stone was in one of two vehicles transporting journalists from the capital to the southern city where a Taliban leader is holed up. One of the vehicles hit a land mine and...

"How badly was he hurt?! Quit dragging it out, you pompous..." Barbara continued shouting at the television.

But word is just coming in that Stone has survived the attack.

"Oh, thank God!" Barbara threw her arms in the air.

It seems Stone suffered only shrapnel wounds.

Barbara folded her hands over her heart. "He's alright! He's alright! Oh my God. Oh, thank you. Thank you." She tried to focus on the rest of the story but her eyes were blurring with tears again.

The first vehicle was hit by an anti-tank mine. Several of the journalists in the van were killed. But those in the second vehicle of the convoy, including Stone, were injured, but not seriously.

Lois tossed to a sound bite of Phoenix President Sloane Davis.

Jack is the true definition of an intrepid reporter...

"You sent him into harm's way, you conniving wench," Barbara talked to the television.

Stone will be flown back to the States to a hospital near his home to recuperate.

Barbara wiped her eyes and exhaled again. "Oh my God."

"Barbara Marie Konig," said Siobhan, getting up from the couch. "Look at me." She took her daughter's arm.

"He could have been killed," said Barbara. She felt delirious. "We thought maybe he had been! But he's okay!"

"And if he had been killed, you, missus, would not have been his war widow."

"Stop it, ma. He's a good friend and colleague. What am I supposed to do? Not care that he was almost killed?"

Siobhan narrowed her eyes at Barbara and walked back into the kitchen to tend to her stew. Barbara sank into the couch. He could have been killed! And if he had been, his last memory of her would have been her stomping off the set, angry with him for accepting an assignment he really couldn't refuse. But Jack was alive and well and so what if she wasn't his *war widow*—okay, so her mother was on to her, that wasn't good—she'd get to see him again and tell him how sorry she was for losing her temper.

CHAPTER 32

From: Jack.Stone@Phoenixnewschannel.com

To: Barbara.King@Phoenixnewschannel.com

What's your e.t.a.? I'd hate to be in the middle of a sponge bath when you arrive.

A couple of days later, Jack was recuperating at a Long Island hospital and Barbara was planning on visiting him. She read his e-mail on the train trip to work that morning. She and Ben were shoulder-to-shoulder in the dirty, red leather two-seater, and she hoped he couldn't read her screen. Ben opened up his copy of the *New York Times,* eschewing the business section in favor of the op-ed page, folding the paper vertically, in the technique of the considerate commuter.

Barbara tapped out a quick reply to Jack.

2-ish. And don't get any ideas about showing me your injury.

The bomb shrapnel had lodged underneath Jack's buttocks; it was an injury that wasn't debilitating, but enough to get you sent home.

After hitting send, Barbara deleted the message stream and decided to tell Ben she was going to the hospital. If she didn't, and he found out about it from her big-mouthed mother, Ben might wonder why she'd kept it from him. "He's doing well but we don't know when he'll be back on air," she explained. If she said he was going to be back the day after tomorrow, Ben might ask why she couldn't wait to see him until then. Thing was, she couldn't wait. As soon as she heard he was back in the States, she sent him a cautious e-mail asking if it would be okay for his sassy-to-a-fault co-anchor to visit him and he happily agreed. And now, in just 8 hours, she would be in his hospital room, sitting next to his bed.

"Since I live closest to the hospital, the guys at work elected me to deliver a get-well package," she explained. "Just some goofy stuff to cheer him up."

"So you're not angry anymore?"

"Well, the guy was wounded. I think I have to let bygones be bygones. I guess I understand why they wouldn't pick me."

Ben put his newspaper across his lap and took her hand. "I sincerely hope you don't have any Baba Wawa aspirations about going over there."

"Well, no. I mean, it's a good way to prove your gravitas, but I'm not sure Sloane cares about that..."

"What I mean, Barb, is you wouldn't want to risk your life for your job. Imagine how scared Jack's wife and daughter must have been."

Barbara hadn't imagined, hadn't thought at all about their reaction. Had his daughter Madeleine cried and carried on, worried sick about her daddy? Had Mrs. Stone wept (without ruining her minimalist makeup) with relief when she found out he was okay? Barbara had thought only about how much she'd miss Jack if he'd been killed. And yet she would have been relegated to the role of the mistress who skulks around at the funeral, hiding behind the headstones.

Ben looked her in the eye. "Promise me that even if they asked you, you wouldn't go. I'm not saying this because I've had my issues with the Phoenix, but really, no job is worth that. We'd be lost without you."

As Barbara walked down the hospital hallway, she brought her wrist to her nose; she wondered if Jack would notice she was wearing his Chanel No. 5. Maybe not, her scent was no match for the hospital's antiseptics, disinfectants, and tasteless-yet-aromatic food. She walked briskly past the other patients' rooms, hoping she wouldn't catch a glimpse of them in their undignified states: gowns yawning open, filled bedpans wedged beneath pockmarked shanks.

Room 242's handwritten sign said, "STONE." Good. No annoyingly friendly roommate with a tragic story. She peered in the room before walking in. And no Mrs. Stone. Phew.

It was a cloudy afternoon and the room's shades were drawn, making it seem later in the afternoon than it was. Barbara walked toward his bed: Jack was sleeping, bare arms folded over the thin white blanket. Dark hair protruded from the collar of his pale aqua blue gown and he had a beard of black sand with a few grains of white sprinkled around his chin. But not a mark on him.

Barbara felt a strong urge to crawl into bed next to him, the way Ryan O'Neal did when Ali MacGraw was dying in *Love Story*. But the fantasy was wrong on too many levels, especially since Ali was his wife's doppelganger. She pulled a chair up to his beside and whispered, "Jack?"

Jack opened his eyes and blinked slowly. "Barbara." He smiled groggily. "Finally."

She hadn't arrived late. Had he wanted her to visit him sooner? "I'm sorry to wake you. But I didn't want you to be startled if you opened your eyes and I was just...you know...here."

"What time is it?" he asked. His eyes were glassy. He inched up in his bed and pushed the button that shifted it into a more upright position.

"Just before two. I'm guessing bath time is over?"

He laughed lazily but she couldn't tell if he remembered the e-mail joke or if he was just happy from pain meds. Jack ran his hand through his hair and turned his body to face her. How could someone who'd been in that wasteland look so good?

"You are a sight for sore eyes," he said.

Barbara's eyes started to well. "Jack, I'm such a jerk, I am so sorry..."

"Hey, good-looking!" A middle-aged, broad-shouldered nurse in hot-pink scrubs suddenly appeared in the doorway of the hospital room. She marched over to the bed and rattled a tiny plastic cup as if it were a martini shaker. "It's happy hour," she said. And then, looking at Barbara, "So, I finally get to meet the lucky woman you're married to?"

Jack cleared his throat. "Well, Janice, this is actually my television wife, my co-anchor Barbara King."

"Oh, Ms. King. I'm sorry. I should have recognized you from television! This charmer over here never mentioned you were coming. We're all big fans here."

"Aw, thanks." Barbara watched as Janice handed Jack a cup of water and the pills which he put on his tongue like a good boy "Is Jack a good patient? He behaving?" Barbara asked.

Janice guffawed. "We wish he wouldn't!" She took Jack's water cup and poured its remains into one of the many poinsettias lined up on the window ledge. "Buzz if you need me, hon." She winked at Jack and was gone.

"Your friend hasn't met Mrs. Stone?" Barbara asked. Could she have possibly not rushed to his bedside?

"When I arrived yesterday, the capable Janice was here to greet me. But Mrs. Stone was not able to arrive until the late-night shift—she flew in from Hong Kong." Jack had mentioned his wife was transitioning into corporate real estate and would have to travel overseas occasionally.

"Oh. I see," said Barbara, hoping that if Mrs. Stone had visited last night, she wouldn't come back again until later.

"Jack," she touched his hand. "I realize you had to go and that you had to keep it a secret. I'm a..."

"I should have told you. I was afraid of your reaction. You are quite feisty when you're upset. There is a history there, Ms. King."

"A long and checkered one. I know." Barbara let out a loud exhale. "Well, if we're friends again, than I can present you with some gifts from the crew." She reached down next to her chair and picked up the large gift bag with the semi-manly argyle pattern. "Allow me to make my presentation."

Jack sat up and moved toward the edge of the bed, closer to her.

Barbara pulled a *New York Post* from the bag. "In case the hot candy striper didn't bring you the newspaper."

"She's one hundred years old. And a he," said Jack, coming to life.

"I'll sum up the article about you. You're intrepid." Barbara put the paper on his night table and continued, "I also brought something to help you wash down those meds." She pulled out a bottle of very fine scotch and held it in front of her as if displaying a product in a television commercial.

"I hope you brought tumblers and ice!" Jack reached for the bottle.

"Not now!" She slapped his hand lightly and put the bottle back in the bag. "I'd do a shot with you, but I don't think your nurse would have much trouble kicking me out of here with her size-11 white clogs."

Next, she displayed a publicity shot of Bruce Hanson. The boys had written on it in Sharpie: *"Dear Jack,* ***Don't*** *get well soon, eh?! Love, Ice Ice Baby*!" Jack let out a hoot. "Bruce wanted to come with me today but we couldn't risk him belly-bumping you."

Barbara was on a roll. She displayed a picture the guys had printed from the internet: a male model looking seductively over one shoulder, wearing nothing but ass-less chaps. "The Phoenix was hoping that you could pose like this in your new publicity shot, you know, to show off your battle scars."

Jack was laughing hard but silently, like he was high. "Thank you for that X-rated presentation. I'll have to hide that photo from the male nurses!"

Barbara was laughing along with him and it struck her again how much she'd missed him, even if it had only been a few days. "Could you do me a favor?" she asked.

"Anything for the woman who brought me liquor and porn."

"Could you *not* go to some place on the map with the bull's-eye on it? You know, I was on the air when the bulletin crossed. I was...we were...so scared...Nobody knew...." Her cheeks grew hot and her voice cracked. "And we had that fight..."

He watched her and tried to look serious, but was still smiling. "You're exceedingly disarming when you're upset."

"I'm just glad you're okay."

"I was lucky. I'm sorry those other reporters weren't."

Barbara cleared her throat and looked up at the clock. She really should hit the L.I.E. and try to make it back for Rory's bus so Siobhan couldn't reprimand her for being late. "Well, I'd love to join you for a Scotch and Percocet, but I better get home. You need anything before I go?"

"No. I am completely ambulatory, with the aid of crutches."

"I'm not, by the way, going to let you show me your scar."

"It's rather unsightly."

"Hope your swim Speedos cover it."

"I should be able to swim again by next week."

"That's good." She didn't want to leave. "You need water or something?"

He looked toward the pitcher on the tray on the side of his bed opposite the one where she was sitting. "There's still some in there. I should be good."

Barbara walked around the bed and adjusted the tray so he'd be able to reach the pitcher. "Alright, I better get going."

She leaned over him and gave him a light kiss on his sandpaper cheek. She was already pulling away when he pulled her toward him and held her. She hugged him back, hard, and slid her hands into the space between his back and his pillow.

"I was so worried about you," she said. Her hair was pressed against his cheek and she felt him inhaling.

"I missed you," he said, squeezing her tighter.

She was wondering what in the world was going to happen next, when she heard footsteps. They weren't coming from rubber clogs and they were closing in rapidly. Barbara pulled back with a start and, as Jack did the same, his elbow hit the water pitcher, knocking it over and onto the floor.

Barbara jumped up. "Oh jeez."

Mrs. Stone, in a tweed suit and pearls, stood in the doorway looking at Barbara and at the pitcher on the floor. Barbara took a step back, away from Jack's bed, to clear the path to him.

Without acknowledging Barbara, Mrs. Stone walked to the bed and kissed Jack on the forehead, pushing his hair back as if he were a kid who'd gotten into a schoolyard brawl. "Jackson," she said, shaking her head.

Barbara looked at the floor where the pitcher lay on its side. The water slowly crept under the bed; soon it would reach Mrs. Stone's Ferragamos. Barbara wished she could hide under the bed.

"Hello, Barbara." she finally deigned to address her. *Hello, Newman.*

Barbara said, "I was just leaving to get to the school bus...but some water spilled—I could get some paper towels or...."

"I'm afraid that was my clumsiness," Jack offered.

"Clean up in aisle three!" Barbara laughed nervously. She felt overheated.

Mrs. Stone pushed the button for the nurse and looking at Jack said, "We'll have someone take care of it."

"I better run," said Barbara and she wanted to run, literally, out of the room. But she walked, and stealing one last look at Jack, noticed that her television makeup had rubbed off on the shoulder of his hospital gown. Have someone take care of that too, Cindy.

CHAPTER 33

Jack's magnet-attracting buttocks also drew viewers to *This Just In*—nearly a million a day since he had come back from Afghanistan. And the rugged war correspondent's near-death experience had landed him on the list of journalists to be feted at the Christmas correspondents' dinner in Washington, D.C.

The morning Barbara opened the large ecru envelope containing the invitation, she did a little dance in her office. Okay, so it was a last-minute invitation, but it was addressed to *Ms. Barbara King and guest,* a bonus ordinarily reserved for prime-time talent. With her contract coming up, the dinner would be a chance to schmooze; she could make nice with Sloane and mention that any dayside show getting prime-time numbers *really belongs in prime time, doesn't it?* Or Barbara would chat with some of the soiree's network executives, making Sloane so nervous she'd offer her a lucrative new deal on the spot.

On a personal level, going to the dinner with Ben might do her good. He could shave that goatee he'd been growing and put on a tux—he always cleaned up nice. And maybe some hotel sex with him would put a stop to her daydreams about consummation on the Craftmatic had Mrs. Stone not shown up when she did.

Invitation before her, Barbara called Ben at his office.

"Can't. CEO's in town," he said.

"Oh no. Are you sure?" If Ben couldn't go, Barbara would have to go stag while Mrs. Stone, the near-war widow, glided through the room on Jack's arm.

"We're all supposed to have dinner with him Thursday." Ben was a stock analyst for a portfolio manager who was no longer "putting up numbers." If the firm fired the PM, Ben would likely be considered a redundancy as the other portfolio managers had analysts of their own. "I have to try to get some face time with the guy."

"I need some face time too," said Barbara. "I can't not go."

"You should go. We might really be needing your job soon."

"Oh no. Really?"

"If they fire us," said Ben. "I won't be too sad."

"Oh, come on, Ben," said Barbara. She knew he hated his job, but they needed their combined income to pay the mortgage, not to mention her parents' expenses.

"I'm serious. I could be done with a master's in two years."

His Bohemian dream again. "Even if you got a degree, how do you know you'd get a teaching job? Don't you have to be published or something? And, what could you make as a poetry professor anyway?"

"Well, I'd have to start as an adjunct, but..."

"An adjunct? That's academia-speak for whale shit at the bottom of the ocean, isn't it?" she asked. She felt mean for being a dream crusher, but he was a hedge fund guy—couldn't he do the math? "I'm sorry. It's a worthy pursuit. And I want you to be happy. I'm just being overly practical, I guess. Just thinking of all our expenses," she added softly.

"Maybe we could consolidate—your parents could move in with us. They're there all the time anyway."

Good God, he'd actually given this serious thought. She couldn't hold back anymore. "What? And be the Joad family all under one roof? I'm sorry Ben, but my mother and I would kill each other in a week. And is this really the time to change careers when you have a family to support?"

"You don't have to get nasty," he said. "I've gotta jump—somebody's waiting on the other line.

"I'm sorry," she said. "I only called about the dinner. I understand if you can't go."

Later that morning, when Jack asked Barbara via top-line if she was going to the dinner, he revealed that Mrs. Stone was traveling and couldn't attend. So the fix was in: she was going alone for an overnight in D.C. in a state of irritation with her husband.

At the Washington Hilton that evening, Barbara walked through the lobby and spotted the escalator—next to it stood a black board with white block letters reading HAPPY HOLIDAYS CORRESPONDENTS! She looked down to the bottom of the escalator where media types and politicians were air kissing, thinking she needed to score political points herself tonight. The ballroom was vast and packed with people she recognized from television: the on-air talent, along with their favorite producers, comprising the dominant demographic. Barbara wouldn't presume anyone recognized her, but as she walked purposefully to the bar, she attracted several admiring smiles. It must have been the head of hair Angelica had given her, all curls to contrast the sleek dress. Barbara ordered a martini, the quickest ticket to loosening up. The bartender poured it, allowing a few ice chips to escape from the jigger, and she had to lower her head to the drink to take her first sip. A direct-from-central-casting, white-haired politician observed her and remarked, "Ice in your martini. That's good luck."

The gin was already doing its job as Barbara walked to the other end of the golden ballroom where another bar was set up and Danko stood, two-fisted, holding a cocktail and a glass of white wine which he handed to Cathryn Collyns.

Barbara approached, asking Danko, "Why aren't you trolling the coat room?"

Danko kissed her, looked her up and down. "Long cool woman in a black dress."

"The Hollies," said Barbara, and Cathryn smiled blankly, probably thinking they were talking about Christmas stuff.

"I was just telling Rip how much I like doing hits on your show." Not to mention sitting in my chair.

"Barb," Rip said, finishing half his drink in one gulp. "Let's talk about tomorrow at some point tonight, k?" Because of the short turnaround, *This Just In* was broadcasting from the D.C. bureau in the morning.

Cathryn touched Rip's arm. "I want to know what you think about this, Rip—for my weekend show I was thinking a home improvement feature might be fun to do, get away from that silly old war..."

Barbara tuned her out, picking up a conversation between Lois Spencer and Bruce Hanson who were nearby. Lois, in a not-to-be-trifled-with satin navy suit, looked bored as she hectored him, "....the telestrator can be used to great effect in war coverage." And to draw genitalia. Bruce nodded sincerely. "Cool," he said, pronouncing it, "Cyool."

Barbara was already down to the soaked olives of her martini as she moved closer to the bar where Stacia Cabrerra was pandering to Ron Kavanagh, Sloane's cherubic henchman. "...and I'd love to start working more political stories into my show..." Barbara smiled at him as she moved up to the bar. He turned away from Stacia and extended his hand, "Hello, Barbara. Ron Kavanagh. I enjoy your work."

"Nice to officially meet you, Ron, and thanks." Already feeling the martini, Barbara ordered a club soda and asked Ron, whose highball glass fit perfectly in his pudgy hand, if he needed another.

"No. I'm good. I was just telling Stacia that in the new year, we'll be ramping up politics."

"Already campaigning for the mid-terms, huh?" said Barbara and Ron nodded, mopping his brow with his cocktail napkin.

"Ron!" Sloane Davis called from halfway down the bar, waving him over to her.

Ron shrugged and left the sweaty napkin on the bar. "Excuse me, Barbara. Duty calls."

Barbara watched as Ron lumbered over to Sloane; she put her arm around him and introduced him to a general, a frequent Phoenix guest. That troika would probably be hatching plans for a new war. The bartender handed Barbara her club soda and she looked over her shoulder to see if maybe Rip had freed himself from Cathryn. Instead, she spotted Jack, who was all the way across the room, but looking right at her.

As they walked toward each other, Jack got a few hearty claps on the back, and a matron in a beaded mother-of-the-bride dress stopped him and reached up to kiss his cheek, then put her hand on her heart. Jack received the kiss, smiling at Barbara with an expression that asked, *What's a guy to do?* Barbara patted her heart and fluttered her eyelashes at him.

When he reached her, they didn't kiss hello. "You made it," she said.

"I had to take the late shuttle in. Arrived at the hotel just fifteen minutes ago." He seemed out of breath. "You look..."

"Jack Stone!" Sloane's political powwow over, she grabbed Jack's arm. "Hello, Barbara," Sloane nodded. "Just wanted to give you a heads up, Jack, they're going to mention you in a montage of the war coverage and probably ask you to stand up." Then, she turned her head from side to side, like a little dog sniffing for a treat. "Gotta run." So much for Barbara's schmooze.

"You look stunning, Ms. King."

"As do you, Mr. Stone."

"Armani." Jack put his hand in his pocket and gave her his best *Zoolander*.

As three notes from a xylophone sounded, they followed the herd into the main ballroom. Barbara walked ahead of Jack, and when she looked over her shoulder to make sure he was there, she noticed him staring at the chiffon lace-up back of her black satin dress. They parted, taking their seats at different tables. With the exception of Ironsides, with whom Barbara refused to make eye contact, Barbara's table was strictly C-list: a former congresswoman, a few Phoenix sales executives, one of the channel's advertisers. Sloane might have invited her, but she'd also taken care to place her at a table that would do Barbara no political good. Barbara could see Jack's table: Sloane and Hanson, Cal and his wife, a muckety-muck from the Phoenix's corporate parent, and the runner-up but clearly more talented contestant from a hit singing show. Lois and Cathryn were seated there too, on either side of Ron Kavanagh.

During the dinner, the lights were dimmed and the war correspondent's video montage was played. First, the narrator told the story of the British correspondent who'd been killed in the attack on Jack's convoy. This gave the anchors in the audience a chance to wear their sad-clown expressions for the C-SPAN cameras. Cathryn wiped a tear. Bruce furrowed his brow. Lois steeled her jaw. Then, the video moved on to Jack's story, featuring footage of him in Kabul, wearing fatigues and stubble. Barbara was surprised to then see a clip of her own first bulletin about the bombing and next, Lois announcing that Jack had survived. Maybe it was reliving those moments; maybe it was the video's piano soundtrack, borrowed from a radio call-in show for the lovelorn; maybe it was the gin. Barbara tried to set her face in an expression of collegial appreciation as the live cameras shined on her. But instead, tears spilled onto her cheek and worse, her attempt to stifle the tear sent moisture on a slow, tickling journey from her nostrils to her glossed lips. She couldn't wipe it, not with the cloth napkin. Luckily, the cameras cut away from her reaction, the video ended, the house lights came back on, and the emcee asked Jack to stand. Once all eyes were on her co-anchor, Barbara pulled a tissue from her clutch and wiped away the evidence of her feelings for Jack.

CHAPTER 34

When the dinner was over, Barbara took the escalator back up to the lobby; she thought she might hobnob at the hotel bar for the after-hours party, since her tablemates had been duds. But Jack was standing at the top of the escalator, flanked by two young Phoenix bookers, their stance at once all Bond girl and all business.

"Barbara King," they said, practically in unison. "We were just getting a limo for Jack to go to the Phoenix after-party. Would you like to join him?" Like two goddesses enticing her to join them in their secret playground.

If she went to the hotel bar, really, what were the odds she'd wind up in conversation with a network executive?

"Ms. King. You really shouldn't let all that glamour go to waste," said Jack, his eyes flitting by the slit in her dress.

"It's *the* after-party!" said the blonde vixen.

"It's a 1970s theme!" said the brunette one.

"Se-ven-ties?" repeated Barbara slowly, looking at Jack. "That's only my favorite decade."

The limo deposited Barbara and Jack at the party and they had to walk down a short flight of stairs to get to the bar, adding to the party's exclusive feel. While there was no disco ball, the room was lighted in purple fluorescence, the white bar surface was sprinkled with bowls of Twizzlers and Smarties, and the Bee Gees' helium harmonies blared over the sound system. Jack's hand pressed against Barbara's back as he guided her to the bar.

Barbara felt as though she'd time-traveled to an era where she wasn't a suburban mother. She was an ingénue at a disco, about to impress Jack with her foxy moves on the dance floor which would soon be filled with amorous couples and slender young men in white unitards.

"What are you drinking?" Jack asked.

"Something 1970s."

"Harvey Wallbanger?

"Perfect!" She clapped like a delighted child.

"Two please," he told the bartender with the fake handlebar mustache.

The first drink, its frosty glass outfitted with orange slice and maraschino cherry went down easily. They ordered a second round, chatting all the while, comparing their tables. Jack said he'd been seated in between Sloane and a general. "It wasn't exactly relaxing."

"I'm glad you got your props, though."

"That was nice. We shouldn't talk about it, though, lest you are overcome again." He paused and grinned. "As you were in the hospital."

"Well, this time, I'm pretty sure the C-SPAN cameras caught it." She plucked the cherry from her drink and threw it on the bar in mock anger. "Damn it, Stone. If you hadn't survived, I would have been stuck with the missing Hanson quadruplet!"

"*Slapshot!*—a masterful piece of 1970s cinema," he laughed. "And speak of the devil."

Barbara twirled her straw in her drink and she and Jack turned their backs to the bar so they could watch the dance floor where the Hustle was breaking out and Bruce Hanson was chatting up Cathryn Collyns. "This just in...," said Barbara.

Jack imitated the whooshing of their bulletin sounder. "A Phoenix News Flash. Tell us what you've learned, Barbara."

"Jack, it would appear that the former archrivals for the title of Most Ambitious New Anchor have joined forces."

"Can you tell us if a peace deal could arise from these negotiations?"

"That's an interesting question, Jack. My journalistic intuition tells me their summit might well lead to a round of tonsil hockey."

Barbara spotted Stacia Cabrerra, in bombshell red, doing a modified tango with one of the sales executives. She'd apparently left her dog-in-a-purse behind.

"Jack, we need to interrupt our coverage to bring our viewers word of an impending attack on the dance floor."

"What are your police sources telling you?"

"They're reporting a canine accessory, not to be confused with an accessory to the crime, is poised to rush the dance floor and attack his mistress' dance partner."

Jack laughed and held up two fingers for a couple more Wallbangers.

"We'll have continuing coverage of the Chihuahuan Crisis, but first, this update from the line dance." As Bruce bumped with Cathryn, Sloane slithered between them, facing Bruce and grinding to "We Are Family."

"It would appear, Barbara, that Davis just back-checked Collyns!"

"It would seem just a matter of time before high-sticking occurs!"

"That's why they call it a game!"

By their third round, Jack and Barbara were doubled over at their own hilarity.

Jack held up his glass for a toast. "To Barbara King, a woman who can deftly handle breaking news, even in a disco."

"To Jack Stone, who can take shrapnel to the arse, but still lace up his boogie shoes."

"Speaking of which," he said, "We've been too busy anchoring to dance ourselves."

"You askin'?"

"I suppose I am," he said, removing his tuxedo jacket and placing it on the barstool.

Jack put his arm around her and led her to the dance floor where he turned her to face him and smiling, took her hands and spun her around, sending the alcohol dancing through her veins. He pulled her toward him, his hands around her waist, fingers brushing the space between the chiffon crisscross of her dress that ended just above the small of her back. Jack dipped her to the howls of the other dancers, and Barbara held on to his shoulders; she could feel the perspiration through his white dress shirt. After several dances like that, the disc jockey said, "We're gonna slow things down a bit now."

Barbara wanted to slow dance with Jack; she imagined resting her head on his chest, leaving her makeup mark as she had in the hospital. They paused for a moment, letting go of each other's hands, catching their breath. He said, "Might another beverage be in order?"

They returned to the bar, and as Jack picked up his jacket, he said, "Sorry, it's vibrating." He retrieved his BlackBerry from the jacket pocket and squinted at it. He seemed as soused as she was.

"'Scuse me, sir. It's 1978 and that gizmo hasn't been invented yet," said Barbara, grabbing the hand holding the BlackBerry.

Jack obediently put the device back in his pocket and smiled dreamily at her. "Where were we?"

Danko appeared out of nowhere. And for a guy who could drink anyone under the table and never appear inebriated, he seemed drunk, too. "Hey. Just sent you guys tomorrow's rundown."

"Where you been all night?" Barbara asked. And how had he managed to plan tomorrow morning's show?

Danko looked at Barbara and Jack's tall drinks and said, "Looks like you two are having a good time."

"Yes. I'd say so," Jack grinned at Barbara.

The two goddess escorts who were now slow dancing with each other caught Danko's eye. "Double fun," he said.

"My favorite Robert Palmer album!" Barbara called after him as Rip sauntered over to the dance floor.

Barbara and Jack ordered another round of Wallbangers and sat at the bar listening to the DJ's selections; he was in a low-tempo groove and Barbara recognized the next song from its first strains. "Oh. Oh. Now this. This, Jack, is one of my favorite songs from my favorite decade. Jack Stone, can you name that tune?"

She sang along with the yearning lyrics about an adulterous couple's secret cafe rendezvous, thinking of her and Jack's own morning meetings.

"You're better at music trivia. You and Danko," said Jack, glancing over his shoulder at Rip, who was now dancing with the Bond girls. "Something regarding a Mrs. Jones?"

"We'll accept that response! 'Me and Mrs. Jones'," said Barbara. "You know, someone once told me that the song was an allegory for heroin addiction, but I don't believe it; he sings it like a man who's in love, who's in pain, ya know?"

"I do know."

"But who sang it?" Barbara quizzed herself. "I can't think of it. Must be the booze." She wanted to dance some more with

Jack, but how could they to such charged lyrics? Sadly, it was time to leave the 1970s.

"Shall we be sensible and call it a night?" Jack asked.

"It's already half-past sensible," she said.

The vixens who'd created a Rip sandwich on the dance floor had somehow disengaged long enough to procure a limo for Jack and Barbara to travel to the boutique hotel where the Phoenix had put them up for the night. Once inside, Jack offered to escort her to her room, "it being a rough neighborhood." As they walked down the hallway to her room, Jack maintained his perfect posture but couldn't walk in a straight line. Barbara held on to his arm and they giggled as she hiccuped.

When they got to her door, Barbara swiped her card key futilely a few times before Jack took it from her hand and got the little green light to flash and the door latch to click open.

She felt woozy.

"That," he said, "was a fun date." Jack leaned against the doorway, one arm pressed against the frame.

"Sure was." Barbara had her back against the door; she looked up at his face, in particular, his mouth.

"Indeed."

"So, the bureau at 7?" she asked.

"Yes. 7." He looked at his watch and blinked. "That's very soon."

She opened the door and started backing into the room and he took a few slow steps away from the door and into the hallway.

"Well, good night, Jack."

"Good night, Barbara. Sweet dreams."

Barbara shut the door and managed to remove her gown and drape it over the desk chair before crawling under the smooth sheets of the queen-sized bed. She didn't even bother removing the surplus pillow; she positioned it lengthwise next to her and draped her arm over it. Jack. Had he wanted to come in? She wanted him to. Badly. Now the best she could do was (for what felt like the millionth time) have a detailed, R-rated fantasy about him in the hopes that it would make her dream about him when she fell asleep. But what would have happened if he had come in? They weren't a couple of teenagers who'd make out and grope each other for a while and then pass out. They were grown-ups. They'd have done it. It. Definitely NC-17 or X territory. She hiccuped again. The clock radio swayed. 3:43. It was better he hadn't come in. She turned off the nightstand lamp. Lights out.

Barbara awoke from a series of knocks on the door. She looked at the night table clock. 3:51. Another knock. Barbara got up and walked over to the door in the dark and looked through the peephole: Jack. She turned into the bathroom and grabbed the white terry cloth robe hanging there. She undid the chain and opened the hotel room door.

"I'm sorry to wake you, but I believe I have the answer to tonight's quiz."

Barbara held the door open and Jack stepped into the room and let door close behind him. Still half asleep and fully drunk, she walked over to the night table and turned the lamp on. Why was he here?

"I assume you were tossing and turning not knowing the answer to that music trivia question." He was still in his tuxedo shirt and pants, the bow tie untied around his neck.

"I...I was," she said, tightening the bathrobe belt around her waist.

Jack took a step toward her and took his BlackBerry out of his pants pocket. "This post-1970s technology tells me the artist is...Billy Paul."

"Right," she nodded slowly. Had he really come to her room to tell her that? "Never trust a guy with two first names," she tried to banter.

"That's true," he said.

"I'm really glad you told me."

Jack put the BlackBerry down on the night table and swallowed. "I thought you'd need to know."

"It would have bothered me..."

Jack moved in and kissed her quickly. Then, as if shocked, he took a step back. They looked at each other. "Barbara," he said and put his arms around her and held her tightly and kissed her hard. She thought her knees might actually buckle, she felt so weak, so...enveloped. He undid the robe's belt and slipped his hands around her waist, just like he had on the dance floor, except this time, there was no fabric separating his touch from her skin. He kissed her just the way she liked to be kissed—long deep kisses, jaws collapsed—whatever else happened, this would be the best part. God, he was positively consuming her. Maybe that's what it was about him: This passion had always been just under the surface. He kissed her hair and neck and shoulders and her mouth again and took her face in his hands, then sat on the bed and pulled her down with him and pushed the robe off of her shoulders. They couldn't get out of their clothes fast enough; they worked as a team, alternating on the buttons of his shirt, then both unfastening his cummerbund. He soloed on pulling his undershirt up and over his head and undoing her bra, but she helped him slide her panties down her legs, grateful they were lace and not Spanx.

They lay on the bed kissing and since they were grown-ups, what happened next was an inevitability. "You're even more beautiful than I dreamed," he said. And really, even if any fit of conscience was going to stop her, who could resist that? So she didn't, and it was even better than anything she'd dreamed.

She had just started to wrap her legs around his back to try to get him even closer, deeper, when Jack's BlackBerry started doing a little dance on the night table's glass top. They ignored it. It continued buzzing. They broke off a kiss. It stopped. He said, "Thank God." They resumed.

They fell asleep for a little while, but woke up when the BlackBerry whirred again briefly, then stopped. Barbara opened her eyes; her head was in the crook of Jack's arm, her nose pressed against his chest. She pulled the sheet up over them and sat up so she could see the clock. *5:07.*

Jack, eyes closed, smiling, asked, "What time is it?"

"Fifty three minutes 'til that alarm goes off," she said, lying back down on her side.

Jack rolled to his side to face her and stroked her arm. "Why don't you re-set it for 6:30? The bureau's close."

"I'm not as impossibly handsome as you. I need to shower, primp..."

"You don't need a thing. You're probably the only female anchor who's completely recognizable without makeup." He slowly brushed her hair from her face. "You even looked ravishing the first day I met you."

"You mean...the foils?" She sat up again, her back turned to him, to grab a tissue from her night table so she could wipe away any smudged makeup.

Jack sat up, too, and lifted her hair from her neck so he could kiss the nape. "I was instantly smitten."

"You're...making fun of me." She let the tissue drop from her hand.

"No, I'm not. I truly was...I don't know..." He pulled her down onto the bed, his arms around her, his chest against her back. Gee whiz, he was good to go again. "...thunderstruck."

"Really?"

"Really." He continued kissing the back of her neck, her shoulders.

Barbara arched her back as he pressed against her. "I thought you were cranky that first time I came in your office," she said.

"Mmmm. I'd like that."

"Huh?"

"If you came in my office."

"Jack...Beauregard?...Stone! That's got to be your middle name, right?"

"I do not have a middle name. And you mean to tell me you've never considered such a scenario?"

"No." He moved his hands from her breasts down to her hips, then ran them down the length of her thighs.

"Not even once?"

"Maybe..." She couldn't talk anymore; she was taking quick, short breaths. "...just once."

"I think about you all the time," he said, turning her on her back, kissing her. He really was the best kisser ever—she almost could have just left it at that. But they didn't. Then the damn BlackBerry buzzed again and a moment later the room phone rang at such a piercing volume, they separated, out of breath. Barbara brought her hands from around his neck to his shoulders. He got up on his hands, still leaning over her and shook his head. The room phone stopped ringing but the BlackBerry started in again. "Someone is trying very hard to get in touch with us." Jack exhaled and, holding her leg for balance, fumbled for the device and read it.

"Damn it," he said.

The room phone rang again and Barbara sat up, grabbing only a corner of the sheets which had been pushed to the bottom of the bed. She picked up the phone.

"Hello?" she said. "No, didn't see it. I was, um, sleeping. Uh-huh. What time? K. I don't know. Maybe he's sleeping? Okay, thanks."

She hung up the phone. "Those hostages have been freed. Danko wants us in the bureau at 6 to anchor a newser at 7."

"Yes, here it is," said Jack, sitting next to her on the bed and showing her the bulletin on his BlackBerry. She inched closer to him, resting her hand on his back.

"Danko says he couldn't find you."

"I guess I better leave," Jack said, stroking her hair. "We can't very well walk into the bureau together." He rose and gathered up his clothes.

"No, we can't." Barbara found her robe on the floor and put it on. She sat on the bed, watching as Jack pulled up his pants and buttoned his shirt.

"I hate to leave," he said and walked toward the bed. Barbara stood up and rested her head on his shoulder, breathing in his perspiration tinged with her Chanel.

Jack took her face in his hands again and gave her a long, deep goodbye kiss. "To be continued," he said. Barbara looked at him, thinking, for the first time, of Ben, and all the times he'd kissed her passionately, and, he'd assumed, exclusively.

CHAPTER 35

Jack, our next guest has a unique perspective on the now-resolved hostage crisis...

...because he himself was once a hostage, Barbara...

...Joining us from D.C. this morning...

...is David Trent, who was among a group of hostages taken in the Middle East...

...during a crisis in the mid-1990s....

...Mr. Trent, thanks for joining us...

Just after 7 o'clock that morning, Jack and Barbara were on the air live from the D.C. bureau's set, a guest seated between them as they waited for a Pentagon news conference to begin. Four American hostages, security contractors held by a shadowy Al-Qaeda offshoot group in Afghanistan, had been rescued by U.S. troops. The headline on the screen behind Jack and Barbara screamed: *SWEET RELEASE!,* as one of the hostages had told his liberators he was dying for a chocolate shake.

Barbara could have used one herself. Excellent hangover food, milkshakes. But there was no remedy for her "love hangover" (she was pretty sure that Diana Ross tune had played in the disco last night). Every time she looked at Jack on the set, she thought of how he'd looked *IN HER BED* just an hour ago.

Sometimes when a guest was answering a question, Barbara let her mind wander to the way he'd moved in for that first electric kiss, the way his lips felt against the skin of her back, the way he'd looked at her with not just lust, but love. But during their 4-hour broadcast, not so much as a flirtation passed between them. Their hours were all ad-libbed and packed with bulletins, news conferences, and guests who sat between them, preventing any games of footsie from breaking out.

They were in their last commercial break before the toss back to New York and *Lois Spencer's America Rises*. Jack looked at Barbara and winked; if anyone saw it, it could have seemed to be just a chummy we-made-it-through-our-show gesture. Feeling punch-drunk now instead of drunk-drunk, she sent him a computer message.

King: *Call for you on line 2, Jack. A Mr. Denny Terrio wondering if you'd be interested in joining his lineup of Solid Gold dancers?*

Jack looked at her out of the corner of his eye as the stage hand wheeled the guest chair away.

Stone: *Only if you'll be my…er…partner again.*

When the show ended, the audio guy stood between them and collected their mics. "Great show."

Barbara looked at Jack and let out a loud exhale.

Jack frowned. "Would you believe I have to hang around the bureau? I was hoping we could make the journey back to headquarters together," he whispered, "but I have one last interview with a D.C. newspaper."

"That's too bad." No mile-high club. She looked at him. *Thunderstruck*. That's how she felt, too.

The studio door swung open and Danko walked onto the set. "Sloane just called."

"Christ. What?" asked Barbara.

"Just called to say 'great show.'"

"Phew," said Barbara.

"Not bad for an inebriated team," said Jack, elbowing Barbara as if she were his football buddy.

"Yeah." Rip studied them. "Sorry I had to hunt you two down last night."

"No sweat!" said Barbara. "No problem!" said Jack, stepping on her line, for the first time that morning.

Danko squinted. "Riiiiiiight." He'd probably seen them leave the party together and knew that Jack was not in his room sleeping when he'd called—those room phones would wake the dead.

The studio door opened again and this time, a D.C. producer poked his head in. "Jack—call for you—*Washington Times?*"

"I guess I'll just see you back in New York," said Jack, addressing both Barbara and Rip.

Barbara barely met Jack's eye as she said, "Yeah. See you back at the ranch!"

On the noon shuttle flight from D.C. to New York, Barbara and Rip sat next to each other and Rip charmed the flight attendant into bringing them two mini vodka bottles each. "One tomato juice will do me," he told her.

"Have a good time with Stone last night?" Rip asked, sucking down the first vodka right from the bottle.

"Yeah, we discoed the night away," she said, pouring both of her vodkas into her plastic cup.

Rip leaned in to her and whispered, "I was talking about the horizontal hulu."

Barbara blinked and took a big swig.

"I tried his room," said Rip. "He wasn't there."

"Well, I left him at the hotel bar."

"Huh." Rip unscrewed his second bottle. "Didn't see him there."

"Well, maybe he...left."

Rip patted her arm. "You're a lousy liar, baby." He downed the second vodka, put on his aviator shades, and fell sound asleep.

Barbara finished her drink and closed her eyes but couldn't sleep; instead she replayed everything from start to its interrupted finish. *To be continued.* She looked at Danko. She wished Jack was sleeping there instead. She craved him, yearned for him. If Jack was next to her now, he'd wake up with that blissful look on his face again, and they'd kiss, discreetly, but then as soon as they got in a cab at the airport they'd throw their arms around each other and tell the driver to step on it and get them to the nearest hotel.

But then what? Where would they tryst from there on? Would she lock the door of her office at breakfast or invite him over to her house for a little diurnal delight? As it stood now, they would be charged with it-was-out-of-town-so-it-doesn't-count, second-degree adultery. A crime of passion, as it were. But if they plotted future rendezvous, the crime would be premeditated, the charge upgraded to first-degree cheating.

If they continued an affair and fell even more deeply in love, would they leave their spouses? She'd have to tell Ben that she loved Jack more than him, but not to feel bad because one day when he was teaching poetry in a wood-paneled room, wearing a corduroy jacket and thoughtfully scratching his chin, he'd find an adoring, patchouli-scented acolyte who'd love nothing more than to drive cross-country with him.

But what about Rory, her flesh and blood? He wouldn't understand why his mom and dad couldn't live together anymore and when he grew older, he'd learn the truth that his mother was a careless slut who couldn't keep her hands off her co-anchor. He'd treat her with thinly-veiled contempt on the days she had custody.

And would Jack leave Mrs. Stone? Sure, part of Jack's ardor could have come from being sex-starved—Cynthia was probably no firecracker in the kip. But she must have some hold on him. Maybe Jack liked maintaining that perfect portrait on display at their Christmas party as much as she did. And maybe he didn't want to shatter his daughter Madeleine's picture of her mom and dad any more than Barbara wanted to hurt her family.

When Barbara got home that Friday afternoon, the house was empty, so like all good adulterers, she took a steaming hot shower. But she wouldn't wash away all of her memories of Jack, so she unpacked her dress and instead of putting it in the dry cleaner pile, hung it in her closet.

She checked her BlackBerry every few minutes. No e-mails from him. But Jack wouldn't send anything foolish electronically and they almost never called each other at home. But he must be thinking of her, missing her.

Barbara called Siobhan on the new cell phone she'd gotten her and said she was exhausted from the trip, would she mind coming over and waiting for Rory's bus? Siobhan agreed and even offered to stay and cook a meal. Barbara was relieved she could rest up before she had to face her mother and play the role of busy business traveler instead of hungover harlot with Jack Stone on her breath.

When Barbara emerged from her nap, she walked downstairs into the kitchen where Rory jumped out of his chair and ran to her. Barbara squeezed him tight and kissed him again and again and again. "I missed you so much!" Ben came up from the downstairs office and joined the hug, kissing the top of Barbara's head. Good thing she'd washed her hair. Barbara smiled up at Ben. She didn't *not* love him: he was smart and sincere and supportive, a wonderful father, and like a son to her parents. Christ, she was living yet another 1970s song: "Torn between Two Lovers." Loving them both *was* breaking all the rules!

"Welcome back, honey, we missed you," he said.

Siobhan, who was setting the dining room table, came into the kitchen to get some napkins. "Hello sleeping beauty," she said. "Enjoy yourself in our nation's capital?"

"I wouldn't say 'enjoyed,' it was busy. That hostage story broke overnight so I had to go to the bureau extra early—that's why I was so tired."

Rory broke away from Barbara's hug. "Gammy says you were at a big party." He turned a cartwheel in the kitchen.

"Why don't you move your Olympics into the living room?" said Siobhan. "Ziti needs another few."

Ben gave Rory a gentle push in the direction of the living room where he started building with the Lincoln Logs and Legos that were scattered about the room. Barbara and Ben sat on the couch and Siobhan followed, taking a seat next to Barbara, wiping her hands on her apron before using the clicking on the TV remote. If her soul sister Bea Arthur wasn't on, Siobhan would probably tune in to an evening entertainment news show.

"How'd it go?" Ben asked Barbara, taking her hand in his, kissing it as they sat on the couch. If he only knew where that hand had been, she thought.

"Truth be told, I didn't get much face-time with Sloane. She was busy schmoozing up. How was your dinner?"

"Okay. I had a benign chat with the big guy, but my PM was a nervous wreck—he took a bath on a big trade just before the close."

"Barbara! They're talking about your party last night!" Siobhan pointed at the screen with the remote, turning up the volume. So C-SPAN hadn't been the only channel to cover the correspondent's dinner—the war reporters' tribute had made it into the lineup of Siobhan's entertainment show. Barbara, Ben and Siobhan all sat up and listened to the perky hostess.

They say politics is showbiz for ugly people. But not at last night's Washington correspondent's dinner, where dashing Phoenix news channel anchor Jack Stone was honored after being wounded in Afghanistan.

That would be Jack Stone, my lover, thought Barbara.

During a video tribute to Stone....

Gosh, he looked good in those clips. Just the right amount of scruff...

...his co-anchor, Barbara King, was visibly emotional.

Yikes.

There she was, cheeks not just moist, but wet with tears. Cut to a clip of someone else's reaction! But no, they were staying on her, the shot of her face getting tighter. Her stomach did a sickening flip as she willed the image away. Finally, they cut away, just before Barbara's nose started running. Jack's publicity shot appeared on the screen behind the entertainment hostess.

Barbara got up from the couch and walked over to the corner of the living room and crouched next to Rory who was knocking down the fort he'd built. "Whatcha makin'?" Barbara felt her mother's eyes searing her back.

"The fort got blown up by bad guys," explained Rory.

Siobhan rose from the couch. "Seems like it was quite the emotional evening."

"I didn't know they were paying tribute to Jack," said Ben.

"Oh, yeah, I forgot they were going to do that." Barbara picked up a Lincoln Log to help Rory rebuild.

"It certainly got you choked up," said Siobhan.

Barbara shot her a look that said, shut up, Ma, and Ben caught it.

Barbara directed her comments to Ben. "You had to see the whole montage they played at the dinner. They paid tribute to a British correspondent who was killed—left behind a pregnant wife and baby girl, I think. Awful. And they showed pictures of the troops who were killed. It was just...really...powerful."

"I'll bet it was," said Siobhan and she gave her beehive a boost and walked into the kitchen.

Ben rose from the couch, walked over to Barbara, and held out his hand to help her up from the floor. "I'm glad to hear they paid tribute to the troops," he said. "They deserve it." He kissed Barbara on the lips. "And I'm glad you're back home."

Barbara was relieved that she'd convinced Ben her display of emotion was elicited by the fallen heroes and not her dashing co-anchor.

The next evening, Barbara picked up Siobhan to go to mass, as was their ritual. Stick to the routine, act normal, Barbara told herself. But she felt more tired today than yesterday and couldn't muster the energy to sing along with the cantor, a plain-looking woman about her age, who cupped her hands and raised them, to encourage the parishioners to participate. The motion irritated Barbara. This woman was probably a faithful wife and devoted mother with a crystal clear conscience whose only time away from her family was spent here in church. Not in a hotel room banging her co-cantor.

Barbara held her prayer book open before her, but she soon closed her eyes and again replayed the clips from the night in D.C.: Jack spinning her on the dance floor, Jack's face when she opened her hotel room door, his eyes closed when they were... Barbara snapped open her eyes and shifted in the pew as she recited the Lord's prayer. *And lead us not in to temptation.* She hadn't been led, she'd gone willingly, and here she was reliving the act in church! As they listened to the final parish announcements, Barbara turned to Siobhan and said, "I thought I might hang around for confession."

"And what do you need to be confessin'?" Siobhan whispered.

"Third Sunday of Advent tomorrow," said Barbara. "You could go too."

"I don't need Father Boring Bill to listen to my sins, which, by the way, are few and far between."

In the old days at church, Barbara and Siobhan bobby-pinned small white lace veils to their hair, and placed their white gloves under the push-button clips installed on the backs of the wooden pews. The clips were long gone and the pews varnished so many times even the imprints had vanished. Teenagers came to mass directly from sports games, in hooded sweatshirts and flip-flops. Grown-ups in jeans. "Common," tsked Siobhan. But most disturbingly, the confessional was now lighted. The priest sat behind a patterned, opaque glass, but you could see him as you walked in, which meant that if he cared to, he could see you too. What was wrong with that pitch black booth all the kids in her catechism class were so scared of? Where was the sliding window that opened only to a netted barrier with a dim amber glow, so you were never seen, just heard, your sins belonging to a disembodied voice?

As soon as Barbara heard the priest's voice, she knew it was Father Bill, the priest who not only had the distinction of being "boring", but was also a dead ringer for Charles Nelson Reilly. His profound but droning homilies were hard to take seriously when Barbara recalled Reilly's campy double entendres on *Match Game* and wondered if Gene Rayburn and those piano-key teeth of his might appear at the altar as Eucharistic minister. Right now though, she took Father Bill plenty seriously as she genuflected in the lighted booth.

"Forgive me Father, for I have sinned, it's been...I'm not sure how long since my last confession."

"Roughly how long?"

"I'm not sure...."

"A month, a year? Five?...."

"I'd be guessing..."

"Ballpark..."

Okay, padre. "Three months. About three."

"Go ahead."

"Well, I've had some harsh arguments with my mother......" She figured she'd start small. Like a squeegee criminal who, by the way, is also as killer.

"Yes, and..." *And?* Had he gotten a look at her and assumed she had a list? She heard him sigh.

"And I was dishonest. "

"Yes?"

"To my husband."

"How so?"

She couldn't confess it. It was the sin of adultery, one of the biggies, on the "Thou Shalt Nots" hit parade, and if she said it out loud, it would be true. Ironically, if only the confessional still had that barrier, she would have felt free to speak of her sin. She'd been kept from sinning in the first place by other barriers: the desk that separated her and Jack at breakfast, the guests who sat between them on the set, the wall between their headboards their first time in D.C. But Barbara had willfully worn them away, scratched at the surface of Jack's cordial façade with her humor, her teasing, and tears. The liquid atmosphere of that night in the disco had finally melted away any remaining inhibition; that sex had never been anything but flimsily contained.

"I suppose I'm guilty of lying by omission," Barbara confessed. "Because I...

"For your penance," he interrupted, obviously having lost interest. "Say three Hail Mary's and one Our Father. Your sins are forgiven."

Just like that. If penance truly cleansed a soul, she'd blown her chance to be forgiven. But why confess anyway? She remembered another tenet of penance from when she was a girl: you weren't supposed to confess unless you were really sorry. And she wasn't. She'd loved every second of it. Both times. She was on the elevator to hell.

Barbara went back to the pew where Siobhan was holding her rosary beads, deep in prayer. She opened one eye when Barbara kneeled next to her.

"That was fast."

Barbara put her head in her hands and said her penance.

On the drive home, when Barbara pulled her minivan into Siobhan's driveway. Siobhan held her purse in her lap primly and said, "Get it off your chest, did you?"

"I don't know what you're talking about," said Barbara wanly.

"I don't know what happened in Washington but I could guess," said Siobhan. "And crying over him again. This time on television!"

"I didn't know the cameras were going to be on me—and by the way, thanks a lot for making Ben suspicious."

"Maybe it's time he woke up and smelled the coffee. I'm having a hard time looking him in the eye, even if you don't."

Barbara didn't look at her mother; she stared straight ahead, gripping the wheel at ten and two. She was glad it was dark in her minivan, darker than in the confessional, and with no C-SPAN cameras shining the light on her guilty, lovelorn expression.

"Cut the engine, Barbara Marie."

Barbara obeyed.

"I'm going to tell you a little tale now and you are going to keep your trap shut and not give me one of your college girl, smarty-pants arguments, and not lose your Irish temper. When I'm done, you'll kiss your old mother good night and drive home."

What in God's name?

"When you were a little girl of 10 and I was working in Bohack's, there was a real charmer who worked there behind the deli counter. Timothy. Black Irish. A real wit. I saw him nearly every day at work and oh, he filled my head with romance and I thought I'd maybe made a mistake marrying your father. I was in love, head over heels. I could barely see straight. And it was just a matter of time before I did something I would have regretted my whole life. Your father has always been a quiet man, a serious man, not a live wire or funny like Tim. But he's a smart one, Hans Konig. Maybe I mentioned Tim's name one too many times at home and the jig was already up. But on a Thursday before Easter, your father left his job in the pits early to buy a leg of lamb for Easter supper. Well, when he came to the store, I was on a break, out in the back lot, sharing a smoke and a laugh with Tim. And Tim kissed me. And who do you suppose comes out into the lot, just at that moment, holding that leg of lamb under his arm? Your father's not a tall man, but he can scare the bejeesus out of you when he wants. Well, he threatened to hit Tim over the head with a leg of lamb—something he'd seen in a Hitchcock TV show. Can you imagine? And when we got home that day he spoke just two words to me: 'Stay away.' And that was the end of that. I asked to have my shift changed so I wouldn't see Tim much anymore. And I'm glad I stayed with your father. But mostly, dear girl, I'm glad I stayed to raise you. You think if you leave your Ben, he's not going to be snatched up? Some pretty young girl will sink her claws into him in no time—believe you me! And then guess what, that girl is going to be raising your boy on the weekends. Rory will be running into her arms at the playground and she'll be tucking him in at night. Don't you think, Barbara, it would be best to just stay away from Mr. Jack

Stone?' Remember what your father says: 'You can't build happiness on top of unhappiness.'"

Barbara gripped the wheel in stunned silence as Siobhan adjusted a bobby pin in her beehive before slamming the minivan door shut.

CHAPTER 36

Jack didn't knock on Barbara's door for breakfast on Monday morning. But maybe that was just because Sloane, via a weekend e-mail, had requested they all attend the morning meeting *in person, in the conference room* so they could review last week's ratings. But then Jack didn't show up for the meeting either, Sloane explaining quickly, "Stone called out this morning. Says he should be back tomorrow."

Where was he? If he was able to pick up his phone to call in sick, why couldn't he have called her? Maybe he'd confessed to Mrs. Stone over the weekend and she was taking him straight to divorce court this morning, after, of course, calling Ben to tell him everything.

Barbara was agitated in hair and makeup. How could he just not come to work today? Angelica took Barbara's hair in her hands, twirling the strands as she looked at Barbara in the mirror. "Heard you two were quite the team."

"What?"

"You and Jack."

"You mean the hostage coverage."

Angelica poked her with her teasing comb. "No, on the dance floor. Heard you two were getting' down and getting' funky."

Barbara felt her neck redden. "And getting' back up again," she joked half-heartedly.

Jane ripped back the curtain and asked, "How long? Do I have time to do a guest first?"

"Go ahead. I just started," Angelica said. Jane put on her new black, owlish glasses and held her hand to Barbara's face. "You look flushed. Are you feeling alright?"

"I'm fine," she said, her voice pitched unnaturally high. Jane closed the curtain and left.

"Is Jack sick?" asked Angelica.

"Dunno."

Angelica sprayed Barbara's hair but then put the styling gel down and her hands on her hips. "You're sure you're okay?"

"Maybe I just look ruddy from all the booze."

Angelica blow-dried Barbara's hair without further questions, but when she turned off the dryer, she whispered in her ear, "Something happen?"

Barbara continued to pretend she didn't understand the questions. "I don't know what happened to him. At the meeting they just said he called out."

Angelica shook her head, exasperated. "No, I mean, did something happen in Washington? Word is you two looked like you were really into each other that night."

"We were just dancing, drinking—everyone was pretty loose," Barbara answered, refusing to meet Angelica's eyes in the mirror.

Angelica looked at her as a mother would when her child won't confess to hitting a sibling. "Barbara, people are talking. Anyone who wasn't at the dinner saw you on that Hollywood show."

"The video they played was really, really sad!"

"How 'bout when you found out Jack was hurt? And since he's been back, when you two say good morning to each other on the set, you can just *feel it* right through the television," she said, tapping the screen with her comb for emphasis. Angelica put her hands on Barbara's shoulders and looked at her in the mirror until Barbara finally met her gaze. "What happened, girl?"

Barbara needed to tell someone, to relieve that weight pressed on her heart.

"I really don't know where he is today and I'm going crazy. We had so much fun together that night and then we said good night, but then he came back to my room and...I should have told him to leave but I didn't...and I didn't want to...I wanted to be with him...I think I....no, I'm pretty sure I'm in love with him. I...I am. Oh, shit. I don't know what to do. I'm a horrible person."

"You're a good person, Barbara. But it happens. You're working with him every day here at this place, looking your finest. It's hard to resist. It's like a great big party here. I'll bet it was an even bigger one down there. But it's not real. Know what I'm sayin'?"

Barbara wondered if what she and Jack felt for each other was real. It sure felt like it. What if they had met before their marriages and children, would they have connected? Definitely. What if they'd worked together on an assembly line minus the glitz and glamour, would they have fallen in love? Probably. And what if they were married to each other and their love wasn't *verboten,* would the sex still be crazy passionate and would the love last? Well, maybe.

Barbara was driving home from the train station after work that day when her cell phone rang. Finally!

"Jack! Where are you? Are you sick?"

"I am driving home from Raleigh, North Carolina." His hometown, where his parents still lived.

"Your folks okay?"

"They're fine."

"So you were just visiting?"

"No. Not exactly. Actually, not at all. I didn't see my parents."

"Then why'd you go?"

"I needed to be alone. To drive. I drove here from D.C. on Friday night. Told Mrs. Stone I was going home. But I've been staying in a hotel. I needed to clear my head."

"Where are you now?"

"On my way back to New York."

"Jack, I..." she wanted to pour her heart out, but the satellite delayed her utterance and Jack continued.

"I have so much I want to say, Barbara, but it's not appropriate for these airwaves."

"When are you back on the schedule?" she asked.

"Tomorrow. May I come by your office in the morning?"

"You don't have to ask." There was a pause and she wondered if the call had dropped out. "Jack?"

"I'm here."

"Jack, we can talk tomorrow, but I don't know if I can do this. I just wish things were different...I wish...that I knew you before."

The next morning, Barbara was at her desk, printing out research she wouldn't be able to focus on. Even though Jack was going to stop by her office, it wouldn't be for breakfast because Sloane had mandated everyone attend the morning meetings *in person until further notice* so they could examine ratings and rundowns every day. As Barbara shuffled her papers into a stack, she heard a knock.

She opened the door to find Jack, a tiny piece of tissue on his nicked chin, hair wet from swimming, duffel in hand." Her face burned. He stepped inside her office and she closed the door. "How are you?"

"I'd be better if we didn't have to attend the morning meeting," he said with a sad smile.

The meeting was starting in minutes. "Yeah, what a drag." God, she wanted to throw herself on top of him.

Barbara's phone rang and she took a step back to see whose number was lighting up. "It's Danko."

"Better answer." Jack gave her a wistful look. "Lord knows he'll try again if you don't."

Barbara's stomach did a flip at his reference to the hotel room. She picked up and told Rip she'd call him right back.

Jack took a step toward her and took her hands in his and cleared his throat. "I worked on a speech over the weekend." He smiled. "You were always the better ad-libber."

"That's not true," she said, moving closer to him as they stood face-to-face.

"What happened in Washington was not a crime of opportunity."

"What do you mean?"

"I mean, I have wanted this for a long time. I told you how I felt when I first met you. But it was more than being thunderstruck, which might seem to connote mere physical attraction. I feel, Barbara, that you and I are...well...this sounds very New Age, but I mean it quite sincerely: soul mates."

Jack looked down as if his teleprompter had gone down, then back up at her and continued. "I know you seem to think I was once some sort of ladies' man, but I truly have never met anyone like you. Warm, funny....and passionate." He sighed. "That night was...." He shook his head. "I cannot help but dream of what a life with you would be like."

"Oh, Jack," she said, bringing her hand to his face. "I've dreamed of that too, but..."

"I know that you are already spoken for. As am I." He rolled his eyes. "And I can see how devoted you are to your family.

When you and I parted in D.C., I said, 'To be continued,' but your face said, 'It won't.'"

"Jack, it's not that I don't want to, I just don't know..."

"Bear with me. I'm reaching the end of my monologue." He took her hands . "Barbara, I love you. But I will honor your wishes, whatever they may be. If you feel we need to be nothing more than friends and colleagues, I shall respect that."

Jack let go of her hands and bowed, then picked up his duffel and left.

Barbara put her head down on her desk and wept. He loved her. *Loved* her! But he understood it would have to end. And it had barely started. And yet, everyone except their spouses knew they were in love. *The Post* would get a hold of it soon if they didn't knock it off. Her mother had tried to scare her straight with her shocking story of love in the parallel universe of the Bohack supermarket. And now Jack was offering her the chance to do the right thing, to stay away.

She wiped her tears and took out her reporter's notebook, ripped off a lined sheet and wrote.

Dear Jack,

There's an old German saying that goes something like this: "You can't build happiness on top of unhappiness." If our families were torn apart, it would be impossible to build a happy life together.

It's going to hurt so much to do it, but I am going to stay away even though I love you very much.

Yours,

Barbara

Barbara cried again, then dried her eyes, put on her suit jacket and went to the conference room. She walked up to Jack, who was already seated at the conference table, and handed him the manila envelope that contained her letter. "I have some research for you."

Jack slowly reached for the envelope; he looked confused.

"Rebuttal research?"

"Ah, yes. Thank you." He got it.

Barbara walked out of the conference room, not looking back at the staff. Go ahead and talk, she thought, you're going to anyway. She went back to her office, packed up and left the Phoenix, calling Danko to say she had an emergency at home and couldn't do the show.

CHAPTER 37

Barbara explained her abrupt departure Tuesday morning to Danko by saying her mother needed a "procedure." In being purposely vague, so the term would conjure lady-parts surgery, she staved off a challenge. And when she got home, Barbara used a different uterine rhetorical device, telling her mother she had a debilitating period and needed rest.

After dinner and wine, and after Rory was tucked in, Ben went upstairs to read and Barbara said she still felt crampy and would stay downstairs again to "watch some TV." A week to go before Christmas, but instead of wrapping gifts while watching a Christmas special, she uncorked a second bottle of red and watched one of the videos carefully selected from her library. The movies' themes were all the same: Impossible Love. *Witness. West Side Story. Casablanca.* Okay, so Jack wasn't a hard-bitten big-city cop and she wasn't a demure Amish widow with a birdhouse that needed fixing. Never mind that Jack wasn't a *boy like that who killed her brother.* And so what if Jack hadn't walked away because Ben needed Barbara at his side to save the world from Nazis. Their love was no less impossible. She popped *Casablanca* in the VCR and poured her wine to the rim. As she watched the final scene, she put a couch pillow over her mouth so Ben wouldn't hear her coughing sobs. Barbara stared through her tears at the man in the fedora on the misty tarmac. They'd always have D.C.

Barbara went to work Wednesday morning with a headache from the wine, compounded by her period, the ovarian retribution for her lies. She was dealing with its unexpected yet welcome arrival, when two young women, probably desk assistants, walked into the bathroom, apparently in mid-conversation. Barbara listened to them from her stall.

He's out on Monday. She's out yesterday? Pu-leese.

I know. And I heard they were practically making out on the dance floor.

Although who could blame her.

Yeah, he looked even hotter out in the field.

I know right?!

Barbara watched them through the cracks of her stall, hoping they'd think whoever was in there for so long was about to unleash the unspeakable. Finally, they finished brushing their hair and putting on their dewy makeup and left. Barbara walked slowly down to the conference room where she and Jack—neither of whom was *out* today—had to attend the morning meeting. It was just as well. "Staying away" obviously meant they couldn't eat breakfast together anymore.

When Barbara walked into the room, Sloane was already sitting at the head of the long oval table, drinking from an iced-coffee cup almost as big as her. She looked up at Barbara and said, "You're back," then typed something into her BlackBerry. Lois and Bruce sat next to each other, Lois on her BlackBerry, Bruce reading the *New York Post* sports page. Cathryn entered the room in a sleeveless yellow dress, ready for a garden party, and said a sunny good morning. No one looked up. Barbara tried to focus on the *New York Times* open before her. She could usually speed-read it and several other papers on the train to work in the morning, but this morning, she had shut her eyes, thinking of Bogey's and Bergman's goodbye.

The conference room door swung open and Jack walked in, his eyes darting around the room, then settling on Barbara. He nodded to her. He had a tiny piece of tissue on his cheek this time—he must have shaved in a rush again, or had he been distracted? If she had been with him in their home, in their shared bathroom, she would have tended to the cut. His wife probably wasn't even there. *I cannot help but dream of what a life with you would be like.*

"Morning, campers!" Jack said way too happily and took a seat directly across the conference table from Barbara. That certainly was cheeky of him to channel Cal when Sloane was in the room, but she was engrossed in her BlackBerry, holding it like a mouse inspecting a piece of cheese.

Barbara looked up from her newspaper and gave Jack a kind smile but then returned to her paper and re-read the same paragraph for a fourth time. They had to act as if they were still friendly or it would mean that—in the parlance of office workers who've indulged in an ill-considered shag—*things had gotten weird.* And she couldn't seem overly friendly, flirty, or familiar with him because that would confirm the gossip that they were in the throes of an affair. Barbara wondered if he was looking at her. All he would see was the newspaper. Was he hitting the bottle at home at night, missing her? *Soul mates.* Barbara lowered the newspaper and looked at Sloane and then over at Jack, who was adjusting his tie and fussing with a shirt button. She remembered unbuttoning one of those. Barbara saw his eyes start to move in her direction and she quickly dropped her head back down into the paper.

Things had gotten weird.

Sloane cleared her throat and put her BlackBerry down. "We'll be issuing a news release about this today, but Ron Kavanagh is going to be joining us full-time, splitting his time between the D.C. bureau and headquarters. He's going to play an integral role not only in prime time, but in daytime programming as well." She glanced at her BlackBerry again. "Okay, so let's hear them. Leads? Where's Danko?"

After the meeting, Barbara went to Rip's office. Scotch-taped to his door was a picture of him in a tux, taken at the correspondents' dinner, standing next to Sloane, whose face had been replaced with Janis Joplin's, cigarette dangling from her mouth. Barbara opened the door: *Rubber Soul* was playing on the turntable. Same old Rip.

"Why weren't you at the meeting?"

"Close the door."

Packing boxes were strewn amid the piles of books and magazines on the floor and Rip's desk was a bigger mess than usual.

"Oh, no. No. Please," she cried. He could not be leaving the Phoenix. Barbara moved the folders that were piled onto the chair facing his desk and sat.

"Yep." Rip reached behind him to turn the volume down on "Norwegian Wood."

"Come on, Rip," she pleaded. She'd talk him out of it.

"I'm telling her this morning. I've thought about it. I can't." Rip leaned back in his chair and clasped his hands behind his head.

Since he'd done such a phenomenal job producing the hostage release coverage in Washington, D.C., Sloane was offering Danko a new position at the Phoenix: managing editor. In Washington. There were two problems with the offer: one, Rip didn't like "managing," and two, he was done with traveling, or in this case, relocating, for a job.

"But it's a promotion, isn't it?" asked Barbara.

"If you have to ask, it isn't," he said, putting his feet up on the desk, on top of some papers. "She wants someone to be Kavanagh's boy."

"I cannot believe she's already thinking about the midterm elections," said Barbara. "Guess she wants to make sure the administration gets a friendly Congress."

Rip held his pen like a cigarette. "It was different with Cal. Sure, he was political—he really believed. But he kept his editorial page separate. Sloane panders...feeds 'em the Kool-Aid 'cause it rates. Bitch won't rest until every last one of us is a prostitute for the party."

"I think this is the part of the movie where you say, 'I'm getting too old for this,' but then I ride shotgun in the squad car and talk you into staying," said Barbara.

Rip laughed wheezily and popped a piece of Nicorette in his mouth. "She wants new blood producing your hours, someone who'll play along."

Then, perhaps getting a jolt from the gum, Rip sat up in his chair and leaned in toward Barbara, his round glasses sliding down to the tip of his nose. "She only offered me the gig because she knew I'd say no."

Barbara reached across his desk and took his hands. "But you're Murray to my Mary." She looked into his eyes. "You can't go."

He squeezed her hands. "I'm pretty sure those two never had a night of Wild Turkey and wild..."

"He wouldn't leave her, is the point. I'm begging, Rip."

"It's no use, baby." Rip got up and walked around his desk and motioned with his hands for her to rise from her chair. "Now, give your old friend-with-an-asterisk a hug." If she hadn't been so emotionally drained from the Jack imbroglio, she would have cried. She hugged him hard.

Barbara looked at Rip's desk where the *Rubber Soul* album cover lay. Side one, track two: "Norwegian Wood (This Bird has Flown)" As she left his office, Rip, feet back up on the desk, sang along.

Later that morning, Barbara sat on the set with Jack, less than a foot away from him, trying not to think about the fact that she was sitting less than a foot away from him. She was dying to send him a computer message, to share her news about Danko. She wondered if Jack was curious about why Rip wasn't in their ears this morning and they were instead stuck with a producer who lisped. But if Barbara started communicating with Jack during the show, that might lead to computer flirting, conduct unbecoming a *colleague and friend.*

Their two hours were busy—a school lockdown was in progress in Florida—and Barbara was grateful to have to focus on the story. During one of the breaks, Jack turned toward Celia for powder and his leg accidentally brushed against Barbara's. "Sorry 'bout that," he said. Barbara thought of his hand pulling the last garment down her thigh that night. "No problem," she said. At the end of the show, Cathryn did a plodding feature story on an astronomical discovery and even donned designer glasses to look smart for her report. Barbara wanted to craft a top-line, something about Uranus, to make Jack laugh. *Warm, funny.* But instead, she pretended to edit copy.

After the show, Barbara was in her office, changing her clothes before leaving the channel for her train home. The phone rang and she jumped. Maybe it was Jack. Maybe he was on his way down to see her, to tell her he couldn't honor her wishes—he couldn't live without her. *And passionate.* In one macho motion, he'd sweep the papers and computer off her desk, grab her, lower her onto it and...

It was Gene's number.

"Phoenix finally fired the first shot," he announced.

"It's about time," said Barbara. Her contract was up at the end of the year, in a little more than a week. She remembered Sloane looking as if a light bulb had appeared over her head when Barbara walked into the meeting that morning.

"Yeah. Sloane David's office called. These pricks just love to wait 'til the last minute."

"Davis, Gene," Barbara corrected. "And that's good, right?" If management liked their on-air personality and all was well, they waited until close to the contract's expiration date, and then initiated a quick back-and-forth before agreeing to a re-up and raise.

Gene continued. "What's-her-chops wouldn't even get on the phone herself. Her *assistant* called to *inform* us that your deal's coming up. Now, here's what you need to do. I want you to..."

"Wait a second—aren't you the one supposed to be doing the negotiating?"

"I will. But you and this Sloane should have a ladies' lunch—it'd be a nice touch—just a couple of gals talking over old times. Tell her how committed you are to the Phoenix, how you'd like to raise your profile and..."

"I get it. And then, you swoop in and do the deal. I'll try, but we aren't exactly girlfriends."

Gene sighed. "Too bad Cal's gone—we'd hammer this thing out in no time."

"Yeah, well, those days are over. I'll call her office," and Barbara did and was astonished when Sloane's assistant told her Ms. Davis had a cancellation and could meet Barbara for lunch tomorrow at Ubon, Sloane's favorite sushi restaurant. Maybe they could be civil to each other and if it went well, Barbara could even broach the topic of a move to prime time—she needed to focus on her career again. But then she wondered if she should pitch it with or without Jack? They were a successful team and Sloane loved Jack so Barbara would be more likely to get a crack at stardom *with* him. Also, this way if she couldn't have him, at least she'd still see him every day. Then again, seeing him was torturous, and if she asked for a solo anchor slot, she'd be moving away from Jack, figuratively and literally. She'd be getting that Bohack shift change her mother had counseled.

After setting up her meeting with Sloane, Barbara took the train home. Ben called her cell phone while the train was in the tunnel, leaving a message saying he was coming home early and that he'd explain when she got home.

Holy fucking shit.

He'd found out. She couldn't call him back and have to share her admission of adultery with the fellow riders on her train car, perhaps prompting the conductor to punch a big "A" on her ticket.

How had Ben caught her? Had someone from the Phoenix who suspected her and Jack called him anonymously? Or maybe after she'd passed out in an alcoholic haze after watching an impossible love-themed movie, she'd cried out Jack's name in her sleep?

And if Ben accused her of having an affair with Jack, would she admit it? That would certainly ruin her marriage and her family. *I can see how devoted you are to your family.* But if she stayed in her marriage out of devotion to her child, but remained secretly, miserably in love with another man, wouldn't Rory eventually pick up on her unhappiness? Don't kids sense when their parents are cordial toward each other, when nary a kiss or a hug or a wink passes between them? Is that the example to set for Rory: Settle down and marry a girl you love and respect, but someone who isn't the love of your life, your....soul mate?

Then again, do people really only have one soul mate? Yes, Jack was bright, witty, sexy, and sexual—Barbara felt, maybe conceitedly so, that Jack was her male counterpart. But the universe was filled with potential soul mates; it was just a matter of whom you happened to meet and when. And when she'd met Ben at homecoming and they'd fallen in love, she probably thought he was her soul mate, albeit in a different way. He wasn't like her, but he complemented her. He appreciated and therefore drew out other aspects of her own personality which she prided herself upon—her discipline, her strong moral compass, her ability to nurture. If she had married Jack long ago and met Ben at the Phoenix, she might well have grown weary of Jack's dazzle and been attracted to Ben's thoughtful, earnest presence.

When Barbara got home, Ben was in his most faded jeans and a tie-dyed shirt, foraging in the fridge.

She tried to sound nonchalant. "Hey, honey," she said, "Didn't want to be one of those annoying passengers who talks on the train." She walked into the kitchen and gave him a kiss on the cheek. "Why are you home? What up?" He didn't look angry.

Ben took her hand and silently led her to the living room couch and sat her down. Oh God. This would be just his style, to drop a bomb calmly.

"They fired me," he said finally, smiling.

"What?! Are you kidding? What happened?!" This was shocking, not just for the news it was, but for the news it wasn't.

"They finally s-canned the portfolio manager and told me they have enough analysts to cover the guys who are still making money."

"Oh my God, Ben. That's horrible," she said, rubbing his back. "I'm so sorry." And so relieved!

"We knew it was coming." Ben continued, matter-of-factly. "They gave me two weeks, but since I was off for Christmas next week anyway, I told them I'd split today."

"You don't seem upset at all," said Barbara. She suddenly felt hot and took off her suit jacket. "I mean, you were hoping to hang in a little longer."

"I know. And they screwed me out of my bonus, which sucks," Ben leaned back into the couch and ran his hands through his hair. "But if I'm being honest, I have to say I feel relieved."

"No bonus? Christ! What are we going to do?" Was he going to tell her this was fate and now he could finally pursue his dream of teaching and writing and he would go back to school to start a new life and then leave her for a fellow faculty member, forcing her into Jack's arms?

"Don't worry. We'll be okay. We have your salary," said Ben. "And I'm going to try to find another job in the business. A couple of weeks ago, I reached out to some old contacts, including one in Boston."

"Boston," she repeated. She didn't want to live there again. It was too cold and didn't pay as much as New York. But what if Ben had to take a job there and she had to stay here and she'd be so lonely that one rainy day Jack would stop by, needing to towel off and...

"Just to network a little. I was thinking we could head up that way Friday after Rory gets home from school—maybe spend the weekend in Amherst." He took her hand in both of his and kissed it. "Our old stomping ground."

"I don't know...Christmas is Tuesday....and Rory will worry about Santa not knowing where to bring the presents and..."

"We'll drive home Sunday night. It'll be nice up there at Christmastime."

"I'd have to finish all the errands, all the wrapping on Monday. I don't know." But maybe this would be just what she needed to stop mooning over Jack. A road trip could be therapeutic and being back on campus might remind her of how she felt about Ben when they first met. Now that he was jobless, they could pull together in the face of adversity and fall in love again. "You're so smart, you'll land something else in no time." Barbara sat up. "Um, I have something to tell you, too."

Ben raised his eyebrows.

"Don't worry, it's good. I think. I have a meeting with Sloane tomorrow to get the ball rolling on a new contract. Lunch, if you can believe it. It would be great to sign a new deal, especially since you're..."

"You can say it, 'unemployed'," Ben laughed.

"In between positions...but it would be good to giddyap and get the deal done."

"You'll be great," Ben said, kissing her cheek.

"Let's hope so. This is Sloane Davis we're talking about."

CHAPTER 38

"I need to look fabulous, but don't pull too hard, my head hurts," Barbara told Angelica on Thursday morning, after filling her in on Rip and Ben. But even if she had a lot of news to chew over, Barbara was still consumed by thoughts of Jack and couldn't resist another cry. She had chosen *Witness* for last night's "Magnum and a Movie."

Before Angelica started styling, she reached into the purse she kept on the console and took out a perfume a bottle and handed it to Barbara.

"What's this for?" Barbara asked.

"Gargle with it, or put it on your neck, whatever," said Angelica. "But you really need to pull it together for your lunch. I got news."

Barbara put a drop of the perfume behind her ear as Angelica turned the blow-dryer on low. "You know those 3-hour drug and alcohol abuse prevention sessions everyone's supposed to go to?"

"Yeah?" It had occurred to Barbara that she might benefit from such a seminar.

"It's 'cause of Bill Hunter," said Angelica, explaining that an audio guy who hated Ironsides' arrogant attitude on the set recently noticed that the old wax figure had accidentally wheeled over the bottle of Goldschlager he stashed under the anchor desk during the show. A stage hand corroborated the allegation, testifying that he'd once noticed a residue of gold flakes when he'd rinsed Ironsides' coffee mug. "Heard he might lose his show, because of a morals something or other?"

"A morals clause in his contract! If they can prove he violated it, Sloane could get rid of him," said Barbara, excitedly sitting up in the chair, then wincing from her headache.

"Nobody knows—you can't say anything."

"I won't, but that's huge!" said Barbara. Holy mackerel. She really needed to be at her best at lunch, especially if prime time was finally, finally opening up. She'd have to find a way to deftly hint at wanting a promotion without letting on that she knew about Ironsides. Before leaving hair and makeup for the set, Barbara gave herself another dab of the perfume.

When Barbara walked onto the set, Jack picked his head up from his computer; she could have sworn he inhaled, perhaps noticing the perfume wasn't her usual scent. She had so much to tell him, but she couldn't. At least she could cut the tension with a little joke. When their lisping producer gave Barbara and Jack a cue—*Thirty theconds!"*—Jack looked at Barbara and smirked, practically begging her to say something. Barbara composed a top-line: *Thufferin' Thuccotash!*. But then deleted it.

Tex offered to bring Barbara a cup of coffee. "How 'bout you, Jack?" Tex asked, wriggling his eyebrows, trying to initiate a conversation between the co-anchors. Without looking up at Tex, Jack and Barbara each muttered "No thanks," and Tex retreated, like a dog denied a game of fetch. Barbara felt bad, but couldn't be jittery from caffeine for her meeting with Sloane.

10:50. Ten minutes to go: 10 more minutes of trying not to look at Jack except when they had to share a read on the two-shot and she had to smile at him, but not too adoringly. As Barbara read through the last section of copy on her computer she noticed her top-line arrow flashing. She took her time clicking it. It was probably just Thylvester the producer.

Stone: *May I bend your ear for a few minutes after the show? I have a Phoenix news flash.*

Jack wanted to talk to her! He couldn't take it anymore, couldn't go on pretending; he was in as wretched a state as she was. *I love you.* Hold on. He'd written "bend your ear," not "bend back your legs." Maybe he'd just caught wind of the Rip or Ironsides news and wanted to share. But Barbara couldn't talk to him after the show; she'd literally have to run off the set to make it downtown to Ubon, Sloane's inconveniently located lair, by high noon.

King: *I have to race out of here today. Can we talk later?*

Stone: *Sure. Okay if I call you this afternoon?*

King: *Try the cell—I might be in transit.*

It was sad, really. Time was when she and Jack would have parsed all their news over breakfast; he would have been the first person she confided in about her contract being up. And if Rip were still around, she'd have known ahead of the lunch what management (Cal) was ready to offer her. But that was then.

Barbara sat at the packed restaurant's tiny square table and had to swing her long legs over to one side. Better that she, and not Gene, was here sitting sidesaddle—she couldn't imagine his gargantuan boots fitting in this cramped space. Barbara shared his wish for a steak house as the locale; she hated self-consciously chic places and was suspicious of sushi from a digestive standpoint. Figures that's all Sloane needed to eat to sustain her 90-pounds-soaking-wet frame.

12:05. Sloane would be purposefully 10 minutes late, a classic power move. Meet me in *my* favorite restaurant and wait for *me*.

What does a sister have to do to get some alcohol around here, Barbara thought as she tried and failed again to catch the waiter's eye. I want my wine—does that make me a raging alcoholic, she wondered. No, she just needed to steady her nerves. She'd stop at one. Where was that little prick waiter? Oh, Christ. She was thinking like Gene. "Excuse me," she said loudly as the waiter passed. Finally. She hoped the restaurant had a heavy pour.

12:07. She could take out her BlackBerry and pretend to be reading an important e-mail, but no, she wasn't going to play that game. It was okay to wait at attention. She wanted Sloane to know this meeting was important to her.

12:14. Sloane arrived, her little heels clicking as she reached their table. "Holiday gridlock alert day," she explained, sitting down and pecking at her BlackBerry. "Just a sec."

Barbara's wine arrived and the waiter smiled at Sloane. "Hi, Ms. Davis. Back so soon?" he asked. "What can I get you this afternoon?"

"Just a club soda," she said without looking at him.

Aw, come on, Sloane. Live a little. Order a double vodka and give me prime time. Barbara forced herself to take only a tiny sip of her wine.

Sloane put the BlackBerry on the table next to the small vase holding a wilting orchid. She smiled tensely.

"This is a nice place," said Barbara. "A big step up from Lord Jeff's, huh?" Maybe if they shared a fond memory of Amherst they could be friends.

"Lord Jeff's?" Sloane's eyes scanned the room as if she were at a party, looking for someone more interesting to talk with.

"Local bar up in Amherst?"

"Oh, that place. I wasn't into that scene."

Sloane's club soda arrived and Barbara held up her wine. "To the Phoenix." Sloane held up her glass but didn't clink with

Barbara's. Barbara took a bigger gulp and thought the only thing that would better subdue her hangover was an accompanying cigarette—a Parliament 100, perhaps, to bring out the chardonnay's fruity overtones.

"So you're contract's just about up," Sloane said.

Barbara chuckled at her abruptness. "It is, and I just want to say, Sloane, that I'm proud of the work we've done at the Phoenix—the numbers are stronger than ever and I want to be a part of the channel's future success." She knew she sounded like a transparent kiss-ass, but she wanted, no, *needed* this deal.

Sloane studied her menu. "Right," she said, running an index finger up and down the seemingly endless list of nasty combinations of fish that were probably still staring at the restaurant patrons from some godforsaken tank. "Let me cut to the chase. Your ratings have been solid so I'm prepared to offer another two-year deal, but with a window after year one."

Barbara looked up from her menu as Sloane looked down at hers. A window meant they could get rid of her in a year, but maybe Gene could talk Sloane out of that. Barbara was dying to ask how much they were offering, but this was supposed to just be a "ladies' lunch."

Sloane put her menu down. "I'll do a 7 percent increase for the first, 10 for the second."

Barbara stifled a "Wow." That was a substantial increase. And Gene had told her that whatever the Phoenix offered, he would try to get the numbers up.

"It's a lot of money, so please don't even thinking about having your agent try to squeeze us for more," said Sloane.

The waiter came and, addressing only Sloane, rattled off the specials. Sloane ordered the fugu, the blowfish, but Barbara was sure she'd once read a Phoenix News Flash about someone dying a slow, twisting death from eating one of those, so she played it safer with a Dynamite tuna roll. Sloane was offering her another deal with a solid increase. Dy-no-mite!

"Well, I'd love to be at the Phoenix for another two years and beyond," said Barbara, taking a healthy dose of the wine.

Sloane seemed puzzled by Barbara; she was probably expecting Barbara the pugilist, fighting for more money right off the bat. "I'm willing to go a little higher on your wardrobe number—wardrobe is adding some more expensive lines to our trunk shows."

Funny, you'd think all that sleeveless whore-wear would be *less* expensive, but hey, great, thought Barbara. "Sounds good," she said. "My rep's office will just have to dot the i's and cross the t's with legal."

"Okay. Good," said Sloane, actually smiling a little. "And I hope you'll be okay with a little travel in the future. We're hoping to be a big presence during the mid-term campaign season and maybe send our anchors to D.C. now and then."

D.C.? With Jack? Oh, dear. "Sounds fantastic," she said.

The waiter brought the sushi and Barbara tasted it—pretty good for something held together by gaffer's tape. A second glass of wine appeared. Barbara felt like George Bailey, smoking one of Old Man Potter's fine cigars, listening to an enticing offer that would put him in the nicest house in town.

"I'd like you to read this," Sloane said, "It's a memo I'm issuing on Monday. It's about your show and a new format and name we'll be debuting the following week. Here." She handed Barbara her BlackBerry. "If it's a hit, I might want to move it to prime time."

Prime time! Yeah, baby! Yeah! This was getting better by the second. Barbara read.

With campaigns shifting into high gear in the new year, a new dayside show makes its debut.

"There You Go Again!" will be two hours of politics, with our pundits and guests engaging in lively, fiery debate.

Ron Kavanagh will provide play-by-play, analyzing the mid-term election campaigns and their strategies. "There You Go Again" will also feature in-depth explorations of the candidates' biographies.

Using our success in prime time as a template, we plan on making the Phoenix the #1 place to be for politics!

"'There You Go Again.' Nice name," said Barbara, re-reading the memo.

Sloane gave a nod toward the memo on the little screen. "It was Ron's idea. Thought it would be a good way of conjuring the 'grand old party's good old days,' in his words."

"Clever," Barbara said, continuing to look at the memo. *Pundits and guests.*

"And you'd, of course, have a new, designated producer for the show. I have a few especially promising ones in mind."

Not a rotating retinue of rookies to replace Rip. Tho long, Thylvester!

"Barbara," said Sloane, leaning in and placing her chopsticks on her plate. "I know you want prime time. You've probably heard the gossip. All I can say right now is I'm looking at the entire programming day and I want to move quickly with this show to see if it'll be a good fit for the 7 o'clock. We need something in the mix other than war and terror."

This was shocking. Not to mention ironic. The kindly Cal, the man who had hired Barbara and liked her, wouldn't give her what she wanted. And now Sloane, her archnemesis, was going to create a hit show for her and make her a prime-time star?

Barbara read the memo a third time, and thought again of how George Bailey had almost gone to work for Potter. Almost.

"Who are 'our pundits'?" she asked, slowly placing the BlackBerry between them.

"Our hosts, our anchors, will be the pundits," Sloane answered casually.

"I don't understand," said Barbara, beginning to understand. She wiped her hand on the napkin on her lap. "The anchors are supposed to be the pundits?"

"That's right. I want you to conduct your interviews as if you're a member of the team, a partisan—your questions and comments should promote the party's philosophy. So instead of asking a candidate, 'What is your position on the tax cut?' you would say, 'This tax cut stands to put money back in the pockets of American workers and yet you, Congressman So-and-So, refuse to support it. Can you sleep at night knowing Americans are being taxed to death?' That sort of thing."

"And who'll present the other side?" Barbara was squeezing her chopsticks; she'd stopped eating.

Sloane laughed a loud, fake laugh. "You're funny, Barbara." She poked at her sushi and sipped her club soda. "The guest can make his case..."

"But you want us, in our questions and demeanor, to...."

"To make him look like an idiot," said Sloane. "Ron will jump in on the interviews, too. I don't know if you've ever seen him in a debate. He's really something." She popped another morsel of fugu into her mouth.

"So it'll be two anchors and Ron, three against one?"

"Well, yes, but anyone who agrees to do the show knows that going in."

"Why would they want to come on the show if they know they're going to take a beating?"

"They get their face on television, we point out that their side is the wrong side, and everybody goes home happy." Sloane, who had stopped eating, too, tapped at the side of her plate with her chopsticks.

"It doesn't sound like any guest from the other side of the aisle is going to be able to get their point across," Barbara offered.

Sloane started to bring her club soda to her lips but then slammed the glass down on the table. "Barbara, let me be clear. We're not trying to be fair. This is not journalism. This is a political show, providing the flag-waving, pork-rind-chewing, Lee Greenwood-loving set with palatable programming. This will rate. And besides, it's not like you've never done this sort of thing before—do I have to remind you again about your special report on Congressman Quagmire?"

"I regretted that," said Barbara, astounded that she'd bring that up after it had almost led to fisticuffs at Jack's party. "Deeply."

"Oh, please." Sloane rolled her eyes. "If you could do that, you can be a pundit!"

No, no, she couldn't. With that mortifying exception, Barbara prided herself on being fair. Maybe imbalanced personally, but always balanced on air. And all she'd ever wanted to do, her entire career, was tell people the news. Tell them what happened at the debate, tell them about the candidates and issues and let them make up their minds all on their own. She liked reporting on politics but never for a second had any desire to work for a campaign. If she became a television pundit, she could never get another job doing straight news again. And even if *There You Go Again!* wound up being a ticket to prime time, no network would hire her to do a traditional news broadcast if she'd been labeled a Phoenix PUNDIT. She wanted to present both sides. Always give everyone a fair shake.

She hadn't seen this coming. Rip had said Sloane was trying to turn everyone into shills, but Barbara didn't think Sloane would try to make dayside more blatantly political than prime time.

And she never guessed that Sloane would hold out an invitation to her to join a glamorous party, but then, just as Barbara was on her way, roll up the red carpet.

But she needed that paycheck. Ben was unemployed. No bonus, for crying out loud! She nearly snapped her chopsticks in half thinking about how she had almost fallen into the trap Sloane had set. She'd almost agreed. But she wouldn't do it. Couldn't. What to do? She needed to think fast. Maybe she could carve out a different role for herself within the show, do news updates or voice-overs for the profiles the memo mentioned. Barbara took a deep breath and through clenched teeth, asked, "What are these biographies all about?"

"That's the best part," said Sloane, her enthusiasm unabated by Barbara's change in tone. "You remember Miletto?"

"Detective Miletto."

"Right. Did those security meetings for us after 9/11. He's been helping Ron get information on one of the democratic candidates in a key race. Rising star. Pretty. Former surgeon. Real do-gooder. Did surgeries for poor, harelipped kids in Central America or some fucking place. Family guy. Wife who gave up a career as an attorney to raise their boys, triplets." Sloane dropped her voice to a whisper, "Well, Miletto got the goods on him. Turns out when the good doctor and his nurse were traveling together, they started a steamy affair."

Exposing politicians' peccadilloes was nothing new in the news business. But these particular details cut too close to the bone for Barbara. And Sloane wanted to pass this muckraking off as candidate "biographies"?

"So the profiles will be hatchet jobs."

Sloane batted her eyelashes. "Now, Barbara, that's not very nice."

Barbara pushed her wine away and sat up in her seat. "Let me make sure I have this straight. You want your anchors, I mean, pundits, to preach the Republican party line, present only one side, have the two pundits hold down the guest while Ron kidney-punches him, and take breaks in between rounds to air skewed, one-sided smears of candidates in order to ruin their livelihood and lives? I'm sorry, Sloane, but shouldn't we leave that to the campaigns?"

"I don't think you've been hearing me," said Sloane, stabbing her sushi now. "We are part of the campaign."

"I understand wanting to add more politics to the mix, but we've had great ratings success with *This Just In,* by just giving people their news, without filters or fluff, remember that?" Barbara's neck felt hot. "Why would you want to turn us into the laughingstock of the industry by becoming Republican party puppets?"

"Laughingstock. They won't be laughing when we get even bigger numbers with this show—it's red meat for our red-state viewers!"

"We don't need to do this to stay on top!"

"What we don't need, Barbara, is you."

Barbara felt the restaurant spinning around her.

"Do you realize," Sloane continued, "the number of anchors who've caught wind of the changes we're making to dayside and have been up my ass day and night, just hoping to get a shot on this show? I could put anyone in your slot. I could script questions for a...for a...." Sloane looked at her plate. "For a blowfish if I had to!" she said, snickering.

"A blowfish might do better than those sycophantic ciphers you've hired." Barbara retorted viciously.

"Alright, Barbara. If you're going to be spiteful, then you should know that the only reason they're not in your chair already is Cal. He gave me a big speech before he left. Your big 'Q' rating. How corporate loves you. And of course, Jack. Jack Stone's always tripping over himself to talk about how much he loooooves co-anchoring with you and I wanted to keep him happy, especially after Afghanistan. I mean, it's fairly obvious to everyone at the Phoenix how *close* you two are. After the bombing, good God! Weeping over him in the greenroom. And at the dinner! But you two have what Cal would call 'crazy chemistry'—whatever's going on between you comes up on that screen and makes people watch to try to figure out if you're fucking. If your numbers weren't so good, I'd have never offered you this opportunity in the first place!"

Sloane looked at her BlackBerry, which was buzzing on the table. "Jack's already on board, by the way."

"What do you mean?" Barbara's stomach twisted. "Have you already talked with him about this show?"

"Yes. We were here last night, in fact."

Dinner?! So that was his Phoenix news flash. And that's why that waiter had said, *Back so soon?*

Sloane was growing calmer the hotter Barbara got. She said smugly, "Jack's agreed to do the show."

Barbara never believed people when they said they felt as though they'd been punched in the stomach upon receiving devastating news. But she felt as though she'd been hit; she wasn't really even seeing Sloane anymore.

"Without knowing who the other players would be?"

"I told him Ron was a definite and that you were a candidate."

"And he accepted?" Barbara was gripping the table now.

"Yes."

"Understanding that he'd be a *pundit?"* Barbara practically spit the word.

"Yes, Barbara, yes, yes, yes."

Et tu, Jack.

Sloane continued, snidely, "Some people don't have a problem having a glamorous job that pays them gobs of money." She looked at her BlackBerry, which was whirring again. "That could be him right now."

Sloane picked the BlackBerry up from the table, and as she was bringing it to her ear, Barbara grabbed Sloane's forearm and squeezed, causing the BlackBerry to drop on the table.

Barbara's chest heaved as she stood up.

"When you speak with Jack, tell him to enjoy his *glamorous* job as a *whore* for the GOP. You can keep your money and your contract and your slutty wardrobe and your DingleBerry and your cherubic little mudslinger and...your sushi."

Barbara picked the BlackBerry off the table and ground it into Sloane's blowfish.

"FUG U, Sloane!"

Barbara threw her napkin on the table as Sloane plucked her device out of the blowfish. Ignoring the stares of the posh clientele, Barbara yanked her purse and coat off the chair and walked out of the restaurant, shoulders back, staring straight ahead, feigning dignity.

CHAPTER 39

Barbara had barely settled into her seat on her train home when her BlackBerry buzzed with an e-mail from Sloane.

To: Barbara.King@Phoenixnewschannel.com

From: Sloane.Davis@Phoenixnewschannel.com

Re: Re:

You are off the schedule. Have Gene Cline contact my office. The Phoenix has arranged the shipment of the contents of your office.

At least Sloane's BlackBerry still worked. Barbara called Gene.

"We're in a real pickle over this sushi business," he said, mixing his food metaphors. He sounded sick with worry. Over his commission.

"She told me to contact your office. To legally sever our agreement?" Barbara asked.

"Morals clause," said Gene.

Barbara had violated it just as surely as if she'd urinated on the set, or, pulled an Ironsides. Maybe she could meet him at the Pepperpot and together, they could cry into a round of Goldschlagers.

Barbara could never go back to the Phoenix again. Some stranger from a moving company would be callously stuffing the picture frames of her family into a cardboard box, along with her suits and shoes, including her prized Jimmy Choos. Jack. Even if he was already sizing Cathryn's feet for a Christmas gift, he had, as promised, tried Barbara on her cell, apparently during the ill-fated lunch.

Hi, Barbara, it's Jack. Was hoping we could chat this afternoon. Call me back on my cell when you can.

To think, when she got his computer message on the set that morning, she'd actually thought he might be calling to tell her he couldn't go on without her. But he was calling to tell her he had agreed to go on. On television. With or without her. Well, she certainly wasn't calling him back. Not from the train. Maybe not ever. And one thing was for sure—now that she was terminated and he was anchoring that sleazy show, they'd never see each other again. That would make it a whole lot easier to stay away.

When Barbara got home, she went straight for the kitchen and poured herself a glass of white wine and sat at the table. Ben came downstairs, poetry in hand; he'd have plenty of time for that now.

When Barbara saw him, she put her head in her hands and burst out crying. "I'm such an idiot!" she said.

Ben walked over to the table and pulled a chair close to hers and sat down. "What happened?"

Through sobs and slugs of the wine, Barbara said, "A Phoenix news flash—we're both unemployed," and told him the whole awful story.

"This is not good," said Ben, stroking his chin. "Shit. Any chance you could get Gene to tell her you were...I don't know... under some sort of personal duress...and that you'd take another position, another shift at the Phoenix?"

"She's already talking with him. About severing my contract." Barbara shook her head. "She always hated me. She only offered me the job because Jack and I get...got...good ratings together."

"I'm glad, and proud of you, that you didn't want to be 'part of the campaign'—that's crazy, so blatant—but it's too bad you couldn't have just told her you'd think about it..."

"Instead of going cuckoo for Cocoa Puffs," said Barbara, finishing the glass of wine and standing up to get a new bottle. "I can't believe it. I'm fired from the Phoenix."

Ben stood up and stopped her at the fridge just as she was pulling out another bottle of white. "Barb, sit down."

They sat at the table and he turned his chair to face her. "You seem so sad lately. Staying up late, watching your, what is it you call 'em, 'chick flicks,' drinking. I know I'm no one to point the finger about getting high here and there, but...then going ballistic the way you did. I don't know. What's bothering you?"

This was her chance to come clean, to confess even if he didn't suspect. Tell him she'd had a fling with Jack but it was over.

"No, I told you, I got my period and was just a little mood-swingy. And as for going off on Sloane, well, she really provoked me. Especially when she told me Jack Stone had already agreed to do the show with or without me. I mean, I thought we were partners."

Ben leaned back in his chair, still holding Barbara's hands. "He agreed to be a pundit?"

"Yeah."

"I thought he was a real reporter. Going into the war zone and all."

"So did I."

"And he said 'yes,' just like that?—I mean, he couldn't have possibly thought you'd do the show, knowing how you are."

Barbara held Ben's hand as he continued. "I know you wouldn't be a pundit any sooner than you would have released those victims names back in Amherst."

Barbara smiled at the memory of her college radio newsroom and her stubborn ethics. And she thought of Ben in his Serpico phase, hosting that jazz show; she'd always hoped to bump into him again. And then she did, and their love developed so naturally. She never had to guess how he felt about her, she never hid behind clever conversation with him. And she knew Ben would have done exactly what she had done in that restaurant: told "the man" to go to hell and then some.

"You know me, Ben," she said softly.

"Besides," he said, exhaling, "I can't say I'm sorry you're not going to be working with him anymore. I always thought he might have had a little crush on you."

A crush. She couldn't shatter Ben's innocence. She couldn't do it, couldn't disappoint him; she was so virtuous in his eyes. And even if their love had been rendered just a glowing ember during the course of her attempted rise at the Phoenix, it certainly could be sparked again, reborn, especially if it didn't have to compete with the conflagration that was Jack.

She put her arms around Ben and said, "We were just really good together on TV."

The next morning, Ben was out running errands and picking up Rory from his last, half-day of school before the Christmas break. Barbara turned her living room television on to catch the last few minutes of her former show.

Coming up on the Phoenix News Channel, we'll be talking live with a soldier just home from Afghanistan and tell you why he's signing up for another tour of duty.

And Jack, don't forget to check out my brand-new blog—Collyns' Corner—where you can find out what I think of the day's news stories! We'll be right back after a quick break!

Barbara grabbed the remote and hit the "off" button—why was she torturing herself by watching Cathryn sitting in her chair next to Jack? Collyns was the heir apparent for her job; she'd have no compunction about hosting *There You Go, Pimping for the GOP, Again.* Cathryn would be sitting next to Jack for two hours every day. Maybe Cathryn and Jack would go to Ubon for drinks with Sloane after work and then take a car home together, just the two of them. Soon, he'd be knocking on her office door for breakfast. And then, at next year's correspondent's dinner.... Christ, she was the jealous television first wife! And it was her own fault. If only she'd daintily dabbed her mouth with her napkin and told Sloane she'd like a little time to consider her fabulous, oh-so-generous offer. But no, she'd gone bonkers.

Barbara went into the kitchen to get some fruit and fill up a water bottle before her run. She would have to stop buying her produce at that chic little fresh market on the way home from the train station. And she would buy get Rory a water bottle instead of spending money on the mini plastic bottles she packed in his lunch. But no, wait, he could bring them home and she could rinse and re-use, a favorite money-saving tactic of Siobhan's. God help me, thought Barbara, these would be the only decisions she'd have to make in the course of a day if she couldn't get another job in broadcasting. It would be lovely not to have to rush off to work and be able to eat the discount-brand frozen waffles with Rory and see him off to school. But then what? Trips to Costco and other tedious tasks would be her raison d'être. *Schedule playdate for Rory. Pack empty tissue box for class build-a-robot project. Find recipe for slow-cook stew.* She'd want to run into a knife in a week's time.

Barbara couldn't finish the orange she'd peeled. Out of Ziplocs—she had better start buying those jumbo boxes. She grabbed the tin foil instead and ran a strip along the serrated edges of the box. She thought of Angelica and the foils she'd put in her hair, the first time she ever set eyes on Jack. Barbara tried not to think about Jack teasing her about the foils when they were in bed together.

Barbara went upstairs to change into her running warm-ups and retrieve her cell phone from her purse. She turned it on to call Angelica. Wooah. Three missed calls from Stone. She wasn't calling him back. She rang the hair-and-makeup studio instead.

Angelica picked up on the first ring "Why'd you have to go bat shit like that?"

"How'd you hear?"

"You didn't see the *Post?*"

Barbara ran down to her kitchen computer and Angelica waited as she logged on.

> ***PHOENIX BIRD FLIES OFF HANDLE IN SUSHI SMASHING SMACKDOWN***
>
> Phoenix news anchor **Barbara King** ruffled feathers in a chic downtown sushi restaurant on Friday. Our spies say she and Phoenix president **Sloane Davis** seemed to be having a leisurely ladies' lunch at **Ubon** when King started shouting and plunged her boss's BlackBerry into her fugu (blowfish), screaming, "**Fug U**!," Puzzled patrons were appalled as the apoplectic King stomped out of the restaurant.
>
> A Phoenix spokesperson would say only that King and the channel had been in contract talks. King's agent, **Gene Cline** would neither confirm nor deny the BlackBerry bashing, but said, "King is a respected

journalist who's helped the Phoenix rise to number one."

The article even had pictures: Barbara's Phoenix publicity shot, a file photo of Gene with his arm around a tiny male sportscaster shrinking from Gene's embrace, and a generic picture of a blow-fish with the caption: ***King's unsuspecting victim***.

"Ang?" Barbara heard Angelica shouting, probably to Jane, "Tell her her hair looks fine parted on that side!"

"I'm here," said Angelica. "That Collyns—does your show for one day and she's already a diva. She made Jane give her extra false lashes today. Before she went out on the set, she said, 'My time to shine!'" Angelica sighed heavily. "Anyway, who cares about her. What happened?"

Barbara gave Angelica the side of the story that wasn't in the article.

"You need to talk to Jack," said Angelica. "I've never seen that man so out of sorts. He comes running down here this morning, I mean running, holding that newspaper. Says Sloane announced at the morning meeting that Barbara King was out today and then she made some little side comment that if anyone wanted to know why, they could read about it in the *Post*. So he comes in here and wants to know if we've heard from you 'cause you're not picking up. Then he goes up to Sloane's office and her assistant tells him Sloane's in a meeting with that Kavanagh guy and when he presses her, the assistant says Barbara King is leaving the Phoenix. And Barbara—he's freakin'—he comes back down here and tells us if you call here, come out to the set right away to tell him."

"I'll call him later," said Barbara. "Maybe. I'm still too angry with him for agreeing to do that show," said Barbara.

"Are you really gone? I mean, no chance, Barbara?" Angelica asked.

"I don't think so."

Angelica's voice was breaking. "Can't you at least please try?"

Barbara hung up, hoping that if she got a job at another channel maybe she could get Angelica to defect with her. But for now, the best she could do was go for that run in Angelica's honor.

When Barbara got back home from her old high school track, she went upstairs and took off her heavy warm-up jacket. But before she got undressed and into the shower, she had to take another look. But make this one her last.

It was in her closet, stashed behind some boxes. Such a clever hiding spot—why, she would have made a worthy drug smuggler. It was a giant plastic sanitary napkin bag, but most of the maxis had been replaced by souvenirs from Jack, including the bottle of Chanel and, pressed into a book, the rose he'd given her the morning after they'd "slept together" on the ride home from the Pepperpot on New Year's Eve. And crumpled in a ball at the bottom of the bag, a lurid trophy: her undergarments from the night in D.C.

She pulled out the bra and inhaled, but unable to detect Jack, gave it and the other affects a proper burial under the pads. She took the blue and pink bag and stuffed it behind some boxes on a higher, harder-to-reach shelf. As Barbara paused at the closet door, the doorbell rang.

Ben wouldn't be back with Rory just yet and Siobhan was out shopping with a friend. Maybe the delivery of a package, a box containing a dead bird from Sloane, now that Barbara had left the Phoenix mafia? She jogged down the stairs and opened the door to find Jack, arms crossed, still in his anchor makeup and suit, no coat despite the cold, his black Mercedes parked at the curb right in front of her house. It wasn't even noon yet. He must have jumped in his car right after he'd said his last words on air and driven like a bat out of hell.

"Why won't you answer your phone?" He was angry. But she was the one who was supposed to be angry with him.

"Shouldn't you be out digging up dirt on candidates for your new show?" she hissed, but let him follow her up the short flight of stairs to her living room.

Jack pushed his hair back and loosened his tie. He sat in the wing chair opposite the couch. He put his elbows on his knees and leaned toward the coffee table in between them, hands clasped. "Barbara, I came here to talk to you, to tell you what happened."

"I think I know what happened, Jack." Barbara crossed her legs, as if she were on the set, wearing a skirt and pumps instead of sweats and running shoes. "Sloane took you out to dinner—Lord knows how many other times she's wined and dined you—and offered you a job pimping for the Republican party with a hooker, I mean, co-anchor, to be named later, and you said yes without knowing or caring if you were going to be working with me." She stood up and put her hands on her hips. "Is that the way it went down, Jack, or did Sloane tell you over dinner that I was definitely not in the picture and that Cathryn was going to be the new..."

"Jesus Christ, Barbara—shut up! Shut up for a goddamned second," he shouted. "Would you please hear me out?"

Barbara wiped the sweat that had re-formed on her forehead. "Okay." She folded her arms.

"I was at the channel late on Thursday, wrapping up a piece on the war, and Sloane called and said she needed to talk to me about something important and would I please join her for a bite to eat. Of course, she insisted on her favorite place, but who was I to argue with the woman who's signing my check? So I obliged. She gave me her pitch for the show and when I asked—before agreeing!—if you had signed on to do the show she said, and this is a direct quote!: 'I'm currently in contract negotiations with Barbara, but we'll be making her an offer she'd be crazy to refuse.'"

"She made me an offer she *knew* I would refuse!"

Jack put his hand up, "Hear me out, Barbara. Sloane absolutely made it sound as though you'd be one of the players. By the way, I didn't even know your contract was up! And yesterday morning on the set, I didn't want you to think I was making some sort of advance, but I wanted to talk to you to tell you about Sloane's proposal and tell you how much I hoped you would agree—even though I suspected you would try to arrange a role for yourself other than pundit. I sensed that would be anathema to you. But you couldn't talk after the show—I didn't know it was because you were having lunch with her! I thought you were just making an excuse to avoid me!"

Boy, she'd never seen him so worked up. Angelica wasn't kidding. He *did* care. He *had* considered her. He thought *she* was avoiding *him*. And his recounting of his meeting with Sloane rang true. Sloane was certainly aware of their chemistry and if she wanted him to agree to do the show, she would have made it sound as though Barbara would be signing on, too. Barbara sank into the couch and sighed. "I didn't know that."

"Now you know," he said, taking a handkerchief out of his pants pocket and wiping the stage makeup off his face.

Barbara sat up again. "But Jack. How could you say yes to being a pundit? That show sounds disgusting. Anathema. Uh, yeah. We might as well go work for the White House. You don't want to do their dirty work for them, do you? Couldn't you have tried to talk her out of it? Don't you want it to be the way it used to be, doing breaking news, cutting up on the set during the commercials like we used to? Are you really going to nail those guests, ruin their lives, and be Ron Kavanagh's bitch? What the hell, Jack?"

"Barbara, listen. It's not the old Phoenix anymore. It hasn't been since the unfortunate turn of events in September. If I don't do the show, she'll get Bruce to do it and stick me on weekends or overnights. Don't think she didn't hint at that during the dinner."

Barbara stood up again. "So let her give it to Bruce. Better than being a pundit."

"I don't want to be relegated to the Siberia of shifts. My deal's not up for another year. I need to play along and I need to make a living."

"You need to maintain a lifestyle, you mean."

"Perhaps that's true."

"So you care more about your image than your integrity. That perfect picture....your perfect wife..."

"Stop it right there, Barbara," he said, jumping up from his chair and walking around the coffee table. "I made it very clear how I feel about you." He grabbed her arms. "I said I would respect your wishes. I said I would be just a co-worker. I was hoping you'd talk me out of it, but you agreed," he said hoarsely. "And so...quickly!"

"I had to....I didn't know what to do," she sputtered, "...I felt I had to make a decision...I wanted to do the right thing, but..." Jack interrupted her by pulling her to him and kissing her. She kissed him back.

The bury-the-memories-of-Jack-in-a-sanitary-pad-bag campaign had lasted all of four minutes.

They broke off the kiss and looked at each other. He took her face in his hands. "I love you."

"I love you, too."

How could she have been so angry with him? Barbara wanted to stay at the Phoenix and see him every day; she'd be miserable if she couldn't just be near him for those two hours. But she had insulted the show and the channel, and had acted like a madwoman, even grabbing Sloane's arm before submerging the BlackBerry and throwing an f-bomb of sorts in the middle of a classy restaurant. Barbara felt lucky Sloane wasn't pressing assault charges.

"My agent says they're terminating me."

Jack stroked her hair. "Listen carefully, Ms. King. I will drive back to the channel right now, demand a meeting with Sloane, and begin brokering a peace. I will offer to meet with her at the Phoenix tomorrow, or a restaurant of her choice, obviously not Ubon—and I will pick you up on my way into the city and escort you to our meeting place and the three of us can reach an accommodation." Jack was talking faster and faster, and had an almost crazed smile on his face. "We can retain the name she's chosen for the show, but you could handle the breaking news—we'll tell her that this plays to your strength anyway—and I could take on the more aggressive interviews and Kavanagh could serve as the pundit-in-chief."

How cute was he? Engineering this shuttle diplomacy to keep her at the Phoenix. Of course, she wanted to give peace a chance, but... "I don't know," she said. "She won't go for it. You read about what I did."

"I can present her with a new BlackBerry at our summit. Come with me tomorrow." He looked at her lustfully and traced his finger along her neck. "After we meet with Sloane we could... stay in Manhattan for a spell."

Barbara heard a car door slam. She took a step back and away from Jack. The door that led from the garage to a back room on the level beneath the living room opened. Jack tightened his tie. Barbara wiped her mouth as Rory ran up the back stairs into the living room and wrapped himself around her.

"Mama, your face is all red," said Rory, looking up at her.

"I was...running outside...it's....cold," she said.

"Hello Jack," said Ben, extending his hand. "What brings you here?"

Jack, posture perfect, had flipped on his anchorman switch. "I was actually driving to a luncheon on Long Island not too far from here and decided to stop by to personally implore your wife to try to mend fences at the Phoenix. I do not believe the situation is irreparable."

Ben laughed and shook his head. "I think you're wrong, man."

Jack checked his watch and said, "Well, I'd best be going." He looked at Barbara. "Please do think about what I said."

CHAPTER 40

The next morning, as the car idled in the driveway, Barbara ran back into the house. They couldn't leave without it, that was for sure. It had just started to snow: the perfect holiday setting for a season which had brought her little joy and no hope. But it was time to get into the spirit. She put up the hood of her coat so her hair wouldn't be damp with snow for the drive.

He was standing next to the car, white flakes shining bright against his dark hair. She handed him the blue and red bag and he threw it in the trunk. She got into the passenger seat.

"Thank you, Mama," came the voice from the back seat.

"We couldn't very well leave without Spidey," she told Rory, smiling at him. His crucial accessory, his backpack with the picture of Spiderman poised to leap into adventure, and all the Legos and Lincoln Logs it contained, would now be making the trip to Amherst.

"Not to be bah humbug," said Barbara, "but the snow?"

"We'll just take it slow," said Ben, patting her hand. "Forecast says we're driving away from it."

"That's good," she said, brushing the snowflakes out of his hair.

Halfway to their old school, halfway back to the start, Barbara drifted off. As she did, she imagined what it would have been like to be seated next to Jack. On a warm day. Top down. On the way to lunch with Sloane. At Ubon. Then on to a hotel.

But she wouldn't be seeing him anymore. It was going to be hard. Worse than hard. But one day, the ache, the near-physical hurt, would start to fade. *I love you, too.*

"Hey, Ror," said Ben, trying to find him in the rearview mirror. "You're going to see your future college soon."

Barbara turned around to see Rory already asleep, slumped in his booster.

"Let's just hope he doesn't wind up unemployed like us," she joked, feeling groggy from barely sleeping the night before.

"Forget the Phoenix, Barb. Really. They never deserved you. And you were only using them to get back to the networks anyhow. Which is where you belong. At a reputable organization. You're really good, Barbara. Not just at breaking news. You understand the issues and can ask smart questions that bring out both sides of the story. You've worked too hard, for too long—remember all those early mornings?—to throw it away to be a pundit for that station which is becoming a joke. Think of Martels. He'd be so proud of you now. I'm so proud of you now. To hell with Sloane." Ben didn't know that Jack had tried desperately to broker a deal with Sloane, but had been laughed at, then screamed at, and then threatened, Sloane telling him, "Bruce Hanson is ready to step in!"

Barbara's phone rang and she bolted upright in her seat. She fumbled for it in her purse—please let it say *Stone*. Sloane had changed her mind. Barbara was going back to the Phoenix. She wouldn't have to miss Jack every day and force herself to forget him.

"Is this the famous sushi slinger?"

"Oh, hello, Gene," Barbara sighed. Ben looked at Barbara and she smiled and rolled her eyes.

"I've got some good news."

"Let's hear it. I could use some." Barbara looked at Ben and he turned down the radio.

"Haven't you checked out that internet?" asked Gene. "You're the talk of the town."

"Oh no."

"Oh yes! Yes indeed. And the competition—the All News Network—is interested. You'll still have to sit on the bench for a while so the Phoenix can't nail you on the non-compete clause. But you could be working for the other guys by spring. Interested?"

"They want me because of my fight with Sloane?...I don't know..." Barbara looked at Ben and shrugged. But the unimaginatively named All News Network did have a reputation for playing it down the middle, in contrast to the Phoenix. Maybe someone there recognized what the Phoenix had become, and admired her pluck in rebelling against Sloane?

"Aw, horsefuck!" Gene snorted. "Who cares why they want you. They're probably willing to pay. I told them I'd get back to them after I talked to you. Listen, this is great, trust me. You're famous."

"Infamous is more like it."

"Look, I don't know this for sure, but they're looking to make their dayside competitive with the Phoenix," Gene snorted again, "You might even wind up going up against your old co-anchor."

Up against Jack. If she took a job with the competition, she'd never ever be up against him again. She'd be forced to stick to her decision to stay clear of him—they'd be members of two rival gangs. A boy like that, who'll kill your...ratings.

"The All News Network, huh," Barbara said for Ben's benefit. He nodded as if to say "not bad." Barbara glanced back at Rory as he slept with a slight smile on his face. "Okay. I'm interested, Gene."

"Oh, and kid? I'm betting we'll get some calls for a response to that bullshit story in the paper. We should come up with a statement."

Barbara paused, then broke into a big smile. "Just tell 'em, Gene,...this bird has flown."

ACKNOWLEDGEMENTS

Thank you to my children, Jennifer, Stephanie, and Rudy, and my mom for putting up with me (in general, but especially while I wrote this). Jen, I'm not sure I would have persevered had you not told me, "It's a legit book, Mom."

Delicia Honen Yard. You are an eagle-eyed proofer and the best friend a gal could have. Thank goodness we bonded over having the same Monkees lunch box back in first grade.

A heartfelt thanks to editor Marlene Adelstein—this would have never shaped up into a novel if it weren't for you. This book has your creative fingerprints all over it. And to Sydney Hilzenrath, whose smart suggestions were invaluable.

Thank you Katherine Fausset at Curtis Brown and Crystal Patriarche at SparkPoint and your wonderful staffs.

To the rock star professors at Sarah Lawrence, especially the amazing Jo Ann Beard, thanks for all your wisdom and encouragement.

Thanks to my buddies Jon and Andrew from Studio L who encouraged me to write by reading my silly e-mails long ago.

And since there's no orchestra prompting me to wrap... David, when I met you 20 years ago, you saved my life.

Made in the USA
Middletown, DE
18 September 2015